# RADICALS

## BOOKS BY NIK KORPON

*The Soul Standard*
*The Rebellion's Last Traitor*
*Queen of the Struggle*
*Old Ghosts*
*Wear Your Home Like a Scar*
*Radicals*

# NIK KORPON

# RADICALS

DOWN&OUT
BOOKS

Down & Out Books
3959 Van Dyke Road, Suite 265
Lutz, FL 33558
DownAndOutBooks.com

The characters and events in this book are fictitious. Any similarity to real persons, living or dead, is coincidental and not intended by the author.

Cover design by JT Lindroos

ISBN: 1-64396-185-3
ISBN-13: 978-1-64396-185-9

*For Colin and Tim, who showed me that my brain wasn't broken, even if they never knew it.*

# 1

They parked the car two blocks down, just past where street-lights spilled weak umbrellas of light over the street, making the broken glass glitter like fallen stars. All three shuffled out, bumping the doors closed with their hips. The summer air was damp enough to touch, thick with the smell of tiny backyard grills and festering garbage. They hurried down the sidewalk, the night thrumming with cars and shouting. The fat man stopped short when a rat scurried out from beneath a car, then kicked a bottle at it, the glass skittering across the pavement.

The man running point snapped his fingers, then set his index finger on his lips before dragging it across his throat.

"It's the middle of the city in the middle of a heat wave," the fat one said. "Ain't no one sleeping."

The point man stopped short, the fat one's gut squished against his sharp elbow. The fat man slapped away the elbow, then straightened his back, his stomach rounding out.

"If people aren't asleep, it's more important that we shut the fuck up and not make any more noise," the lead said. "Everyone stays quiet, we complete the mission, and everyone's happy. Got me?"

"Be careful, son," the short man said to the fat one. "He'll take your nuts, you don't watch your mouth."

The fat man started to respond, then caught his tongue, and nodded forward. "Are we going or what?" he said to the lead.

1

The point turned without a word and continued. Two hundred yards out, Community Health Medical Clinic—housed in a converted row home—sat quietly between a boarded-up Chinese restaurant and a darkened pawnshop, its metal gate drawn down tight. The moon silvered the windows, making it hard to see inside. The lack of visibility could have complicated the mission, if they hadn't already obtained the staff schedule, security plans, and three weeks' worth of camera footage of the lone watchman. Places like this, they made hacking as easy as breathing.

Standing at the corner, awash in jaundiced light, they pulled down their balaclavas and the group split.


Raymond Cody slapped his feet on the desk and opened his latest issue of *Popular Mechanics* beneath the lamp. His daughter had got him a subscription as a Father's Day gift, and he'd gone to the library to read whatever back issues they had on hand. Really, it was a gift for Raymond's grandson, who was spending the summer weekdays with Raymond while his mother worked. He'd gotten into computers and gadgets over the last year at school and talked about them endlessly. Giga-this, pixel-ready that, slam-zoom-something or other. It was all Greek to Raymond; his TV still had knobs. So the magazine was like a monthly Rosetta Stone to understand hyper-connected teenagers and a good way to spend night shifts at a tiny clinic on the Westside.

Raymond took the top off his coffee and blew at the steam. He loved spending days with the boy, especially because it took some pressure off his mother, but the long days and work-filled nights were beginning to wear on him. Normally, he'd spend most of the weekend in the basement, planing boards for a dresser or working table legs on his lathe. These days, he felt like he could lie down as soon as his daughter left the block and not get up until she came back the next week. The boy's one saving grace was that the teenager liked to sleep till noon, so Raymond could catch a little rest when his shift ended. True, the boy would be up all hours, but he was a good kid and Raymond trusted him to make the right decisions. Until summer's end, Raymond was spending his nights with his new best friend, Juan Valdez.

Inside the clinic, the short man crept down the hallway. The tile floor needed a wash, speckled with dirt and other things he wasn't willing to wager a guess on, but a clean floor would have made for a squeaky floor, and so he was grateful for that. He passed four exam rooms, some sterile white with only a framed motivational poster as decoration, others painted with gaudy but fading rainbows and clowns.

He paused at the edge of the hallway, listening for the guard, then risked a glance. The Center hummed quietly with the sound of the whirring computer fans in the server room off to the side. He'd been surprised to see the layout of the place, at its open floor plan and abundance of half-walls—save for the closed-off examination rooms—but he figured it was a cost-saving measure, and done with the help of the very people it would serve. Beyond the guard, the short man saw the sharp shadow of the point man and the bulbous one behind him.

The point raised his hand. They raised theirs in response. He dropped it and they moved.

Raymond was halfway through an article about using torpedo technology for self-driving cars when he heard a squeak. He set his magazine against his chest to listen a minute, but heard nothing else. *Probably a mouse,* he thought, though having vermin in a supposedly sterile environment wouldn't sit well with the Center's director. Not his problem now, though. He went back to his article.

But two paragraphs down, he heard another noise, something like a swishing. He set his magazine on the table and grabbed his Maglite to investigate. He headed toward the hall-way with the examination rooms.

The Maglite's beam pierced the darkness of the first exam room. Nothing unusual in the corners, or behind the door. Nothing except for that creepy clown painted on the wall. He understood it was supposed to be cheery, put kids at ease and whatnot, but every time he saw that clown he expected it to take off its face and expose teeth like a giant anglerfish. Raymond moved on to the second room, then paused outside the third, listening. The clinic lay quiet, and he began to wonder if he was just hearing things, the way his old partner used to when they were on stakeouts. That old boy either had supersonic hearing or had kissed the bottle one too many times.

To be safe, Raymond cleared the rest of the rooms. Each was silent and still as a tomb. He closed the door to the fourth and headed back to his post in the main room.


"This isn't going to work," the fat man said to the point. "This place isn't big enough."

"We have to try." The point heard a door close down the hallway.

"Trying's going to get someone shot."

He whirled around to face the fat one. "No one's getting shot. Just relax and stay quiet and everything will be fine."

They crept across the main office toward the servers. *He's right,* the point thought as the second door closed. This place looked bigger in the security footage than in real life. The idea was to get in and out without anyone noticing—draw the guard away, hit the servers, and be gone before he came back—but there wasn't enough space to distract him, get him away from the main area. And besides, once a single screen lit up, the guard would be able to see it over the half-walls from his post. He'd had reservations about the plan, but they didn't have any other options; if they wanted to get in the castle, this was the door they had to use. This job was bigger than them. It was for the Harper twins; it was for the people.

As they approached the server area, a third door closed. They stopped short. One exam room left.

"Told you," the fat man said.

The lead could hear the smirk in the prick's voice as the final door slipped closed.

The footsteps tracked into the main office and the chair creaked as the guard sat with a sigh. His feet landed on the table.

"Okay," the point said. "We'll have to improvise." But as he went to turn back, the fat man was already moving forward. The point grabbed at the fat one but he was too far away. Calling to him would make too much noise. Choking him—while cathartic—might alert the guard. Plus, he weighed a ton. Instead, he strafed along the half-walls, approaching the guard, ready to spring up behind him, cinch his elbow around his throat, and put him out.

Then the red dot appeared on the guard's chest.

As he scurried to get in close to the guard, the point promised himself he was going to kick that fat ass in his pencil-dick as soon as they got outside.

It took the guard a couple seconds to notice it, then a few more to understand what it was before jumping out of his chair. He went to dive under the desk, seeking cover, when the point man wrapped one thick arm around the guard, pressed a cloth against his mouth with the other. He guided the guard's body down to the tile floor, resting him gently.

When the guard was fully out, the point man stood and cracked his neck.

The short man stepped forward, assuming control of the situation. "Tape him up."

"On it," the point man said.

"Not you. Him."

"But—" the fat man started.

"But nothing. You watch one TV show and you think you're a criminal genius?" He snatched the laser pointer from the man's pudgy hands on the way to the servers, shoved it into his pocket, and pulled out a thumb drive. "Make sure he's comfortable and keep a lookout. We've got work to do."

Raymond Cody's eyelids flickered open. His lips slapped together, trying to find moisture. He started to call out, but caught himself as images slammed against him. The red dot, the man choking him, the rag. He stayed quiet and shut his eyes, in case someone was close and had a mind to finish the job. He listened to the noises, determining position, number, temperament. Raymond wagered there were at least two of them, both men. There was a bunch of clacking and a voice farther away, on the other side of the office. Labored breathing behind him, thick inhalations through a busted nose, maybe ten feet away. So make that three perps. He let his eyes crack open.

Blue light shone on two faces in the server area, both hunched over a computer and rapidly typing, pointing at things on the screen. He had no idea what they were doing but doubted it was particularly good. Could they steal money that way? Maybe they were hacking into the clinic's accounts, a pretty low move, stealing from a nonprofit.

A few minutes later, the two finished the computer work. The third one set something on the security desk. Raymond closed his eyes when they turned toward the main office.

They stopped beside him, one pressing his fingers against Raymond's neck, checking his pulse. He reflexively swallowed, kicked himself for it as soon as it happened.

"You don't have to pretend to be out," the man said.

Raymond opened his eyes. A short man crouched down a hair, a black balaclava covering his face.

"You feel okay?" he said.

"Head's fuzzy."

"It'll be like that a bit. Are you comfortable?"

Raymond looked down—his wrists duct-taped to the chair's arms, his ankles to its legs, his torso to its back—and motioned with his hands.

"Sorry, not much else I can do," the man said. "You don't have circulation issues or anything do you?"

"I'm not that old," Raymond said. "And would it matter if I did?"

The man cocked his head. "Good point. But there's no reason for you to be unnecessarily uncomfortable. You haven't done anything. In fact, everything we're doing is for you."

"And what's that?"

"You'll see." The man stood. From his demeanor, Raymond expected him to be much taller, not a squat five-foot-six. "A few days from now, when everything starts happening, remember what I said."

The three of them made for the door before Raymond called out. "What about when I have to piss?"

"You're not that old, right? Hold it." The man laughed once before walking out.

The clinic was quiet once more, computers humming, air ducts rattling. Raymond sat in the dim light, flexed his fingers, and sighed hard.

"Holding."

# 2

Jay Brodsky punched the button on the car radio to change the station. He couldn't handle listening to more coverage of the Harper twins, who were both afflicted by the same congenital disease, the name and nature of which totally escaped Jay. But the big story was that their mother's insurance company had determined it was a pre-existing condition and could therefore deny payment, forcing the mother to choose which twin received the life-saving procedure. As the twins' health worsened, the mother had to make the worst, most painful choice a parent ever could: decide which child would live and which one would die.

Jay didn't have kids but damn near teared up every time he heard the story. Even two weeks after the story broke, news outlets continued to cover it. Jay figured they would have moved on to a different tragedy already. He turned left and came face to face with a colorful mural that took up the whole side of a building. *Justice for the Harpers* ran across the bottom of the painting on a cloth banner, with *No Healthcare? Go to Hell* and other slogans written around the edges.

So instead of listening to coverage of dying children, Jay was now listening to meteorologists' vast and varied predictions for the path of Hurricane Donovan—where it would make landfall, how strong it would be, what the damage might be. Jay sighed hard and turned off the radio completely, opting to spend the rest of his commute in silence instead.

Jay walked through the FBI field office in downtown Baltimore, down hallways with bureaucratic gray carpet, along white walls pocked with black scuffs, past groups of men with stale coffee breath and Danish crumbs on their untailored Men's Wearhouse suit jackets arguing emphatically about the Orioles' playoff prospects, all the way down to the end of the hall where he badged in to the Cyber Crimes division. He placed his lunch in the fridge, the same he had every day: peppered turkey sandwich, Muenster cheese, an apple, a handful of pretzels, a small container of raw almonds. A woman he'd been dating laughed one night when she opened his refrigerator and saw four brown paper bags sitting in a row, his lunches for the week. She asked if he labeled them for each day. He'd laughed, said, *Of course not, they're all the same. Just like breakfast.* He pointed to the shelf below with four six-packs of Greek yogurt—strawberry and honey—beside two bottles of orange juice with pulp and two cartons of eggs. She just blinked and excused herself. That relationship didn't last long either. He'd always had trouble explaining the need for routine to girlfriends, which was part of the reason he'd simply stopped dating a couple years ago. It wasn't that he was OCD or a control freak, but more that he couldn't *not* be in control in order to keep his tics reined in. It was a fine distinction that was either understood or not. His sister, Sam, understood it. She'd taken care of him when he was younger, made sure the Tourette's didn't consume him whole. And for the last seven years, in her absence, he was trying— with mixed results—to keep it at bay.

Jay slid into his cubicle.

"Yo, you watch it yet?" Special Agent Ari Yemin said as he poked his head around the divider wall.

Jay glanced up at him. "Watch what?"

"The video about the room."

"What are you talking about?" Jay picked up a report sitting on his desk, a sticky note affixed to the top. *Look at this ASAP.*

Yemin rolled his chair into Jay's cubicle. "Dude, I sent you the video about redoing the kids' room. The one with the X-wing bed and speeder bike rocker? Here, look." He brought something up on his phone.

"No really, it's—"

Jay sighed as Yemin tapped his phone against Jay's, transferring an image of some blueprints.

"Now you can look at them." Yemin's face was long and angular over his rumpled Oxford, his cheeks gaunt, though Jay rarely saw him not snacking on something at his desk. Jay did his best not to cringe at all the almond skins and stray raisins littering the papers and floor. Yemin's father was Turkish and his mother was Sicilian. With his dark skin and close-cropped brown hair, he regularly got called a terrorist and, despite the FBI badge, got tons of side-eye when going through TSA security. Jay knew he'd grown up in New Jersey and was more worried about rolling a d20 with his kids than daisy-chaining C-4. "You said you'd help me build it."

"I forgot, I'm sorry. I'll watch it tonight." Jay split the folder open and began scanning the specifics. Break-in at Community Health, a small Westside community medical clinic. Nothing stolen. No one hurt. Only a strange computer graphic displayed on the monitors. "But I still don't think they're ready for it. Or at least won't appreciate it."

"Doesn't matter if they're ready." Yemin's oldest boy was seven and his twin daughters—*oops babies*—were three. "You make them ready. They grow up in *Star Wars*, they'll love it whether they want to or not."

"Ah, the classic nature versus nurture argument." Jay flipped to the next page, which detailed how the perps had accessed the server of the clinic and wiped all the billing records, setting the company's ledger back to zero. *That's unexpected,* Jay thought. Hackers always looked for personal information. Patient ID numbers, Social Security numbers, addresses, things that could be used to create false personas. "You're not showing them the prequels are you?"

"My job as a parent is to protect them from evil, not give them the CGI version of it." Yemin shook his head, like he was amazed Jay could even ask that. "Besides, in these plans? The bed glows. I got a rope of blue LEDs to string along the bottom. How can they not like it?"

"Kids do like glowing things. Least, I assume they do. Cats do, according to videos." Jay went further into the report, skimming over the details of two dozen additional clinics that had reported the same issues, minus the break-in. Jay flipped back to the first page and checked the dates. *This spread across twenty-some clinics within two days?*

"There's not much difference." Yemin started to say more but stopped short and stood up, held his hand out. "Sir."

Jay stood by reflex and turned to face Assistant Special Agent in Charge Brett Dalworth, the man who supervised their squad.

Dalworth looked to Yemin, and said, "Give us a minute?" Yemin grabbed his stained coffee cup and went for a refill.

ASAC Dalworth had lobbied for Jay to be stationed at the Baltimore office when he came out of Quantico after working with the ACLU for a few years. It was an unorthodox move— normally agents would be assigned someplace other than the district they applied through. But Jay had finished near the top of his class and cyber agents with a background in programming were in demand, so Dalworth called in a few favors. Handpicked for the position, Jay felt a strange combination of having a bit of leeway with Dalworth while also needing constantly to impress him and live up to his estimation.

"Everything okay, sir?"

Dalworth pulled Yemin's chair over, brushed off the bits, nodded for Jay to sit as well. He ran his hand through his thick gray hair, something that, pushing his late sixties, he was inordinately proud of. *My grandfather died at ninety-five,* he'd told

Jay before, *could've mopped your house with his head*. Jay wondered sometimes if that was the eccentricity of living in Baltimore for forty-plus years.

"We missed you this weekend," he said to Jay. "Annie even made that god-awful Jell-O pudding you like."

"You know I only ate it because you wouldn't and I didn't want her to feel bad. And now she makes it every time."

"When you've been married forty years, you don't have to eat the shitty dessert. Smart move on your part, though."

Jay nodded, the compliment a small consolation. Dalworth's wife was one of the sweetest women Jay had ever met and he sometimes wondered what his life would've been like if he'd grown up with a mother like her instead of his own mother, but none of that changed the fact that two scoops of that pudding threatened to throw him into diabetic shock.

Dalworth shrugged. "I put your care package in the fridge next to your lunch."

"Care package?"

"Jell-O pudding. From Annie." He said it as if it were the most obvious thing. "Anyway. You have a look at that hack?"

Jay motioned with the folder in hand. "The broad strokes. What are we thinking?"

"That's what I came to ask you."

Jay cleared his throat and began to leaf through it once more. "First thought would be a virus, maybe with hyper-specific coding that lets them target only the billing records. I've never seen something like this before, but that doesn't mean there's anything unique about it. Maybe there's some kind of AI component to it or something. I'll have to look at it closer before I can say more."

"It is strange, isn't it?"

"Everything's strange until you've seen it a couple times."

"Jay, these places were hacked and billing records deleted and the only thing we have to go on is a cartoon ghost displayed on the monitors."

"It's sixteen-bit animation, not a cartoon," Jay said. "They're different."

"Whatever." Dalworth crossed his arms. "You see what connects them?"

Jay creased his eyebrows and reexamined the reports. "All part of the Hopkins network. The virus could easily pass through an intranet."

"Not that."

A moment later, Jay looked up from the paper. "Each clinic is serviced by Bay State Insurance or Tidewater Mutual?"

Dalworth raised an eyebrow.

"They're the two largest insurers in Maryland," Jay said. "That's not too weird."

"How many accounts have been affected?"

"Couple hundred at each site."

"And more than twenty sites—"

"Means thousands of accounts, all with only those two insurers. Not nationwide like Exemplar, not any of the small local places. And all in less than two days."

Jay chewed on his lip. "That is strange." His right finger twitched. He lined it up with the edge of the paper, blinked once with his right eye, once with his left. "Has the virus or whatever infected their mainframes?"

Dalworth breathed a laugh. "They're conducting an 'internal review' and will get back to us."

Jay could hear the air quotes around *internal review*. "Maybe we could actually figure something out for them if they let us do our job."

"Your lips, god's ear," Dalworth said, standing. "Look into it, will you?"

"I'll get on it right now."

Dalworth clapped Jay's shoulder, then paused a second. "Not to bring up a sore subject, but IT mentioned a few"—he paused, searching for a diplomatic way to say it—"searches with your ID on it."

Jay swallowed. "I don't know what they're talking about but I'm sure it's not a problem."

"I get that this is a difficult week. It was seven years on Tuesday, right?"

"Monday, but everything's fine." Jay snapped it out before Dalworth could say anymore but realized it sounded more aggressive than he intended. "I'm good, sir."

Dalworth held his look a long beat before rapping his knuckles on the edge of the cubicle. "Let me know when you find something. And don't leave that pudding in the fridge. Somehow, she'll know."

Jay arranged the piles of papers, saw the invisible line coming off the corners of them and intersecting at a ninety-degree angle in the exact middle of his laptop.

"It's fine. I'm fine." Jay fired up his laptop, telling himself to breathe and keep his Tourette's under control.

As Yemin walked back to his cubicle, he watched Jay correct the angles of the papers while the machine connected to the Bureau's server. "What're you doing there, buddy?"

"Logging on." Jay handed Yemin the incident report. "You want to do me a favor and call an AUSA—try Gutierrez, she's usually in early—and get them to subpoena every affected clinic and get their server records? Thanks, sweetheart."

Yemin took the paper without looking at it, kept his eyes on Jay. "Seriously, I got three kids, I recognize evasion when I see it."

Jay popped in his earbuds and turned on Cock Sparrer—a punk band Sam loved when they were growing up—even though he knew it was probably a poor choice, given it was the anniversary of Sam's disappearance. Or rather, when she walked out the door, seemingly evaporating into the ether, leaving no information with her girlfriend and few leads for Jay to follow.

He pushed those thoughts aside and got back to navigating through the server, looking for the video investigators had taken of the animated ghost.

He could feel Yemin hovering behind him but knew if he ignored him long enough, he'd eventually give up.

Jay found the file and double-clicked. A graphic appeared on the monitor—a skeleton draped in a deep-red cloak, slightly pixelated like the old sixteen-bit video games. Its jaw opened and closed like it was laughing.

He recognized it immediately.

Jay's right eye twitched twice. He blinked his left twice.

It was the Crimson Ghost.

# 3

Twenty-three red dots were scattered across the projection map in the Field Office conference room, like Baltimore had caught chicken pox over the past forty-eight hours. Some spread over the Westside, some on the East, several clumped around the main Hopkins medical campuses. Each dot represented a site whose computer system had been compromised, whose billing records had been completely wiped, whose monitors displayed only a sixteen-bit skeleton wearing a red cloak.

Jay's initial thought: virus. Of course it was a virus, because viruses spread, and spread rapidly. But viruses also spread randomly. This wave was targeted, methodical, only affecting the billing departments, nothing pertaining to patient care or patient records.

The method of infection also suggested a virus, especially as no other clinics had reported break-ins. They made their way into Community Health, then infected the other places through the intranet. But there was no indication the other locations had downloaded any malignant files.

*All that aside, what are they looking for? What's the point of this?* Jay thought as he sat at the conference room table, his eyes flicking among his laptop screen, the projection map, and two tablets running analysis on the skeleton's code. Beside them were squared-off piles of printed tech specs and logs tracing the user flow from one IP address to another, the top edge of each stack creating a straight line across the table. If he squinted hard enough, the disparate pieces of the case started to track, but he lost focus of the connections when he took a bird's-eye view.

Jay picked up the locust sitting on his desk and stared at it. Forensics had found it on the security desk at Community Health but got nothing from it, nothing from the site either. Whoever pulled these jobs wanted to send some kind of message with the locust—you wouldn't leave such a thing behind otherwise—but the message was as inscrutable as what they wanted.

The only thing Jay was sure of was the ghost itself. Growing up, he'd seen it on dozens of his sister's records and shirts, all for The Misfits, another of her favorite bands. Every time he looked at the image, he felt a quick jab in the soft spot between his ribs, felt a longing to pause this investigation and continue searching for Sam, to find out where she'd gone and what she did. Dalworth's IT mole could go to Hell.

"You know this is what a serial killer's garage looks like, right?" Yemin stood in the doorway behind Jay.

"If anyone would know, it'd be you."

Yemin settled himself into a chair with a long sigh. "So. What do we got now?"

"Where do I start?"

Yemin pointed at the table, three screens filled with various incarnations of the skeleton.

"Image referencing brought back a bunch of stuff, mostly bad tattoos. I'll get to that in a minute. I tracked the original image to the broadside of a film called *The Crimson Ghost*, a Republic Pictures serial from 1946 in which a mysterious villain"—Jay lowered his voice—"the eponymous Crimson Ghost, is determined to steal a counter-atomic device known as Cyclotrode X, which can short out any electrical device."

"Which is exactly what our guys did. Froze computers and servers. So we're looking for a cell of terrorist film nerds?"

"There are other people who would recognize the ghost's face." Jay picked up a tablet and flipped to a new window, displaying multiple photos of a horror-punk band, their faces painted corpse-white and black with long, jet-black hair. "Band called the Misfits. Their logo is the Crimson Ghost skull, hence the plethora of stick-and-poke tattoos in the image search. They do the whole 'Teenagers from Mars' meets pop-punk thing with some low-budget fifties sci-fi thrown in."

"I wrote my first program in C-plus-plus when I was thirteen and I don't understand anything you just said."

Jay shook his head. "Typical teenage rebellion stuff. Walk by Hot Topic and half the kids inside will have Misfits or Slayer shirts on. It doesn't mean anything in this context."

"That skull would be cool airbrushed on the side of a van," Yemin said. "Maybe they just like the way it looks."

Jay figured it was more likely they were drawing on the plot of the movie, but that didn't explain their ultimate goal. Shorting out electrical devices wasn't quite analogous with selectively deleting records.

"Yeah, maybe. However"—Jay thumbed through the papers for the ones he wanted, then arranged them in front of Yemin—"this might have legs."

Jay noticed Yemin watching him adjust the papers to get them straight, but Yemin didn't press him. "IP address logs?"

"I had the techs get into the various servers and run analysis on the logs, see who's coming from where, temporal signatures, how long they're on, all that. At least, as much as two people can do."

Yemin scanned the list, his lips moving as he talked to himself. "And it's the usual lot."

"Right. China, North Korea, Russia, Iran."

"Aka roll call for terrorism."

"Right. But we're not seeing any activity from Yemen, Syria, Nigeria. However—" Jay said, his tone implying *wait for it.*

Yemin tapped his finger on a line of code. "But then there's a few hits from Venezuela, Ukraine, Cuba." He leaned back in his chair, steepled his fingers together and set them against his lips.

18

"It's the same people who are always trying to get in, probing for soft spots."

"Or maybe they're trying to look like they're the same people to throw us off. See these hits? It's evenings and weekends, US time."

"Which means it's daytime in China."

"Right, but they're only on for two or three hours at a pop, then longer on weekends. If it was China trying to get in, they'd be banging on the door for eight, nine hours straight during the week and quiet the other days, because even state-sanctioned hackers get the weekends off. And if this was coming from the Middle East, there wouldn't be so much activity on Friday and Saturday because of the holy days. And that aside, what kind of terrorist organization—state sanctioned or lone wolf—breaks into Community Health in Sandtown?"

Yemin arched an eyebrow. "Some kid in Caracas—one who might crib the skull logo of an American punk band because it looks cool—accidentally showing up on our list doesn't mean it's not someone else trying to get in."

"Exactly," Jay said. "If they were using Tor or another kind of onion routing—which, ostensibly, any decent hacker or cyber operative would be—they could bury their location through thousands of reroutes and we wouldn't pick up their original location in the first place. All of them would dead-end in Zimbabwe, Bolivia, Tibet, Sri Lanka, someplace random with no interest in hacking the US."

Sometimes Jay wondered what it would have been like thirty years ago, collecting intelligence without having to sift through hundreds of thousands of entries from programs like Tor, which allowed someone to bounce their signal off communication satellites around the world to hide their location.

"Next question," Jay said. "Most hackers want to make a point, even if it's just that things need to be destroyed. So what are they trying to say? Why target billing records?"

Jay looked up at the room's drop-ceiling. It was a midnight

sky in reverse, depthless points of darkness amid a field of blinding white. At times, Jay thought it was an apt metaphor for the Bureau itself.

"Health care is a lot of money. Maybe they want to disrupt the economy," Yemin said. "Or shake the public's faith in their cyber security. You know how upset everyone gets when there's a breach."

"Yeah. For two days. Before they change all their accounts to *password2* instead of *password1*. There's a reason they're attacking billing records." Jay stood and stretched his back. *Breathe, be aware, count.* "What if they think they're creating goodwill? Like, they're helping wipe out debt to show they're on the people's side so that…no one complains? Give them extra money to buy stuff? I don't know."

Yemin sighed. "Me neither. Something doesn't add up."

"Right. So what's their next move?" Jay cupped his chin, ran his fingers over his cheeks while staring at the map. "What if it actually is creating goodwill for their cause, so that when they attack—"

"They have public support." Yemin pressed his fingers against his eyelids. "We should run this by Dalworth. Not that these people are going nuclear or anything, but with that plotline?"

"Yeah, I know, I know."

Someone knocked on the conference room door. Jay and Yemin turned in their chairs to find Jeanie standing there, her face dappled with sweat. She was the new tech they'd finally been able to hire, after months of pleading and cajoling, and even then only because she was fresh out of college and the department could pay her nothing.

"Agent Brodsky," she said, her breath rushing in and out. "You need to hear this."

# 4

Jay and Yemin followed Jeanie down the hallway, weaving around slow-moving packs of suited agents, dodging a mop bucket sitting in the middle of the tile floor with no attendant around. She impressed Jay with how quickly and nimbly she moved, especially given the heels she wore. He would break his neck five times a day if he had to wear them.

Just past the kitchen, they banked right and stopped at the second door, a cramped room filled with servers, corkboards, and a computer for each analyst. Algorithms were scribbled on a digital wipe-board, next to a crude drawing that could have been an alien or one of the techs with elephantiasis. Numbers and something like a heartbeat flashed on a few screens.

Darragh, the other tech, looked up at Jay, then over at Jeanie, his eyes nervous and maybe a little scared.

"What do we need to hear?" Jay said as he sat down with Yemin alongside.

Jeanie cleared her throat. "We were running analyses, as you asked, when Darragh put his earbuds into the wrong laptop."

Jay glanced at him.

"I didn't want to disturb anyone with my music. I wasn't watching Netflix or anything." Darragh's voice was as timid as his appearance.

"I'm sure Jeanie appreciates that," Jay said. "What happened when you plugged in?"

21

Darragh handed him the earbuds. He took one and gave the other to Yemin, pressed his finger in the empty ear but had to breathe through the feeling of being out of balance.

A tinny, metallic voice ended a word, then there was silence. Some kind of whoosh, like a robot inhaling, then the voice spoke again. *Your time is over. Our time is now. We will break their chains. We will laugh as you burn and dance on the ashes of your empire.* Another pause, the same whoosh, then repeat.

Jay took the earbud out, calmly set it on the table, and thanked the techs for alerting him. "We need to go to Dalworth. This is a terrorist threat."

Yemin sighed and nodded.

This wasn't some bullshit Nigerian prince scam. Something was starting. Jay didn't know what, but he knew it was about to get much worse. This was an intent to attack. This was someone who wanted to kill them.

Jay blinked right, left, left—

*Stop it,* he thought, closing his eyes. *Just stop.*

# 5

Oscar Forlán sat behind his desk, scrolling through data trends on his laptop, his right ear throbbing slightly after spending the last two hours with a phone pressed between his shoulder and head. His clients were worried, and rightfully so: the hack of a small community clinic in west Baltimore had spread through two dozen other clinics within the Hopkins medical system. If these hackers could find their way inside one of the largest medical systems in the state, each client was convinced they would be next.

As founder and CEO of Amaru Cyber Storage, he knew it was incumbent on him to assure each client—from the small organic market in Virginia Beach to the Fortune 500 used-car dealership with locations in twelve states—that he and his entire staff were closely monitoring the situation and, no, there was not a chance they would be affected.

Still, he couldn't blame them for being concerned. Data breaches and identity theft were running rampant these days, as everything was online. No one could be bothered to create unique passwords for each account so one password that generally contained a pet's name or a birthdate spanned everything from Hulu to bank accounts to mortgage records. Any hacker worth their salt could access and own an account through a simple dictionary attack, and generally in less time than it took to spell the word *dictionary*. Which is why Forlán impressed upon his clients the need to use multi-word phrases with a combination of upper- and lower-case letters and frequent symbol substitutions. It was a pain for the client to keep track of, he understood, but it also ensured their safety, which had helped Forlán's business double in size every two years for the last decade and change. Forlán thought that was a testament to his character—especially as most new clients came as referrals from existing clients—proof that he was not only thoughtful and thorough, but also ethical.

Seven years earlier, Amaru Cyber had been offered the opportunity to take on a large portion of Philip Morris's storage and security needs. The company had been facing yet more backlash and was looking to bolster its image in the Richmond community. Two of Forlán's market advisors insisted this client could quadruple the size of their company and make them millionaires many times over. Forlán had a moral issue with Philip Morris—not necessarily with smoking, because that was a personal choice he wouldn't impede, but because of the constant lying and deception employed by its PR staff and its practice of targeting young users. At the same time, he knew some of his clients had business practices that dipped below his own high moral ground.

But for all of his advisors' bullet points and spreadsheets, Forlán kept asking the same questions: Why? Why do we need to quadruple? Why do we need more money? Why does our stock price need to go up even more? We can provide our clients with consistent, reliable, personal service and give our employees living wages and health benefits and the assurance that, even if they aren't doing something explicitly positive, they aren't hurting anyone. They could feel good about where their money came from.

*What difference would it make to anyone other than me if I had millions of dollars more?* he'd asked one advisor. *What could I possibly buy that would make my life so much better than it is now?*

And so they turned down the contract. By that Christmas,

they'd signed on four new midsize clients, hired ten new employees, and given everyone a four-thousand-dollar bonus. Their stock price ended up higher than the advisors had predicted during their Philip Morris pitch.

Forlán's phone buzzed. He took a deep breath before answering.

"Mister Forlán," his assistant Megan said, "Mister Taiari is on line two for you."

"I'll take it in here."

"Can I get you anything?"

"A maté would be wonderful. No sugar, extra strong."

"Long day?" She let out a short laugh.

"Nothing I didn't expect, and nothing we can't provide."

The smile was audible in her voice. "I'll bring in the tea. Anything else?"

His cell phone buzzed in his pocket. "Yes. We'll keep monitoring everything, but reach out to people. Let them know our assistance is available to anyone who needs it."

"Done and done," she said.

Forlán thanked her and checked his phone.

*We good for tonight?*

His lips curled in a slight smile. He texted back, *We've been ready for years.*

*Hasta la lucha.*

*Mátalo,* Forlán texted. Kill it.

He set his phone down, then picked up the office line. "Monsieur Taiari, *bonjour,*" he said. "*Comment ça va?*"

# 6

ASAC Dalworth removed the earbuds and placed them on the laptop, now sitting on his desk beside a few photos of Annie and their kids and grandchildren. Framed commendations hung on the walls, as well as photos of Dalworth with old, white men—dignitaries, heads of other offices. He sank into his leather chair, knitted his fingers together, and took a deep breath.

"That's scary," Dalworth said.

"We need to figure out who's doing this and where they're going to hit next," Jay replied. "Headquarters of an insurance company? Hopkins Hospital?"

"You're doubting yourself," Dalworth said to Jay after a moment. Jay pressed his palms against his eyes and exhaled.

Yemin jumped in for him. "Agent Brodsky and I have been going back and forth on this and there's something we can't quite square."

"I can't square why my son insists on eating tofu bacon," Dalworth said, "but he still does it."

"It's just," Jay started to say, then changed direction. "The IP addresses tracking back to known enemies, the tokens left at the scene, the ominous recording. All of it feels like a threat—a warning—but that one image keeps popping up. Why would ISIS, Boko Haram, or North Korea reference a B-movie from the Fifties? And without any kind of explicit demand?"

"The question we need to answer isn't why, but when and

where." He stood and held out his hand. End of conversation. "Thank you in advance, gentlemen."

Jay and Yemin shook his hand and turned to leave when Dalworth called Jay's name. Yemin went into the hallway.

"You sure you can handle this?" Dalworth asked.

"I'm fine. I promise."

He looked at Jay a long minute. "I know you've got a lot on your mind with your sister, plus hearing that you're using Bureau resources—*again*—for personal matters—"

"I'm fine. Sir. I told you before."

"I get that you want to know, and that not knowing eats at you. If you're not up to this, just say so. You can always step back. I'll give Yemin lead and you can pick up the next one when you're feeling better."

"This is my case. I'll work it till it's finished."

"Is there anything else I need to know about?"

Jay swallowed, shoved his hands inside his pockets to keep them still, and kept Dalworth's level stare.

"I'm fine, sir."

Dalworth appraised him a moment longer before nodding.

Jay left the office and caught up with Yemin, walking most of the way down the hallway in silence.

Finally, Yemin let out a loud sigh. "You have any idea where to start with this?"

"Yeah," Jay lied.

# 7

The moon hung low over the rocky edge of the mountains, illuminating the street while casting pallid light on them. Cicadas, crickets, and frogs filled the night. Bright spots reflected off watching eyes in the darkness of the trees. There was rustling in shrubbery near the ground.

"Wasn't there a target that's not in *Deliverance* country?" the fat man said.

The point man hushed him. "I said no talking. It's too quiet. Someone could hear."

"There's no one out here to hear."

"How many times do we have to say this?" the short man said.

The fat man grumbled to himself as he stepped over a large rock in the lot. They'd parked next to the small strip mall—or what passed for a strip mall in Pentress, West Virginia, which was three conjoined stores on the side of a one-lane road with a liquor store across the street. Somewhere off in the distance, a wolf howled, its voice echoing through the night. He thought it was actually kind of cool, until a second wolf answered.

The target was a small office that housed Patrick & Sons Insurance Company, nestled between a gas station/bait shop and a nail salon. Dwight Patrick, proprietor of the company, made his living offering mining companies coverage, often undercutting other local companies, sometimes far enough that it was to his own detriment just so he could get more business. But the recent fracking boom meant he could afford to do it, because he'd amassed such a client list that he became the de facto insurance provider for new employees and companies, slowly suffocating the competition. And once there were few options remaining, he could not only raise rates but begin to amend the policies, filling them with loopholes and conditional language that curried favor with the company providing the insurance. *May* and *could* became his two favorite words, even above the names of his children. But what moved him to the top of their list was the fallout from a worksite accident two years ago.

As renewable energy became more feasible, a local mining outfit started to cut corners in order to save money, pushing off renovations and avoiding safety checks that would surely shut them down.

When one faulty machine threw a spark in a mine with no exhaust fans, it turned into scores of dead miners with hundreds more injured. The mining outfit was clearly at fault, but since Dwight Patrick had inserted his two favorite words into every policy, it helped his provider decline almost all the claims, saving them upward of two million dollars—and giving him some sort of perceived privileged status—on the backs of dead miners.

The short man crouched before the front door and unzipped a leather case, pulling out two thin pieces of metal and sliding them inside the lock. A minute of manipulation, then the short, hard click. He went inside and the fat one slipped in behind him, leaving the strongest member outside as lookout.


When he left the station twenty minutes ago, Deputy Sheriff Robert Sweeney knew with one hundred percent certainty that he could make it home without having to stop. But that was twenty minutes ago. Right now, guiding his Crown Vic around the winding Monongalia County back roads that were barely a car wide, he could feel that last coffee swishing back and forth in his bladder. Were he in his personal car, he'd have no problem pulling over and watering the daisies. But whipping it out beside his county-issue vehicle felt wrong. Didn't matter that he hadn't passed another car in ten miles. The principle remained. He could hear his wife chiding him, saying if he didn't want to piss his uniform, he shouldn't have moved all the way out here with the cows and coyotes. She wasn't really a city girl—no one could mistake Morgantown for a thriving metropolis—but all the sky got to be a bit much for her sometimes. He liked it out here, though, where the air was clean and he needed binoculars to see the nearest neighbor.

He hit a pothole and the car shuddered. He squeezed his muscles tight, barely keeping it all in. That pretty much sealed it. He figured it'd be better to hope no one drove by than to walk into his house with piss-soaked trousers. He pulled over on a ridge a couple hundred feet before a valley, stepped out into the air, and unzipped. As he stood there, a wolf howled in the distance. He loved the sound of that, the freedom of it, especially when a second wolf answered.

Once finished, he zipped up and stepped back to his Crown Vic. Then a flash caught the corner of his eye. He paused and squinted. It looked like it came from one of the cluster of stores below, but they were all dark, save the liquor store across the street with its dim security lighting. He glanced up, thought maybe it was the moon's reflection or a passing airplane. Then he saw it again in the center window. Dwight Patrick's place. He flipped the lock off his holster and set off on foot.


While the fat man paced circles between the roughly upholstered chairs ringing the linoleum sitting area, the short man booted up Patrick's computer and got to work.

He was halfway through the installation when he heard a grunt outside. Everyone froze.

"Everything okay out there?"

A thin whisper from across the room. "Dunno."

He clicked off his Maglite and turned off the monitor, letting his eyes adjust to the dark. A couple seconds later, a shadow passed by the front window.

*Shit,* he thought.

In a loud whisper he thought wouldn't be heard outside, he said, "Get ready."

The man leaned on the corner like he was waiting for a girl-friend to meet him, his rear foot kicked up and resting against the cedar-shingled wall, thumbs slung in his belt loops. Deputy Sheriff Sweeney crouched down and took a wide, loping arc, staying below the patches of shrubbery until he got to the rear of the building. He crept along the wall to the corner, then paused and listened. Insects thrumming, communicating in clicks and snaps. Wild animals rustling, searching for food. He wagered a peek around the corner and saw the man, still against the wall in his pose. Sweeney figured the distance to be about twenty feet, which meant if he moved quickly and quietly, or if the man was slow, he could reach the man before he'd be able to signal for help. It was a gamble, sure, but standing here and waiting was the other option, and that wasn't no kind of option. He touched the handle of his service weapon by reflex, then moved.

The man barely had time to look up as Sweeney drove his shoulder into the man's stomach. He grunted hard and hit the ground, gasping for breath like a fish yanked from the water.

"You're going to be okay. Your air will come back," Sweeney said in a hard whisper. "How many are inside?"

The man formed some sort of word. Sweeney wasn't sure he really heard it, hoped not, for the man's sake. He leaned closer, told the man he was going to need to repeat that. The man cleared his throat, swallowed.

"Fuck you, pig," he spit.

"That's what I thought you said." Sweeney leaned back, saw

the moonlight glint off the man's smile, then buried his fist in the man's face. His head snapped back and to the side and he quickly went dark.

Sweeney pulled himself to his feet, unholstered his weapon, and stepped over to the door, gently testing it. Unlocked. He turned the knob quiet as a stolen breath and eased the door open. No sound. He hunkered down to make less of a target of himself, then slid through the crack into the office.

Darkness hung heavy, no movement or shapes looming in the corner. The office faced north, and so the moonlight couldn't get in. No streetlights in this area either. He made a mental note to suggest that to the community association, see if they could write it off as citizen safety and get a tax benefit. In the small office off to the side, a computer fan hummed. He took two steps in that direction when a yell erupted, a bear's roar. A mass of black rushed at him, a giant tackled him. A bright-white spark as his head hit something metal, then nothing.

"Christ, don't kill him!" The short man yanked at the fat man's arm, dragging him back. "The hell is wrong with you?"

"I was taking care of it." He shook his hand off, looked down at the man slumped beneath him. "Oh, shit."

"Shit what?" the short man said. "Shit. What."

The fat man pointed at the patch on the unconscious man's shoulder. "Cop."

The short man crouched beside the body, pressed his finger against the underside of his chin a few seconds. "He'll live." He stood up and returned to the computer, flipped on the monitor.

Perfect timing. Install complete. He ejected the thumb drive, slipped it into his pocket, and went into the sitting area. He pointed at the sheriff, and said to the fat man, "Pick him up and lay him on the chairs. No need for him to have a stiff neck to go with the migraine."

When they exited the insurance office, he saw the other

member of the group propping himself up on the side of the building, his face split open.

"Pig sucker-punched me," he said.

The short man crouched down. "That wasn't a sucker-punch. This is," he said as he slapped his fist against the other man's cheek. When the man howled in pain, the short man quieted it with a cupped hand. He leaned in close. "You weren't paying attention and almost cost us the mission. If we're going to do this, we need one hundred percent commitment. This is too important."

The man spit blood in the dirt. "Yeah. I know. That's why I asked you to help."

"You needed my help because I'm the best programmer you know and you wouldn't be able to pull off something like this without me." He nodded to the fat man. "Help him up. We need to ghost."

"Wait a sec," the fat man said as he pulled up his injured partner. "I think we should make another stop. I saw something on the way in."

"We stick to the mission," the short man said. "You know how Teniente is."

"Yeah," the fat man said. "But I think she'll *really* like this."

# 8

Jay had spent the last hour with his earbuds in, foot tapping rapidly, listening to a Canadian thrash-punk band called Left for Dead on YouTube because he'd been up so late last night re-alphabetizing his record collection from *I* to *L* that he'd forgotten to rip the record onto his phone. A brass locust statue stared at Jay from atop three piles of neatly stacked tech spec and IP flow printouts. He'd been sifting through various chat rooms and message forums, looking for anything related to *The Crimson Ghost* or Cyclotrode X. Mostly what he found was stupid hardcore kids selling old records for exorbitant amounts of money to other kids just like them.

*What kind of asshole would pay a thousand dollars for a record?* Jay thought. *You take that* Walk Among Us *record to any normal person? They'd give you ten bucks for it or tell you they already had it on iTunes.*

Jay had even dipped into the dark web—or at least the small section he could access by establishing a proxy IP address and posing as some miscreant. It was unfortunate, tragic even, that smugglers and pederasts and drug dealers had free range of the dark and deep webs via peer-to-peer networks, while he remained penned into hell's half-acre by a picket fence constructed of legal precedent. Even that small bit had to fall within certain parameters while the Bureau collected evidence, lest the P2P networks catch wind of it and get the whole case thrown out on grounds of entrapment. Sometimes it was enough to make Jay wonder why they even tried when the odds were stacked so high against them, but that's what they did: try.

Though the dark web was verboten for work, he'd spent a lot of time trolling it in his search for Sam. At first, he used the Bureau's resources, starting with running credit cards, which was a long shot, given she was severely against banks and credit card companies and preferred to use cash, or better yet, barter to pay for things. Then he'd searched through used-car shops and activist groups in areas where she had friends, using facial recognition to scan photos posted on social media from shows her friends' bands played. Every time he traveled for work, he'd be vigilant in train stations, airport bars, slowing his car when passing bus stations to look for a tall, thin woman with bright neck tattoos.

When none of that panned out, he turned to the dark web. Scouring leftist chat rooms for any avatars that resembled The Savages, the punk band Sam sang in, or Kat Savage, her stage name. Sifting through anarcho-syndicalist and Marxist message boards for any mention of Plants Not Profits, Baltimore, anything that might lead him to her. He didn't need to prove any of this in a courtroom; he just needed to find her. But even after surfacing from the depths of the dark web, he'd always return empty-handed.

The frustration of not being able to find one goddamned lead coupled with the lack of completion in alphabetizing scratched at the inside of his head but he did his best to ignore it. Something about alphabetizing, sorting, organizing, keeping things ordered, it all helped to sedate the low-flying panic attack he constantly felt inside his head.

He tried to explain it to Sam once, when they were living with their grandmother after their mom died. Jay didn't know then that before he was thirty, he would lose his mother, father, and sister. All were for different reasons, and all of them hurt, but where his mother and father had faded with time, Sam's absence became more pronounced every year. Their grandmother hadn't been that nice a woman to start—subtly judgmental, prone to backhanded compliments, convinced Jay's father was stealing from her—and she only got worse after her daughter's death, like she thought the suicide reflected poorly on her, showed some deficiency in her own parenting.

It didn't help that their father very well could've been stealing from their grandmother. They'd cut off contact with him after he showed up to the funeral blackout drunk and tried to fight the funeral director for using too many flowers, screaming at the poor woman that she was trying to rip him off. Years later, after he'd dried out, he tried to get back in touch with them, but both Jay and Sam agreed they wanted nothing to do with him. At the time, it seemed very logical. He was toxic; they didn't need him around. But then Sam walked out and cut off contact with Jay, and he began to wonder if she was trying to tell him something. Sam was the one person in whom he'd confided, and her leaving—knowing everything that Jay was dealing with—stung in a way he couldn't articulate.

Jay had wanted to give her a peek at the buzzing and whirling that constantly happened inside his skull, to help her understand why he was the way he was. They were walking to a punk show one night and he pointed at the sidewalk and said, "You don't step on the cracks, because step on the crack and break your mother's back, right?"

She shrugged. "Sure, kid."

Then he said to imagine that lines came from the corners and quartered the square, like cutting a sandwich into small triangles, and he couldn't step on those either.

"Blow that up, Sam, and when you're riding in the car and pass a telephone pole, you have to blink. Say it's your right eye. So at the next pole, you have to blink your left eye. The next pole, left eye again, next pole right eye, because that's four times and it completes the pattern.

"But that's only one pattern; you have to do it again, but go left, right, right, left, but that's only two sets, and it has to be four for it to be correct, and to follow the larger pattern, you have to do left, right, right, left, then right, left, left, right. Once that's all done, you have to close your eyes and try to calm your breathing because you can actually feel your heart thumping inside your chest at the thought of blinking one more time because that pattern of four sets of four blinks is bulging at the seams and ready to spill out into an even larger pattern that will definitely, without a doubt, consume you whole.

"But then it's not just poles, it's holding out your pinkie and looking past it so that there are two ghost versions—a right-eye version and a left-eye one—and you have to line it up with a sidewalk curb or the straight edge of a counter, then blink right, left, left, right, et cetera, and somewhere after the migraine from constant blinking sets in, you realize there are just too many straight lines in the world.

"Now imagine all that going on inside your head," he told her, "but you can't tell anyone about it because they'll look at you like you're insane, and you've already got a mother who killed herself so you don't need more to make you stand out like a freak."

"Mom didn't kill herself," Sam said for what felt like the thousandth time in the past few weeks. She'd always been convinced that someone had killed their mother—because of the big bruise on her temple—and it was covered up as a suicide.

"I'm not arguing about this anymore, Sam," Jay said. "Cops said she did. Evidence says she did."

"You always believe the cops?"

Jay didn't bother responding. He hadn't examined the scene or anything and had never sought out the autopsy photos—because who would?—but he trusted those who had. Their mother had been acting increasingly erratic in the years leading up to her suicide. At the time, Jay had been too young to understand it, but looking back, he could see why she'd slowly unraveled. Supporting two small kids virtually by herself. A husband who wasn't around much, and was generally drunk when he was there. None of it excused what she did, but he'd spent years trying to figure her out, to pinpoint the exact moment she felt it was easier to die than take care of her children and all it had got him was anxiety attacks and hangovers. He struggled with it for a few years until he eventually realized he'd never really know why she did it, and instead shifted to trying to make peace with it, even if Sam couldn't. Or wouldn't. They continued down the sidewalk for several quiet moments.

Sam glanced up at him as they walked, maybe working something out in her head. Finally, she said, "Look, kid, you *are* a freak." She shrugged and wrapped her arm around him. "But normal's pretty boring anyway."

Jay felt a slow tearing sensation creeping up his throat at the tender thought of Sam and bit down on the edge of his tongue to stanch it when his music suddenly went dead. Immediately, he focused on his laptop, afraid that somehow, someone had bypassed his secure connection and started shutting down his machine. Then he heard the song coming from the small computer speakers and saw ASAC Dalworth, plug-end of the cord dangling from his hand. A woman stood beside him. Nearly as tall as Dalworth. Light-brown skin, dark hair with streaks of blonde scattered through it.

"At least pretend you care about the rest of us," Dalworth said.

Jay snapped out of it.

"I figured you for Hootie and the Blowfish," she said, "not Blow-up-a-Church."

Jay raised his eyebrows. "Why do you think I was wearing headphones?"

Dalworth motioned toward her. "Jay Brodsky, this is Special Agent Paloma Vargas, from the Pittsburgh office. Agent Vargas, Agent Brodsky."

"Nice to meet you." She shook his hand. Her skin was soft but Jay nearly winced at her grip.

"Sorry to hear that, Agent Vargas," he said.

"Pardon me?" She cocked her head.

Jay shrugged. "You know. Pittsburgh."

"Ah." Agent Vargas nodded. "Says the man who lives in Baltimore."

Jay paused a second, then said, "Touché."

Dalworth cleared his throat. "Agent Vargas was on the Roshetnikov Brothers casino case."

Jay arched his eyebrows. "Impressive."

"Agent Vargas is from Domestic Terrorism. She'll be assisting us on this case."

"Great," Jay said.

Dalworth turned to Vargas. "Agent Brodsky has been leading the team in scouring the field as to the identity of the group but hasn't unearthed anything yet."

Jay held his hands up. "We know plenty about them. We're just looking for the clue that pulls it all together."

Dalworth gave a tight smile and handed Jay another folder. "Maybe this will help."

Jay flew through the pages, talking to himself as he read the details of the Patrick & Sons hack.

Once he finished, he closed the folder and looked up. "It's the same goddamned thing. The ghosts, the locust, the billing records." Jay tossed it on his desk and ran his fingers through his hair, pulling on it until he felt pressure at the roots. Blinked his right eye, his left, his left, his right.

"Except they haven't found a way into the Bay State or Tidewater systems proper." Dalworth cleared his throat. "Yet."

Jay's head drooped. "When did this happen?"

"I heard something today from a source. The CEOs have ordered an internal investigation to avoid investor panic, but my source sounded pretty worried."

Agent Vargas laughed to herself. "Imagine what we could do if we were allowed to do our job."

"As of now, this new hack has already infiltrated seven other locations. Two other insurance brokers and five community clinics."

"Any connection to Bay State or Tidewater?"

"No. This one's Exemplar, but they're the largest in the country, so that's not terribly surprising."

"I know you're going for encouraging but…," Jay said.

Dalworth continued. "Only other difference is a responding officer was assaulted during this break-in—he's fine, just happened to be passing by during the incident—and this one didn't seem random, like Community Health did. Remember the mine explosion in West Virginia, what, two years ago? This Patrick guy backed most of them and inserted—how would you say it?—*convenient* language that allowed his provider to deny everyone's claims."

"Even though it was the mine's fault."

Dalworth nodded. "Not saying that's why they hit this place, but it's something to keep in mind."

Jay leaned back in his chair, thinking a moment. "This is a big step. They've crossed state lines."

"Crossing state lines does help our case."

"No," Jay said. "I mean that they're showing us what they can do."

"If they can do it in one state, they can do it in any state," Vargas said.

Jay nodded. "*Every* state."

"Well, that's why Agent Vargas is here. And Pentress, West Virginia, is four hours away so I'd suggest you get moving."

"Who's going to swear for the warrants?"

Dalworth looked around. "Where's your life partner?"

Jay shrugged.

Dalworth scratched his chin. "Give him a call, see if he can. If not, I will." Jay cocked his head, slightly taken aback by his ASAC's involvement. "The healthcare industry accounts for about twenty percent of the nation's economy. So you can imagine we have a lot of eyes on us right now. You two need to get out there,

40

and we don't have time to sit and play pocket pool while these jokers are running around out there."

"Thanks for the help," Jay said.

Dalworth nodded to Vargas. "Agent Vargas, thank you for coming, and I appreciate ASAC Hart loaning you out. Let me know if I can do anything else for you."

She shook his hand. Then he turned on his heels and left.

It didn't surprise Jay to see another agent, and if he had to have a ride-along, he could do worse. At least he wouldn't have to listen to Yemin yammer on for hours about building a bed for his kids. Jay made a mental note to watch that X-wing video when he got back.

"Agent Vargas," Jay said, "you ready to see God's country?"

# 9

It took Jay a few calls to track down Yemin, who answered with, "What favor do you need now and how soon will you help me build this if I do it?" It had cost Jay a weekend in the near future, but by the time they passed Hagerstown, Jay had the warrants in motion and had brought Vargas up to speed.

"What do you think this is about?" Vargas dug through her purse, unearthing a pack of tissues, cell phone, a rolled-up reusable bag, and a compact umbrella into her lap before finally pulling out a granola bar. She dumped the contents back in, opened the bar, and dropped the wrapper on the floor.

Jay glanced down at the wrapper, his lips twitching. "Didn't we just spend twenty minutes talking about this?"

"I understand what is happening with the case. What I'm saying is, what do they want? Why are they doing it?"

"Does it matter?" Jay took the ramp where I-70 split off to I-68, heading west.

"You don't want to know what makes them work? You don't think that helps you track them?"

"I'm not as concerned in why as in what and when." Jay glanced at the wrapper again. They had known each other three hours. Over the years, Jay had learned to keep a stoic face and contain his tics. Unless he was incredibly tired or stressed, most people didn't notice the arranging, the patterns, the oddness. Sam's presence had been the bulwark against whatever black shadows lapped inside his skull, and it got worse every year around this time, but this time it felt especially difficult. It'd be nice to have a fresh start with someone, especially someone like Vargas. Still, there were lines and then there were lines. "There's a plastic bag behind your seat I use for trash."

"Okay." She bit into the bar, crumbs sticking to her lips. Jay looked at her. "Right," she said, and stuck the wrapper in the bag.

"Sorry, it's just, you know...," Jay trailed off. He didn't want to be a pain in the ass so soon after meeting her, but knew he'd see nothing but the wrapper for the remainder of the drive if it weren't put away. He held his pinkie out, lined it up with the white line on the side of the road, blinked right, left, left, right. In the corner of his eye, he saw her watching him. Finally, she got back to the point.

"What I'm saying is, we're looking for something that unites these hacks, correct? Are these socially motivated? Is that why they hit this asshole who denied everyone's claims? Or is that incidental and they targeted him because he's a predatory agent with a lot of clients and he's a soft touch and they're actually trying to throw the economy into chaos?"

"Isn't that splitting hairs? They still wiped everything out. Every day they go free increases the chance that they can hit other states and turn this into a national crisis. Or shit, even a global one. You saw what happened during the Lehman Brothers crash. Everyone got hurt. A lot of people still haven't recovered."

"That's ominous."

"Ominous, sure, but also possible."

"No," Vargas said, pointing out her window. "That. Beginning of Hurricane Donovan?"

Jay glanced out the passenger side and saw a thick mass of black clouds strafing between mountain peaks, stretching across the highway.

"Hurricane isn't supposed to make landfall for a few more

days. I'm hoping it skips north of us," Jay said. "There's a saying in Maryland that if you don't like the weather, just wait five minutes and it'll change. It was never this bad when I was a kid, though. Unpredictable patterns. More violence and destruction. Tearing things down and uprooting what used to be planted. It's getting really dangerous."

"We're still talking about weather, right?"

Jay peeled back the lid of the coffee he'd bought at Sheetz when they stopped for gas, and blew off some steam before taking a sip. It tasted like old socks fished from the bottom of a planter after a rainstorm, then wrung out and baked in the sun. They had to get off the road when the band of storms tore through, the rain falling so hard and fast that Jay couldn't go more than twenty-five and, even that slow, full-speed windshield wipers were as useless as if they were turned off. He figured if they had time to kill, coffee would be a good way to kill it, especially after the long drive.

"Who was that in your wallet?" Vargas said when they got back in the car. "If you don't mind me asking."

Jay stiffened, didn't realize she'd seen the photo inside the gas station. "Family photo. Mostly."

"You mind if I see it?"

Jay swallowed. He never showed it to anyone, just carried it for personal reasons, some small way to remain close to his mother and sister. But not showing it to her would make him seem even weirder after the granola bar wrapper, so he pulled his wallet from his pocket, slipped out the photo.

They were at a protest—which seemed to be where they spent every weekend—this one against the Reagan administration selling arms to Iran, holding illustrated signs of Reagan with a nuclear bomb sticking through the fly of his pants. Jay was on his mom's shoulders, Sam standing beside them. She looked about ten, smiling wide with that gap between her front two teeth. This photo was taken about ten minutes before the riot police opened a fire hose on the protestors, knocking Jay from his mom's shoulders, which is how he got the scar on the back of his head, now covered by his hair. Every time Jay looked at the photo, he discovered something new—the freckles on his mother's cheek, a new sign he hadn't seen, the man behind them checking out his mother, a piece of food stuck to Sam's face. It was the last photo they'd taken together; his mom would kill herself later that night. He would've expected everything about the situation surrounding the photo to be vivid in his mind, being so momentous, but the whole scene felt nebulous. A memory of a memory.

"This is your sister?"

Jay nodded.

"Your mother's beautiful. You all look really happy. You still close?"

Jay chewed on the inside of his cheek. "Mom died when I was young. I haven't seen Sam for a while."

Vargas started to say something, as if wanting to ask what happened, but graciously cut herself short. She breathed out a quick laugh. "You were a cute kid."

"Thanks?"

"What happened?" She opened the bag of Utz crab chips Jay had bought for her. Jay slid the photo back into his wallet, fighting back a smile.

"It's a tragedy you've never had those before." He nodded at the chips. "You're obviously not from Maryland. So where are you from?"

"Born in El Salvador but moved here when I was little to get away from all the problems there. Ended up in El Paso for a while, then I got assigned to Pittsburgh after Quantico."

She tilted the bag toward him, offering to share. He couldn't resist. To Baltimorons like him, Old Bay might as well have dope mixed in it.

"So Pittsburgh is the Bureau's fault," Jay said, taking the

ramp to Route 7, which would lead them to Pentress.

"You should've figured that. One way or another," she said, wiping her hands on a napkin, then making a show of putting it all in the trash bag, "the government is screwing us over."

"You would've gotten along well with my family." Jay turned up the volume on the radio before she could ask what he meant.

NPR was playing a story about the Baltimore hack and how it had spread within the insurance providers. There was a clip from Ron Kuzak, CEO of Tidewater Mutual, giving the usual line about everything being under control and their customers' privacy being the most important thing, but Jay could hear in his voice that he was damn terrified. Probably livid, as well, that someone had leaked information about the incursion to the press so Tidewater couldn't bury it. The reporter went on to outline the impacts of a national economic crisis were this to spread further.

They needed to get a bead on this before every fourteen-year-old who'd watched *Mr. Robot* too many times fancied himself the chosen one and took on The Man. And before the Crimson Ghosts decided it was time to end the beta testing and show the country what they were capable of.

# 10

Jay had hoped the group would slip up as the stakes got higher, but as he stood in front of the monitor, staring at the skeleton draped in a red robe and laughing at him, he knew they wouldn't be so lucky.

He and Vargas had already walked through the insurance office, interviewed both employees and the owner, and they had zero fingerprints, zero frames of security footage, and zero additional leads. Sure, Dwight Patrick had pissed off a lot of locals over the years, but this had to be the same group as the health clinic hack. There was no other explanation.

"That really is creepy," Vargas said.

"You've heard the recording, right?"

Vargas nodded. "Seeing it in real life is different, though. Standing in this office, knowing they were here, going through this guy's stuff, typing away on that keyboard, watching the virus upload and disappear into the ether. And they were standing right here less than twelve hours ago."

"We're going to get them, Vargas," he said, laying his hand on her shoulder, then immediately removing it. "They have to slip sometime, and when they do, we'll be there."

Vargas gave a slight smile. "I appreciate the pep talk—"

"No problem."

"But I wasn't asking for it. I'm angry, not upset." She cupped his chin in a patronizing way. Jay fought against a smile—both because he was embarrassed and because her skin was warm—but lost.

"Fair enough."

She patted him on the cheek and told him to question the sheriff while she took care of the CPU and locust sculpture.

While Vargas bagged up the evidence, Jay went outside to speak with the deputy sheriff who'd called it in. Younger guy, probably a few years under Jay. Well-built, too, and sporting a sizable gash on the side of his head and a constellation of bruises on the right side of his face. Jay wasn't sure if the fatness beneath his lip was swelling or chaw.

"I should see the other guy, right?" Jay said.

"Hell, I hope you do. Then hold him back a minute so I can tune him up."

"Be careful who you say that to."

"I don't give a good goddamn who hears it." Sweeney spit from the side of his mouth, a brown arc that splattered on the ground beside another dark splotch.

Jay squinted against the sun, held his right hand like a shelf over his eyes. He hated wearing sunglasses because he thought they made him look like an FBI douche, but damned if they wouldn't be nice right now. Even with all the mountains and pine trees stretching up toward the brilliant blue sky, there were no buildings to block out the light, and he felt like he was being interrogated by God. He imagined black clouds working their way toward Baltimore.

"I read that it was dark, so you couldn't see much," Jay said, "but is there anything else you can remember about it?"

Sweeney shook his head. "Just that it was three of them. The strong one watched outside. Short one inside. An obese one with him." He paused. "That's impolite, even if the asshole did try to crush me. He wasn't obese, more like Texas-big, like he's proud to have his name on the wall for eating a seventy-two-ounce steak in one sitting."

Jay laughed. An evocative description, though he didn't think it would help much on a *Wanted* poster. Still, the descriptions matched the ones Raymond Cody had given at Community Health, which was something to work with. Jay handed Sweeney his card. "You think of anything else, you let me know."

As he was walking back to the car, Vargas nudged his arm, nodded at the liquor store across the street.

"I'm driving." Jay held up his hands. "But I won't tell Dalworth if you need a nip."

Vargas shook her head, then set the evidence bag on the back seat floor. "I don't day-drink." She shut the car door. "But while I'm over there questioning the owner—who most likely has a security tape—I'd be happy to pick up some Zima for you."

"Very kind of you, hon. But if you were any kind of detective, you'd know I'm the white-zin-with-three-ice-cubes type."

Vargas smirked. "You are such a dick."

Jay was still watching her cross the street when Dwight Patrick called his name, hustled up behind him.

"Agent Brodsky," he said, laying a hand on Jay's shoulder as he caught his breath. Red splotches covered the man's cheeks beneath a thin coating of rust-colored whiskers. "What do I do now?"

Jay reached up and squeezed the opposite shoulder, balancing out. He nodded across the street. "Agent Vargas and I will continue the investigation. I'd suggest you get your office back in order, file all the necessary paperwork with the banks and whoever else needs to be involved. It'll be hard, I'm sure, but you need to try to move past this and get on with your life."

"I'm just supposed to sit on my hands and let these shitheels ride around the county with my information?"

Jay shook his head. "We don't know what their motive was, or what they were looking for, or what they now own."

"I'll tell you what they—"

"What I'm saying, Mister Patrick, is that we need to work the investigation, and that will take time."

Dwight Patrick chewed on his lip like it was a rubber band. "What am I supposed to do? What about my business, my family?"

Jay had never found an easy way to have this conversation. No matter how tactful his words, there was nothing he could say or do that would unwind the tape, present a different outcome for the victims, even if the victim did seem to be a prick.

"Honestly, sir? That's between you and the insurance company. You still have my card, right?" The man nodded. "We'll keep you updated as best we can. They'll have our report to draw on, but figuring out all that is their specialty. If you run into any issues with them, or if you see anything happening around here, you give me a call. I've got no sway with the insurance, but I can—and will—catch the people who did this. That I can promise you."

That seemed to help a little, set Patrick's shoulders at ease, but that was about the end of it for Jay. He knew the insurance companies might try to screw the man—though he was sure Dwight Patrick would do his best to screw them first—but all Jay could do was live up to his promise. And he intended to.


By the time he got over to the liquor store, Vargas was already crouched behind the counter, scanning the security tape. Jay nodded at the older man standing behind her, shook his hand, and flashed credentials.

"I appreciate you letting us use your equipment," he said.

The man ran his hand over his close-cropped hair, a thin blanket of ash.

"You lock them up, they won't be coming by my store and I won't have to shoot them in the ass, so I figure y'all're doing me the favor."

Jay couldn't argue with that logic.

"The deputy's description matches the one I got at Community Health. Anything promising over here?" he said to Vargas.

The camera, attached to the back wall, looked out over the store's shelves and halfway across the street. Jay figured they wouldn't get lucky enough to see the opposite parking lot, but maybe they could get a partial plate, or at the very least, the make and model.

"Not yet. Got about thirty minutes till the deputy's call comes in."

The three of them stood there watching, their eyes loose as the night sped by beneath the orange tint of the store's security lighting. The occasional glow of headlights. The flash of a deer passing by the window.

Vargas hit play and said, "And here we go."

The screen remained the same for a few seconds before the red reflection cast on the window turned to white.

"They're in the car and backing up," she said. A dark shape moved past the camera, then a lighter circle. "Rear wheel driving past, and gone. Shit, nothing."

She turned to look up at Jay. Jay pinched his bottom lip and shook his head.

"Play it back."

He crouched down beside her, both of them with their noses a couple inches from the monitor.

The sixth time the car backed up, Jay grabbed Vargas's arm. "Pause it."

She hit pause, then backed up a couple frames. "What? I don't see anything."

"There." Jay leaned forward, his forehead nearly on the screen, and touched the center of the white glow. "A reflection."

Vargas got close and looked a minute. She shook her head. "A reflection of the reversing lights?"

"Look in the middle." He pulled out his phone and snapped a few pictures, then stood and took a few of the view from the store for context and positioning. "It's faint, but it's there."

"I still don't get it," she said.

Jay flipped back to his photos and found the clearest one,

enlarged it for her. She crowded close to see, and he could smell the cocoa butter lotion on her skin, a faint chocolate smell. She took his phone from him and enlarged the picture to the max, then shook her head and clucked her tongue.

"You lucky bastard," she said.

"Got to be good to get lucky," he said, stepping outside. He emailed the photo to Jeanie, then called the field office and was forwarded to the techs' room.

"Jeanie, this is Agent Brodsky. I just sent you a photo of a license plate. Can you run it through NCIC and see what pings?"

"Absolutely. Are you out of the office?"

"For most of the day, yeah. Call my cell. But you're going to need some image sharpening and enhancement for confirmation. Sorry, the photo's pretty grainy, but I think I can get a read on it." Jay squinted and read off the numbers and letters. "Double-check it but that should be pretty close. Just run the adjacent plates."

"No problem," she said. "Call you when I have something."

As soon as Jay hung up, his phone rang again.

"Hey, sweetheart."

"You ain't going to be loving me so much in a minute," Yemin said. "Just got word there was another hack."

Jay felt a sinking sensation in his stomach. "Please tell me it's not in Pennsylvania or something."

"No, it's in Maryland. Outside Frederick, actually."

"But?"

"It's a furrier. You know, like fur coats and hats and shit."

"Yeah, Ari, I can figure that out from the name. Did this just happen?"

"Happened last night, about eleven-thirty. Buechner Furriers. Or Furrier. I don't know how that works. Anyway, they hacked the computer and left the Ghost calling card. But," Yemin said, "to get in, they threw a brick through the window, then trashed the place."

*That's different,* Jay thought. *And not disciplined like the other two hacks were.*

"Fake blood thrown all over the furs, ghost faces painted on the mannequins."

"Jesus Christ." He heard bells tinkling, Vargas walking out of the liquor store with a paper bag in her hand. Jay cocked his head.

"But the good news is: local pulled a footprint. Looks like a boot, size eleven to thirteen, but Forensics is working on it right now."

"Great. Send me the information and we'll check it on our way back."

Jay hung up.

"You did good," she said, handing him the bag with a straight face. "Thought you deserved a treat."

Jay pulled out a bottle of wine. White zin. He tried not to smile but couldn't help it.

"You forgot the ice cubes," he said.

She nodded at the phone in Jay's hand. "Who was that?"

"Yemin. Apparently, there was another hack last night. Buechner Furriers, outside Frederick."

"I have to say, that's a kind of terrorist strike I've never seen."

Her tone made Jay flash back to dinner-table conversation from his childhood, his mother and father giving impassioned speeches about post-colonialism and the need for self-rule. He'd been too young to understand what they were saying, but even then he could tell their conversations never quite synced, more like they just wanted someone else to hear their opinions so they'd feel validated. He shook off the memory.

"What do furs and insurance have to do with each other?" Vargas said.

Jay shrugged. "Let's go find out."

# 11

"This," Vargas said, the car now back on the interstate with the sun behind them, "this complicates things."

"Actually, I'm thinking it might clarify things a little."

Vargas bit the edge of a fingernail. "Explain."

"The Crimson Ghosts hit a medical clinic—"

"Wait, what?"

"What?"

"Is that what they're calling themselves?" Vargas spit a piece of nail out the window.

"Well, no, it's kind of a shorthand I made up."

"That's derivative, don't you think?"

Jay chose not to comment. "Regardless, the Crimson Ghosts hit the clinic, infecting the server and erasing all the billing records. We get a brass locust and a skeleton with a creepy message. That infection spreads to twenty-two other sites within a few days—"

"Serviced by two gigantic insurance companies."

"Correct. And now spread across to another state, increasing the odds that this will go national and completely fuck us up."

"Motives include terrorism and maybe some kind of social commentary?"

"Definitely social commentary. The furrier has absolutely nothing to with the other two hacks. They don't offer insurance and there's no direct pipeline to a company. They bank with a local federal credit union, so there's no hope of, say, spreading into Wells Fargo like they did Tidewater. This one is personal, especially with them painting the mannequins."

"Which is likely why they slipped up and left a footprint." Vargas rubbed her temples. "This new thing, though—especially if you look at it within the context of them erasing all those insurance payments and letting people get a fresh start—that starts tipping it toward being a home-grown activist group we need to monitor."

Jay shook his head. "Activism is just politically correct terrorism."

"You are such a cynic."

Jay took a long breath and leaned forward against the wheel. He felt a sharp jab of nostalgia, this conversation feeling awfully familiar. "I'm a realist."

He glanced over at her. "You know who the Sandinistas are?"

"You know El Salvador and Nicaragua are different countries?"

"Just answer the question."

"Of course."

"They took up arms to defend themselves and the people against a dictator. So were they terrorists or activists?"

Vargas moved away. "For being a federal agent, you're pretty shit when it comes to nuance. I know where you're going to try to take this, but you have to remember the Crimson Ghosts haven't killed anyone."

"Not yet. But again, you saw what happened a couple years ago with the crash. People lost their damn minds. Destabilizing things again—when they aren't particularly stable anyway—and creating a constant state of alert for new terrorist attacks? It wouldn't take much to push people from vigilance into full-on panic."

"We are not there yet." Vargas closed her eyes. Jay watched her take a few breaths. "Instead, can we please focus on our case to keep things from getting to that point? Starting with what we know about Buechner."

"They sell fur coats and are located near Frederick."

"That's not what I meant." Vargas dumped her purse on her lap and extracted her phone. She left everything in her lap and asked Jay to spell the name while she searched.

The conversation gave Jay an eerie sense of déjà vu. He couldn't count how many times he'd had variations of this argument with Sam, most of the time while they were working with Plants Not Profits, a grassroots organization that served vegan food to the needy in the city, because what else were they going to do while standing behind a table for six hours?

They worked with the group a lot anyway when they were teens, but had a tradition to make sure they volunteered on the anniversary of their mother's death, to commemorate her passing with service, as she would've liked. This time, on the tenth anniversary, they were working the table beneath a bright-blue July sky. He'd turned sixteen a few months earlier, and Sam was scheduled to head out on a three-week tour in a few days, crossing the country and edging up into Canada with Jesuseater, one of the biggest bands in the area—and her favorite. Their singer had been picked up on an outstanding warrant and the band had asked Sam to fill in. It would be the first time Sam and Jay had been apart for more than a day.

Sam was busy giving out anarchist literature to people while Jay scooped bowls of ginger sweet pepper rice and casserole with carrots, potato, and eggplant, annoyed she was railing against the inherent hierarchy of capitalism while he did all the grunt work. It didn't help that Sam kept using several phrases he'd heard their mom use. Her presence still hung heavy, even years later, from inspiring Sam to level-up her activism to the turquoise earrings she'd taken to wearing.

"It's informing the public of their rights and providing them alternate choices." Sam saw Jay's deadpan look and stuck out her tongue. She raised her arms and gestured around. "And besides, what better thing to do today than this? It's a gorgeous day, we're helping people, and Mom is looking down on this and loving it."

Jay plopped a serving of rice into a man's paper bowl and gave him a fake smile. "If she loved it so much, she should've stayed. She could've done it all the time."

Jay saw Sam deflate. He felt bad, but part of him was relieved. Why should he be the only one upset?

"She just wanted what we all want, JJ," she said. "Freedom."

"Shut the fuck up. How does killing yourself equal freedom?"

"Maybe freedom's not the right word. Something closer to liberation. You don't understand what it's like to be a woman," she said. "To feel the pressure to look pretty and act smart—but not too pretty or too smart—and stay feminine but be able to hold your own against the boys and be cool but not too cool because that could be slutty."

"So?"

"So? You wake up three days in a row wearing the same clothes and no one blinks." She pointed at his blue T-shirt and khaki shorts. "But she had to raise two crazy-ass kids pretty much by herself, while making enough money to let us eat and keep us clothed and safe, and then try to keep some shadow of her former life so she felt like herself. You just have no idea."

Jay motioned at the patches on her black denim sleeveless vest and combat boots. "Apparently you don't worry about those expectations too much."

Sam barked out a laugh. "Fuck that noise. It's my life, I live it my way."

"This is not about feminism, and it is not about politics."

"The personal is political."

Jay scoffed. "Put it on a back patch, okay?"

"She was an inspiration. She might've been taken from us—"

"She committed suicide."

Sam repeated herself for effect, putting special emphasis on every word. "She might've been taken from us but we were still lucky to have her. Remember what she said? *Maldito sea el soldado que vuelva las armas contra su pueblo.* Cursed is the soldier who turns arms against his people."

"Jesus Christ, you don't even speak Spanish. You just memorize lines because you think you're...Chick Guevara or something."

"Hey, I'm learning. And I don't have to speak it to understand its truth."

"Here's some truth: she could've lived and stayed with us, or killed herself and left us. And which did she choose? There's your truth."

"JJ," she said, but had nothing to follow with.

"Whatever. It doesn't matter," Jay said. "Everyone leaves anyway. Everyone ends up alone."

Sam just stared at him, chewing on her bottom lip.

Jay popped the serving tray from its holder. "We need more rice," he said as he walked away.

Later that afternoon, back at the church basement that acted as the Plants Not Profits headquarters, Jay was scrubbing pots when Sam came up beside him.

"I talked to Rico," Sam said, sliding another serving dish into the soapy water. "Shauna from War on Women is going to sing for them."

Jay dropped the sponge into the water. "What?"

"It's a better fit, really. Her voice is deeper than mine. And if I scream every night, I'll blow out my voice within a week."

"Sam, no," Jay said, shaking his head.

"It's fine. It's already done. This is Rico's last tour with them anyway. He's getting tired of that band and wants to focus more on The Savages when they get back. We'll get our shit together and start touring in a year or two."

*Once I leave for college,* Jay thought.

"Sam," Jay said again.

Sam wrapped her arms around Jay, squeezing him tight. He remembered the way the shaved side of her head itched his nose and the lingering smell of sweat.

"I have to put away the rest of the food before the rats get it." She turned and walked up the worn wooden steps of the church basement. Jay stood there, feeling relieved that she was staying, and feeling like a gigantic asshole for feeling relieved.

But looking back on it, Jay thought, it was the beginning of the end.

Vargas spoke up, snapping Jay to attention.

"What? Yeah, I'm listening."

Vargas creased her eyebrows, cleared her throat. "Apparently the Buechner store has been hit three times in the last five years. Firebombed twice, cinder block through the front window once, after which all the furs were covered with red paint."

"But no record of the painted faces?"

"Correct." Vargas mumbled to herself as she skimmed her phone. In front of them, the buildings of Cumberland rose from the trees. They always gave Jay a distinctly Russian feeling, with their bulbous, onion-shaped caps and gold paint. It was totally incongruent with the rest of the Maryland countryside, which wasn't completely unexpected, given Marylanders' eclectic tastes. "All three previous attacks were suspected to be initiated by the ADB."

Jay nodded, remembering Sam talking about them years ago. "Animal Defense Bloc. Like PETA on steroids."

Vargas gave him a look, lips pursed and eyebrow cocked. "Yes, I know. Founded in 1981 by Chris Louis. Active in forty countries. Responsible for hundreds of bombings and arson attacks in the US and worldwide. Wearers of the same black balaclavas our Ghosts are so fond of, as are the IRA."

"Maybe the IRA is moving in on the lucrative Maryland fur business."

"At least we'd have priors then. Even though the Ghosts weren't involved with the prior attacks, at least not in this kind of way, we can reasonably say there might be overlap, no?" Vargas returned to her phone. "In all three attacks on Buechner, only one person was ever convicted. Luke Jennings."

"It's worth a try. Where is he now?"

Vargas glanced up, looked out the window, and smiled. "Take the next exit."

Jay gave the *yes, ma'am* nod as they passed a sign on the side of the road: *Federal Correctional Institution, Cumberland.*

# 12

Jay and Vargas sat in the middle of a row of blue plastic chairs in the visitor waiting room, the whole thing bolted into a concrete floor painted gray. The walls were stark white, only a few finger-print smears on them.

"They've redone the place," Vargas said, surveying the room and nodding with approval. "Looks a lot better."

Jay leaned back and looked at her. "Excuse me?"

"It's hard to find a single man out there." She said it so deadpan that Jay almost had trouble deciding if she was being sarcastic or candid. She glanced at him from the corner of her eye and smirked. "I started in Organized Crime, which brought me into Domestic Terrorism. There's a guy in here, Little Vic Amuso, he was boss of the Lucchese family."

Jay's head dropped a touch. "You took out the head of the Lucchese family?"

"Me?" She laughed. "Hell no. He went away in the early Nineties. But we suspected he'd ordered a hit on the foreman of a stevedore union. Amuso thought the guy was 'losing' ship-ments and then selling them to some Haitians in Brooklyn."

"You get him for it?"

Vargas shook her head. "The witness said he forgot what the guy looked like."

"They got to him."

"No, he had Alzheimer's." A buzzing sound. Vargas reached

61

for her phone.

"Really? Alzheimer's?" Jay said.

"No, of course they got to him." Vargas cursed to herself as she saw the number on her phone. "I have to take this," she said, then stepped out of the waiting area.

Jay leaned forward, resting his forearms on his knees, and realized he was watching her leave. He stood up and went to the visitation desk, separated from the rest of the waiting area by a two-inch-thick piece of Plexiglass.

When the man behind the desk finished his phone call, Jay said, "I need a list of everyone who has visited Luke Jennings."

"What month?" the clerk said.

Jay stared through the man. "All of them."

It took the clerk a little while to get the list, something Jay thought more indicative of the employment requirements than the reams of visitors Jennings had. Part of him wanted to get the man to unlock the door so he could do it himself. It would have been faster.

Jay skimmed through the list. Five different Jenningses, likely all relatives. One Father Bergman, which Jay thought odd. He paused on one name, Patrick Felder, letting it float around his head. It sounded familiar but he couldn't place it. Maybe an old case, someone he'd interviewed once. He underlined the name as a reminder to look into it later, then continued scanning, flipping to the second page.

He froze on the third name. Blinked a couple times, then returned to the first page as if there had been something he'd missed, but no, the name was still there, pulsing in jet-black ink.

*Breathe, be aware, count.*

It didn't help.

Kiki Laughton.

It was his mother's maiden name—nickname and maiden name, actually—but she had been dead nearly twenty years. Only two people would ever know that name. One was his father, who moved to western Massachusetts years ago, and to whom Jay hadn't spoken in nearly three decades.

The other was Sam.

His skin prickled, feeling Sam's presence everywhere, a reflexive, comforting sensation that quickly dissipated when he understood the context.

Why the fuck did his sister visit Luke Jennings three months ago, in a prison less than two hours from Baltimore, after she hadn't spoken to her brother in seven years? Sure, they hadn't ended on good terms, but blood was still blood, so why had she chosen this shitbird over her own brother?

Jay's chest quivered, rose and fell. He flicked the base of his neck four times on the right with his right hand, four times on the left with his left. There was some explanation for it. Jennings—or whatever he was involved in—must have been related to Sam's disappearance. Did she go stay with him after she left? Were they having an affair? Was that why Sam's girlfriend had been so weirded out when Jay had gone to their apartment searching for her after she hadn't answered his calls? None of it made sense to him. He extended his pinkie and lined it up over the edge of the paper. *Right, left, left, right. Breathe, be aware, count. Breathe, be aware, count.*

"What's that?" Vargas said, her voice suddenly next to him. Jay nearly jumped. He flipped back to the first page to keep Sam's name hidden.

He looked up from the papers. The skin around Vargas's eyes looked red, as if she'd been pressing on them. Her mouth tighter than usual.

"Everything okay?" Jay said.

"I'm fine. What's that?"

"Checking the visitor log." Jay lowered the papers to his side, slid his other hand in his pocket to keep it still. "What's wrong?"

"I said I'm fine."

Jay loosened his posture, putting on a faint smile. "I'll figure it out. You probably don't know this about me, but I am equipped with keen deductive skills."

She stepped into him, her hips swaying, almost sensual, and put her face inches from his, close enough he could see the soft lines at the edges of her lips. She laid a hand in the middle of his chest.

"Will you be able to deduct my foot from your ass if you don't drop it?"

Jay pursed his lips. "So nothing's wrong, then."

"Exactly." She patted his cheek.

A voice called out behind them. "Agent Vargas, Agent Brodsky?"

"Right here," Vargas said.

As she turned, Jay ripped the second page off and stuffed it in his back pocket, then followed Vargas into the visitation room. He didn't have the urge to touch his chest, felt no need to rebalance.

# 13

A spider web wove beneath a cascade of skulls down Luke Jennings's arms—one skull with a mohawk, one with an axe in its forehead, another overlaid by an American flag pattern, which Jay figured was supposed to be some kind of political statement. Resting below that, a faded dragon and something Jay thought was a wizard but had spread out and hued so far green it was unrecognizable. His knuckles read ACAB—All Cops Are Bastards, an old punk saying. He slouched forward, elbows resting on the stainless-steel ledge of the visitation booth, the phone hanging loosely from his fingertips.

"I know you?" he said into the mouthpiece. His jet-black hair was slicked back off his forehead, and his cheeks had a rosy hue despite his spending the last two years in jail, though the underside of his chin wobbled when he spoke.

Jay introduced himself and Vargas, showed their credentials. "We need to know what you know about Buechner Furriers."

Jennings cocked his head. "Is this a double jeopardy kind of thing? Y'all can't lock me up for what I'm already locked up for."

"Double jeopardy is when you're acquitted," Vargas said. "Answer the question, Mister Jennings."

Jennings arched an eyebrow, looked at Jay, and bobbled his head, as if saying *nice catch*.

"Buechner Furriers was recently attacked," Jay said. "The

ADB previously claimed responsibility, but you're the only one who went down for it."

"Whoa, whoa." Jennings held a hand up. "I'm not ADB. I never said that."

"I know," Jay said. "That was a smart move on your lawyer's part, separating you from them. They would've gotten you labeled a terrorist, sent you to some black site in backwater Russia. But you did work with them."

"Buechner got hit again, with a cyber-attack thrown in this time, and we need to know who might have done it," Vargas said. "That's where you come in."

"I've been inside two years. What the hell do I know about it?"

"You knew people who were interested before. I'm sure you still hear stuff," Jay said. "Someone who's angry, a couple people looking for work…"

Vargas picked up on the rhythm. "You give us some help, point us to a couple people, we can talk to a judge and see about getting your sentence reduced." Vargas paused a moment, letting it sink in. "But this is all conditional on you giving us real names of real people. No runaround horseshit, got me?"

"I give you names and you'll get me out early?" Jennings barked out a laugh, ran his hand over his hair. "Number one, I snitch on someone in the ADB, they'll get word inside and I'll get a sharpened chicken bone in the shower."

"That would be ironic," Jay said.

"Number two, why the hell would I want to get out early? In here, I tattoo half the inmates and no one messes with me." Jennings pressed a finger against the smeared Plexiglass separating them. "Out there? I was sleeping in a squat and eating food from trash cans. Shit, I love it in here. I might cut someone just to stick around longer."

Jay leaned back in his seat while Jennings mugged it up, gloating before the agents. Vargas held her hand over the mouthpiece and glanced at Jay. "Now what?"

"Did Patrick Felder have anything to do with it?" he said to Jennings.

The flinch was slight, but enough that Jay knew he'd hit something.

"I don't even know who that is," Jennings said.

Jay bit the inside of his lip, uncomfortable with bringing his sister into this when he didn't know how she fit in, especially with Vargas sitting right there.

"You know Matty Pants?" Jay said, throwing out a punk rock name he knew from years ago.

"That dude's like a hundred twenty."

"Ben Wah?"

"Seriously?" Jennings laughed. "You know he runs his own butcher shop, right?"

"What about Kat Savage? She have anything to do with it?"

Jennings's smile flatlined. Jay's stomach sank.

Kat Savage was Sam's stage name.

"I got nothing to say to you, man." Jennings pushed the words through his teeth.

"Okay, that's fine," Jay said. "While you stay quiet, I'll give my buddy Angel over at DOJ a call, see about getting your cell flipped, machines confiscated, maybe spend a couple weeks in the hole. We'll see how many packs of ramen you get after that."

Jay started to hang up the phone, but Jennings nearly jumped from his seat.

"Okay," he said, holding up his hand. "Okay, Jesus Christ, you don't have to be a dick about it."

"What about her?"

Vargas whispered to him, "Who the hell is she?" Jay shook his head, waiting for Jennings.

"Kat Savage." Jennings shook his head and whistled, his face seemingly lighter at the mere thought of her. Jay ground his teeth, her signature on the visitor log pulsing inside his skull. "Man, if you thought she was intense on stage, spend a night with her. Jesus, I thought my dick was going to break off the way she was going at me—"

Jay sprang from his chair, jumping toward the Plexiglas, his arm held back. Vargas jumped up and grabbed his forearm, dragging him back to the metal seat. She threw his arm back, squaring up. *What is your deal?* she mouthed.

"We get it, you know her," Jay snapped. The muscles of Vargas's jaw flexed and writhed under her skin. Jay swallowed hard, trying to compose himself. "In regards to Buechner, to activism, how do you know her?"

Jennings let go a long sigh. "I met Kat about fifteen years ago. Used to see her band play. My buddy Jorge's band toured with them a couple times. We'd hang out, get lit, you know how that goes. Well, she wouldn't, but the rest of us did. Anyway, I started going to Plants Not Profits with her. We made vegan food and gave it out to homeless people. With all of the corporate interests in agriculture, their priorities—"

"Stay on topic, Che," Jay said.

Jennings glared at Jay before continuing. "After a while, we went our separate ways. I got more involved in animal rights for a while, organizing, protesting, that kind of thing. But again, I'm not in ADB. You need to get that."

"What about Kat?"

"I ran into her at a Cock Sparrer show in Philly three years ago, not long before I came in. They were doing a reunion tour. She said she'd left Plants Not Profits because she was frustrated with the whole thing."

"Because she wasn't making a difference?" Jay said.

Jennings clucked his tongue. "Wasn't making a big enough difference."

Jay felt a chill pass over him, remembering saying that line during the last conversation he had with Sam, as if he had inadvertently planted the seed that would destroy their relationship.

Jennings continued. "Whole reason she started the damn chapter in the first place was to do something bigger, make a bigger impact."

"She started the chapter?" Jay felt the room spin slightly. How many times had he gone there with Sam and he never realized she'd started their group?

"Who else would've done it? We were all too lazy. Or stoned. She saw what they were doing down in Chiapas and wanted to bring some of that north. Anyway, turned out there were too many municipal regulations controlling what they could give out and when. Getting their tables shut down because they were giving out voter registration stuff even though city council passed resolutions that made it damn near impossible for those people to register to vote. That woman was all pie-in-the-sky, take over the world and smash the state and to hell with anyone who stood in her way. She was a damn Anti-Flag song come to life, but with a nice, tight ass."

Jay ground his back teeth, twice on the right, twice on the left. "But neither she nor Patrick Felder had anything to do with the latest Buechner attack?"

"Look, I told you, man, I don't know shit. These guys in here ain't worried about testing perfume on animals. Hell, most of them are animals." Jennings shook his head. "But I'll tell you what. You get a bunch of angry vegans together, what's the first thing you think they're going to hit?"

# 14

Luke Jennings stood in the middle of his cell, his head still reeling after the visit from the agents. What the hell had happened to bring some federals to his doorstep, asking about ancient history? The guard locked the door, pausing a moment outside the bars.

"When you going to finish my arm?" he said to Jennings.

"I don't know, man." He sat on the edge of the thin mattress, the sheets rustling under him, and ran his hands over his hair. "Come at me later."

The guard leaned forward. "You want your packages to keep coming in, you need to finish my shit."

"I said I'd finish it, all right? Just not right now." Jennings felt his jaw tense up, listening to this mouth-breathing redneck harass him about a tattoo that was stupid in the first place—an Indian chief head with a confederate flag flapping behind it.

The guard tapped his baton against the bar, wood dinging on metal. "You got a lot of mouth for someone with a lot of debt. Maybe someone needs to fill that mouth for you again, keep you from talking back."

"Look, Kirby." The words threatened to rush out but Jennings bit them back. The last thing he needed was to piss off one of his two pipelines to the outside. And he could get rid of the man quicker if he just placated him. He forced himself to give half a smile. "How's next week looking for you?"

The guard stood quiet a beat and stared at Jennings, as if

running through his mental calendar. He coughed up something wet, scrunched his nose, then swallowed it. "I'll let you know."

Jennings closed his eyes and concentrated on the pressure building in his fists, then started counting. When he reached one hundred, he took a quick look into the hallway, made sure it was empty, then kneeled beside his bed and fished out the iPhone from beneath the mattress. He dialed a number.

"Heads up," he said when a man answered. "I just had some visitors. Two FBI agents."

"What were their names?" the man said.

"Vargas and Brodsky."

"What did they want?"

"Asked about the Buechner bombings a couple years back, then said there was a cyber-attack there recently and wanted me to give them names. Mentioned you and Kat. No idea what else they have but I thought you should know."

"We'll take care of it," the man said before hanging up.

A few seconds later, Kirby appeared in front of the cell. "Next week won't work. Book me the week after," he said, then walked away.


Patrick Felder ended the call and tapped his phone against his chin. FBI was visiting Jennings? Not necessarily surprising, but it did make things interesting. At the least, it indicated they were closing in. He walked from the kitchen into the house's compact, austere living room—just a large television, several framed photos, and a colorful knitted blanket on the walls, and one rough-hewn end table on the hardwood floor—and over to where a man sat on a couch that looked decades old, watching birds at the suet feeder hanging outside his window.

"That was Luke Jennings," Felder said.

"That's a name I haven't heard in a while."

"He just got a visit from two FBI. Vargas and Brodsky."

"Interesting," Oscar Forlán said. "What did they want?"

"Asking about Buechner. They also mentioned my name and Kat's."

Forlán exhaled hard through his nose, shook his head. "I told you that was a bad idea. That's why we have a plan, so we have something to follow. You go off-script, you get caught."

"There's nothing linking us to that. We're careful. We always are."

Forlán nodded out the back porch, toward the woman on the patio, leaning against the railing that prevented someone from tripping and falling five feet into the water, cigarette in hand, a slow stream of smoke leaking from her lips as she watched the boats ferry tourists from Fell's Point around the harbor to Federal Hill.

"You wanted to be in charge of field operations, no? Then you won't mind telling her?"

Felder swallowed hard, considering the proposition for a moment.

"I didn't think so. Even if they don't know anything, they know names, which is enough to make me worry. I'd say remember that next time, but there won't be a next time. Understood?" Forlán exhaled hard as he pushed himself up off the couch. "Now go track their phones and clean up the mess you made."

Felder nodded before grabbing his keys and leaving the house. Forlán slid the glass door to the side and stepped outside to inform his teniente of the visit.

# 15

"What the hell was that?" Vargas said as they exited the prison.

"What?" Jay headed toward the car.

"You know damn well what I'm talking about. Patrick Felder? Kat Savage? Whoever those clown names were? Questioning a potential informant without telling your partner anything? Is that how you do things in Baltimore because—"

"Hey," Jay said. "Look, I'm sorry. I wasn't trying to keep you out of anything, okay? I saw Felder's name on the visitor log and it sounded familiar."

"And the others? Matty Pants? Kat Savage? Do any of them have real names?"

"Felder's the one I wanted to know about but when I started throwing out names of old punks from way back when—lots of punks in ADB—Savage was the one he responded to. I figured I'd stay with her, see if anything came of it."

"So that's why you freaked out?"

Jay ran his fingers through his hair. "Kat was a local legend of the punk scene. I saw her band play a bunch of times when I was younger. You ever had music become transcendent for you?"

"When I was fourteen I used to get stoned and listen to Pink Floyd."

"And you question my musical tastes?" Jay shook his head. "That's what it was like watching them when I was a kid. But I grew out of that a long time ago. Thought I'd test the waters, see if Jennings would rattle."

"You were the one who looked upset."

Jay clicked the key fob to unlock the doors. "That band meant a lot to me when I was young and hearing that shitbird talk about her like that kind of pissed me off, okay? It's no big deal. I didn't even know if she was still around." He tossed the keys to her. "Can you drive? I need to do some work."

"That's fine. But I'm going to need some caffeine. This travel is wearing me down."

"Let's stop at a coffee shop in town. I can't do Sheetz again. That place is as much a result as a brand." Jay climbed into the car, but he still heard Vargas say *It's shocking you're single* under her breath.


Jay booted up his laptop, then plugged in the air card and connected to his cell phone's signal, creating a hot spot while Vargas drove.

"We are in agreement that Jennings is full of shit, right?" she said.

"Absolutely." Jay brought up the secure portal and logged into the Bureau's server, eventually navigating to NCIC, their database. What worried Jay wasn't that Jennings was full of shit, but that he was involved. It also meant Sam could most certainly be involved, given her activism, her work with Plants Not Profits, the way she saw punk rock as a means of social revolution, and the sheer number of her belongings that featured the Crimson Ghost. The thought chilled Jay. "The question is how he fits into everything else. No way he could be directly involved with the hack. Assuming he's telling any version of the truth about tattooing half the prison, he's probably curried some favor with guards, but you can't smuggle in a laptop between your cheeks."

"That said," Vargas replied, Jay already knowing where she was going, "five'll get you ten he has a phone inside his cell."

"And having a phone would give a concrete record of who he talks to and a reason to tap it," Jay said, already running Jennings's name.

"Is this the exit?" Vargas said.

He glanced up. "Turn left at the end. There's a place called Café Mark a couple blocks down that got good reviews online."

"You know those are all paid for, right?"

A window popped up on Jay's monitor. "Found it," he said as he opened it.

Vargas glanced over. "What pinged?"

Jay shook his head. "It's blank."

"You haven't even run it yet."

Jay tapped his monitor out of reflex and Vargas leaned over, squinting at the bright-white type against a black background. Jay noticed a small scar that started halfway in the middle of her neck and ran up into her black hair, then reflexively touched the one on his head.

"You should watch the road, I'll take care of this."

It didn't matter. Vargas already understood the situation. "Goddamn cell phone companies." She sighed hard. "Run it through LexisNexis anyway, just in case."

When the cell phone companies had begun declaring their phones to be personal property—meaning the company only provided the hardware and had no access to the information inside the device—they'd put a big wall around a swath of information agents could use to help break cases. Most cyber criminals figured this out ages ago and realized that, if they made phone calls, the Feds could track them through public record via telecom companies. But texting, using encrypted messaging apps, even chatting through an Xbox, they all provided a secure way to talk.

Sure, the Bureau could try to find a back door or farm the work out to a variety of cyber companies or hackers, but as soon as they breached one, the company would rewrite security protocols and close that door, so the Bureau would effectively be doing quality control for the very thing that caused them so many problems. When an attack occurred—a mass shooting, a suicide bomber, a large-scale data breach—social media and newspapers lit up with more examples of how government intelligence was lacking. As with the picket fence around the dark web, protecting privacy and personal freedom from intrusion stacked the deck against Jay, who had to defend those rights while skirting around them in order to protect people. If Jay didn't have enough static filling his head already, trying to reconcile this might have driven him crazy.

So the telecom search had come back predictably blank. Jay could feel the grains of sand slipping past, measuring the time wasted. He leaned back in his seat and stretched his hands over his head, held out his pinkie over passing telephone poles. *Right, left, left, right. Left, right, right, left. Left, right, right, left.*

"Felder and Savage got a reaction from Jennings," Vargas said. "Run them."

"If there's nothing for Jennings, there won't be for them."

"Humor me," Vargas said, slowing as she approached Café Mark. Jay searched for Felder, then paused and typed in "Selvage" to ensure nothing would ping.

"Nada for either."

There was no street parking, so Vargas passed the café and continued for a few blocks, pulling into a small lot nestled among the old brick buildings. She parked but kept the engine running. Jay pressed his palms against his eyes. *Think, man, think. You are smarter than them. You can do this.* He heard his mother's voice in his head one early morning, disappointed that he'd questioned the importance of protesting after she'd woken him up when it was still dark outside. *Everyone, everything, is connected to every other thing, even if only by one point,* she said, *but that one point can change the world.* It sounded equal parts prophetic and horseshit at the time, but there was some merit to it. *What is that point here, then?*

"Brodsky, that thing Jennings said, about what the angry

vegans would hit. ADB was suspected in those bombings. There are lots of angry vegans in ADB."

"Yes."

"But you said there are also a lot of old punks in ADB. Ones who might've known Jennings."

"Ones who also would've listened to the Misfits, whose logo happens to be a crimson ghost," he said.

"Search NCIC for known associates of ADB," Vargas said. "Twenty bucks says Felder or Savage shows up."

"Already on it."

"Kat Savage isn't her real name, is it?"

Jay squinted as he scanned the list, running his tongue along the inside of his teeth. "No, probably not. But Plants Not Profits and ADB have different MOs."

"What, one's politically correct and the other isn't?" Vargas tried to hide her smile, but Jay could hear it in her voice.

"One feeds people who need food, the other bombs people who buy fur. Whether those people deserve it or not, that's a different conversation."

"Your head is a complicated place, isn't it?" Vargas said to him, but Jay chose not to respond.

"Got one for Patrick, partial for a Robert Ryan Felder." Jay's fingertips tingled with anticipation as he continued, the energy of the chase palpable in his body. *I'm going to find out who you are.* He tapped and clicked. "Young Patrick was picked up for fighting and public intoxication, not to mention disturbing the peace, assaulting an officer, and resisting arrest twice during public demonstrations."

Jay half-laughed and shook his head.

"What? Don't tell me he's two cells over from Jennings."

"No, he's free. But I would've put a hundred bucks on him being arrested at an anti-cop protest."

"So where was it?"

Jay glanced up at Vargas. "A rally in support of the IBEW."

"The labor union?"

Jay nodded. "That was not how I thought that would play out. One younger sister, deceased, cancer. One older brother, Eric Felder."

Jay scanned through the rest of it but found little else.

"What about Savage?" Vargas said.

"Nothing."

"Well shit." Vargas turned off the engine and sat there.

Jay clicked on Robert Felder.

The screen showed a brief summary: his name, date of birth, the usual smattering of misdemeanor offenses—vandalism and public intoxication—but then one charge for possession with attempt to distribute. But what caught Jay's eye was in the header. *AKA/Bobby Milk. AKA/Droopy Dick. AKA/Dumpy.*

*Dumpy?* Jay thought. *How many guys in Baltimore are called* Dumpy? *There's no way—*

Vargas nudged Jay.

"You there?" She looked at him. "Can you look up Eric Felder on his own? No cross-referencing."

Jay cleared the search and typed in Eric Felder's name. That last name wasn't very common, and Robert being related to Patrick and Eric *would* help connect some of these pieces. The signal wavered a moment, stalling the search. Jay looked around the car. "Couldn't you have parked out in the open, maybe not in between a bunch of buildings?"

Vargas checked her phone. "I have four bars."

The search came back online. Jay said, "Eric Christopher Felder. Currently works in IT for IBM."

"I like that."

Jay paused, scanning farther down. "Some minor juvie charges—vandalism, disturbing the peace—likely what prompted Mister Felder to get himself together and on the straight and narrow, after which he went to two technical colleges for computer science."

"I like that even more."

"Nothing much else that's interesting."

"Anything about Savage in his?"

"Nope." Jay slid the laptop into its case and hid it beneath the seat.

"I'm going to hit the restroom," Vargas said. "It's going to be a long drive. And I think we need to go chat with Mister Felder when we get back."

Jay agreed, but with which Mr. Felder?

Jay bought them coffees, then stood by the counter, playing on his phone while he waited for Vargas to return. He was halfway through an article with an updated trajectory of the incoming hurricane—which was tracking closer and closer to barreling up the Chesapeake Bay and hitting Baltimore head-on—when he heard a faint but familiar voice. He looked up, scanned the area, trying to locate the source. Two teenagers—black shirts, black jeans, black shoes—huddled around a laptop at a café table, pointing at the video playing and giving little cheers of support.

Jay hurried over behind them.

"Dude, what are you doing?" one of the boys said, his shoulders hunched and protective. The other hit pause. "Step off, pervert."

Jay flashed his badge. "I need you to play that video again."

The boy muttered *narc* then hit play. A pixelated Crimson Ghost came on the screen, its mouth moving but words obscured.

"Turn it up."

"What are you, deaf, old man?" The teenagers snickered. Jay sighed. He wanted to say *You'll be like this too because I guarantee you don't wear headphones at shows* but ignored it. The boy turned up the volume three clicks.

"...we've tried voting. We've tried incremental change, and we've tried to change the hearts and minds of our representatives. We appealed to their sense of goodness, but none of that succeeded because the system is set up to reward selfishness, to offer resources to those who already possess an abundance, to promote those who kneel before their masters rather than protect those whom they are supposed to represent. This will no longer stand."

Jay felt someone behind him.

"What the hell is this?" Vargas said.

The Ghost continued. "This system is designed to propagate itself like a tumor, and like a tumor, there is only one way to fix it. We will remove it. We will eradicate it. We will destroy the conditions that allow it to flourish. We will no longer be subject to their yokes, no longer be held by their chains. The people should command and the government should obey. Here, it doesn't, and so we will unite, and we will destroy. This is the end of our manifesto."

Just as the video ended, Jay heard the voice again, at a table to his right: *appealed to their sense of goodness...* Then again at a table on the other side of the room, playing on a phone: *We present to you our manifesto, our plan for radical change.*

"This is not good," Vargas said. "This is..."

"An escalation and a warning," Jay said and held out his hand. "Keys, please. We need to get back now."

She tossed them to him. "Hope you drive fast."

The sun shone on their backs as they left the café and hurried to the car, their shadows creeping longer on the sidewalk as evening settled in around the edges, but Jay still felt cold, and not just from the Ghosts' newest threat. *Dumpy,* he kept thinking. Could it really be *the* Dumpy? Everything was connected even if he couldn't see how.

Something about what they said stuck out to him. *The people should command and the government should obey.* It sounded like the usual leftist rhetoric but also pinged something inside his head.

Vargas said, "Dalworth is going to shit a brick when he—"

She grunted and flew forward as a man in a hooded sweatshirt barreled into both of them. Jay hurtled forward, flinging out his hands to break the fall and roll onto his side but wasn't fast enough. His forehead cracked against the concrete sidewalk, keys skittering away.

The man howled as Vargas stomped his ankle. He swung his elbow back toward her, aiming for her nose, but she side-stepped and hooked her own elbow inside his, ramming her knee into his, then yanking her arm down as she dropped her hip and flung him over her back. His arms bent at an obscene angle as he landed, sprawled out like a skydiver who forgot to pull the cord.

Jay pushed himself off the ground just as Vargas brought up her foot, probably to bury it in the fallen man's crotch. Jay saw another man appear behind her but couldn't shout quick enough. The man rammed his shoulder into Vargas's back, sending her careening forward. Jay threw his arm out, catching her around the waist before she ground her face across the sidewalk, and she crashed into him, her knee jamming into his ribs. They tumbled to the ground and her forehead brushed his cheek. He thought it was strange that he noticed the scent of her perfume in that moment.

Vargas rolled off and pushed herself up to fight back, but the two had disappeared.

"Bastards," she yelled at the empty street.

"Call the locals," Jay grunted as he pushed himself up to his knees. "Get someone to pick them up."

Vargas slapped at her pockets, looked over the ground, ducked down to check beneath a parked car. "They stole my Bureau phone."

"And spilled my coffee." Jay snatched the keys from the sidewalk and jingled them. "But at least we don't have to walk."

"Shit, you could walk. My ass would take a cab."

He took her hand and she pulled him to his feet. "They didn't teach that fighting in the academy."

"Krav maga," she said. "A girl's got to know how to defend herself these days."

"You have to show me how to do that."

"Maybe you buy dinner and I'll show you a couple things."

Jay winced as he pressed his fingers against his forehead, the tips coming back tinted red. "The only possible outcomes of alcohol and jiu-jitsu are a broken nose or someone getting pregnant."

"Poor baby." Vargas gave a thin smile and tapped his cheek. "You've already gotten hurt once today."

# 16

Yemin nodded at the scratches on Jay's forehead and looked over to Vargas. "He mouthing off to you? He does that sometimes. Just got to keep him in his place."

"I did, obviously," Vargas said.

"You two can go to hell," Jay said.

"Rain check, I'm late to pick up the kids."

"Any word on the print at the furrier, Yemin?" Vargas said.

"Came back inconclusive, as far as the model. But it's pretty obvious it's a big boot."

"And we're sure it's not the owner's?"

"She's a seventy-five-year-old woman, so I'm guessing not." Yemin knocked on the cubicle divider and walked off. Jay gave a begrudging wave.

"If you're worried about jeopardizing your meaningful second career as a male model," Vargas said, "you should learn to take a punch."

"You and Yemin are probably soulmates. Asshole buddies." He plopped down into his chair with a long sigh. "Now, where are we?"

"C'mon, Brodsky," Vargas said. "The license plate?"

Between seeing his sister's name on the prison register and a man nicknamed Dumpy listed in NCIC, the license plate had slipped from the front of his mind. He grabbed the phone on his desk and called the techs' office. Darragh answered. "This is Agent

Brodsky. Is Jeanie there?"

"No, sir. She had to leave early."

"I sent her a photo of a license plate to run through NCIC. Any word on it?"

Darragh shuffled through papers on the other end. "No, sir. Nothing popped for the numbers you gave us, and the photo was pretty grainy. We sent it out for image enhancement but they're busy. It might be a while. I'll let you know as soon as we hear something."

"You don't know any graphic designers, do you?"

"Um, no." Darragh waited a beat. "Why?"

"Never mind. Call down again and make sure they know this is a rush," Jay said, then hung up.

"You're trying to Photoshop-zoom a license plate?" Vargas laughed.

"I'll try anything that helps. Not everyone has the full resources of the Bureau at their fingertips."

"Seriously?" Vargas leaned back, her eyebrows raised. "At least you have techs to do the analysis for you. Someone in our office botches a red-ball case, they become the new tech until someone else screws up."

"You could always transfer down here." Jay didn't realize what he'd said until the words hit his ears. He felt his cheeks flush, fought the urge to blink.

"This case, though," she said, a slight smile tugging at the edges of her lips, not acknowledging his comment but not rejecting it either.

Dalworth cleared his throat behind them. Jay and Vargas hopped to their feet. Dalworth nodded at Jay's forehead. "You give Agent Vargas some lip?"

Jay closed his eyes and sighed. "No, sir. Two guys tried to mug us. Made off with Agent Vargas's Bureau phone."

Dalworth's face shifted into something like concern. "You filed a report, right?"

"We were busy working the lead we found," Vargas said.

"I'll file before I leave tonight."

"ASAP. They'll need to wipe it." Dalworth nodded at Jay. "Where are we at?"

"Jesus. Where to start."

Vargas motioned between herself and Jay. "Patrick and Sons falls right in line with the other hack, though there is the possible moral angle—"

"I'd say it's more than possible."

"You're not wrong." Vargas licked her teeth. "The sheriff's deputy gave us descriptions that are consistent with the Community Health hack. Everything else correlates. But this is where it gets interesting." She nodded at Jay.

"On their way back from the Patrick hack, they stopped by Buechner Furriers outside Frederick."

"A furrier?" Dalworth said. "Why?"

Jay and Vargas smiled.

"Yes, you two are cute," Dalworth barked, "but what's the connection?"

"The perps are the connection," Jay said, fighting to keep his face from blushing. "This falls completely outside their mission."

"Which is another thing we found today," Vargas said.

"One thing at a time." Dalworth crossed his arms.

"The furrier was sloppy, emotional. It was a personal vendetta they were settling—mostly like the animal liberation break-ins over the past few years but they also painted all the mannequins with ghost faces."

"So there is a connection?" Dalworth said.

Jay shrugged. "Maybe not explicitly, but I'd wager there's some kind of overlap. We got a photo of the car from a liquor store across the street from Patrick and Sons. They're trying to pull the plates now, but the resolution is shit."

"Then get down there yourself and start looking." Jay started to respond but Dalworth held up a grip of reports before dropping them on Jay's desk. "More intrusions, all stemming from Patrick and Sons. And don't think you're the only one who noticed what crossing state lines means. I've fielded a dozen frantic calls today and I expect more tomorrow. We're chasing after a group we can't identify, which may be days from unleashing an assault this country has never seen before."

"They haven't physically attacked anyone yet."

"They trashed the furrier. How long you think before that moves to people? How long before they figure out how to move the virus from the Tidewater or Bay State mainframe in Maryland to the Virginia one, then North Carolina, then South Carolina and Tennessee, wherever the hell they are? They've infected dozens of sites and wiped millions and millions of dollars. I'm not a fan of high insurance premiums either, but healthcare is a big chunk of the nation's economy. What do you think will happen once they wipe all that out? I give it two days, three at the max, before the Director brings himself in here and burns our office to the ground." He pointed at the reports on Jay's desk. "You figure out who's doing this now, because it's not long before all of us are going to be fighting for who gets to sing 'Happy Birthday' at Olive Garden." Dalworth glanced at Vargas, said, "File that report," then turned around and left.

They both watched Dalworth until he was gone. Vargas glanced over at Jay, their eyes meeting a long minute, like they were waiting for the other to speak. Finally, Vargas said, "He's kind of a dick, isn't he?"

Jay shrugged. "He's a real good guy once you get to know him. As long as you don't get on his bad side..." Jay let Vargas fill in the blank. He motioned at the stack of reports on his desk. "Want me to take those?"

"We can split them."

"Aren't you going to fill out your phone report?"

Vargas glanced over to the door where Dalworth had been. "Which would you do, work the case or dance to the organ grinder music?"

"We'll split them," he said.

Jay scanned the list of handles of the intruding systems, where they could be recovered. The biggest case of his career, and he couldn't figure this out? To hell with that. He was not going to let the Ghosts win. Order and structure would prevail. He was going to nail these sons of bitches.

As he looked at the flow logs, he recognized several of the signatures, all coming from conspicuously antagonistic countries—the same as the previous hack and, if he wasn't mistaken, two in common with a movie studio hack a couple years earlier.

"These guys have a small toolkit to draw from," he said to Vargas, "and they're starting to repeat themselves."

"What do you mean?" Vargas said, looking up from her stack.

"Look at this guy. His handle is *Tupac the Second*, the second coming of Tupac or something."

"Maybe Tupac isn't actually dead," Vargas said. "He's gone digital."

"But would any North Korean or ISIS hacker go by Tupac? You don't hide behind something like that. Do WhiteRose, or PixelPimp69. Something stupid and innocuous. These people are throwing up signals that look like routine intrusions from hostile countries, trying to get our attention. Why?"

"What if it's some kid in Syria?" Vargas said. "He thinks he's a gangster, so he uses Tupac as a handle?"

"Yemin said the same thing about the Crimson Ghost skull." He flipped through pages again as he spoke. "But what if it's misdirection instead? Same idea as Buechner, but get us to chase people instead of markets."

"What are they directing us away from?" She waved her ream of reports. "We know their targets."

Jay shook his head, feeling the static building inside at every roadblock and double-back they had encountered since this case started.

Back up. Reboot. Look at it from a different point.

Fifteen sites infected just yesterday alone. The insurance

company hack was spreading faster, wider, smarter, than the previous hack. Jay's fingers twitched. His sister's name on the prison visitor log. He tapped his right heel against his left ankle, then left against right. *Breathe, be aware, count.* Dumpy Felder listed as an ADB associate. Did it again, but opposite, a set of two, then switched again. *Breathe, be aware.* The Ghosts spreading across the net, soon the country, mocking Jay as they did it. *Sets of four. Patterns. Breathe.* What if the patterns that lurked in the dark shadows of his gray matter were the same as the pattern of this infection spreading—like, in Sam's absence, without his regular routine in place, he'd unleashed an exponential amount of destruction because he couldn't keep his structures in place, and what he really needed was closure with Sam, to make things right with her no matter how many years it had been and stop himself from spinning out of orbit and not stopping this hack in time. *Breathe.*

Vargas set her papers down and excused herself. Jay squared off the piles of papers and pulled out his phone while waiting for her to go out of sight, opening up an incognito window and searching the phrases *people command* and *government obeys*. The first instance: a hand-painted sign in Chiapas. Specifically, at the entrance to territory controlled by the Zapatistas. Maybe it was coincidence that Jennings mentioned something about Sam being interested in what was happening to Chiapas.

But all Jay's training had taught him coincidence was anything but. And Sam *had* mentioned she was learning Spanish.

He put his phone away and moved to his laptop before Vargas came back, bringing up the database, searching for a few minutes for instances of Dumpy Felder. The name was flagged in two files, both in the basement archives, neither yet digitized, thank god. He checked his watch—Archives should still be open—then typed the file numbers into his phone, just as Vargas came around the corner to Jay's cubicle.

"We're not going to find anything else sifting through this," she said. "I need to eat, but then let's go talk to Felder. He's our best lead right now."

Jay almost said *which one?* but caught himself. "We have one lead and you're thinking about dinner?" But Jay also felt his stomach grumble too.

Vargas gathered her purse. "I get really grumpy when I'm hungry."

"Are you hungry all the time?"

Vargas rolled her eyes. "How about that dinner we talked about?"

"As much as I'd love to get my ass kicked by you on a full stomach, I have to take care of something."

"Your loss." She clucked her tongue. *Actually,* Jay thought, *it was.* "Meet back here in thirty?"

He nodded and she turned to leave, then paused and looked back at him.

"Hey, Brodsky?" she said, standing near the door. "I get why you have such a hard-on for these guys, that they're one move ahead of you at every step. I've had cases like this and they are so frustrating you want to scream or break something."

Jay conceded. "I won't lie, it is messing with me a little."

"Letting them get inside your head means they're winning," Vargas said. "We'll catch them."

Jay swallowed twice, then nodded.

Vargas said, "See you soon, tiger," and left.

Jay waited until he heard the elevator door ding closed before he grabbed his things and headed for the stairs.

# 17

Jay took the steps all the way to the basement, exiting the door and hurrying to the archive room. An old-timer, wide as he was tall, sat behind the gated window, face down in his book. His bald head was liver-spotted, and tufts of white stuck out of his ears, as if all the hair had migrated down the man's skull.

"Help you?" the old man said without looking up from his book.

"Need to check out two files, please." Jay scrolled through his phone to find the numbers, then jotted them down on a piece of paper and slid it over to the man.

The old man barely looked at the paper before asking, "You got your ASAC's say-so?"

Jay straightened his back, spread his chest a bit. "You have a badge, sir?"

"No, I do not. If I did, I wouldn't be down here reading late at night, would I?"

The man continued to point his face at his book. Jay was honestly curious what book could be so damn captivating.

"I do have a badge. And I'm asking—politely, for the last time—for you to get me my files so I can leave you to your stories."

The man leaned the book down. Jay saw part of the cover— *Eddie Coyle*—but didn't recognize it.

"You need permission to look at CI files, son."

"CI files? Felder was an informant?"

"Correct." The man cleared his throat with a wet gurgle, then swallowed it. "So, do you?"

Jay checked his watch. He wanted time to look at this before Vargas got back. "Would you mind," Jay said, checking the man's name tag, "Norman, grabbing the files while I call up to my ASAC? I know it's not protocol but I'm in kind of a hurry."

Norman considered Jay for a minute, then sloughed off his chair, thumb still holding his place in the book. "Make your call," he shouted over his shoulder.

Once Norman had gone into the stacks, Jay brought up the browser on his phone and searched "Eddie Coyle," reading what he could in the time Norman was gone.

Norman came back no more than four minutes later, set the files down on the counter. One was two inches thick and the other only a few pages. Judging by the paper quality, they were both more than thirty years old. Norman raised his eyebrows in lieu of a question.

"Straight to voicemail. He's on a call."

Except for a slight puff of air through the lips, Norman's expression didn't change. Jay wasn't sure if that was a good thing or not.

"Let me ask you, though, while we're waiting." Jay nodded at the book cover. "I know this might sound like heresy, but I prefer the movie to the book. What do you think?"

Norman blinked twice, his eyelids tinted purple.

"What do I think?" Norman finally said. "I think, *no shit*. I think, *Bobby Mitchum*."

Jay nodded sagely, totally agreeing with whatever the man was saying.

"I think, *this kid is bullshitting me*," Norman nodded, "but I admire his chutzpah and his Google-machine skills."

Jay shrugged.

Norman slid the folders beneath the metal gate. "I think you better have these back to me by tomorrow. No later."

Sticking the folders beneath his arm, Jay told Norman he would do just that. As he turned to leave, Norman spoke up again.

"I also think you better have a decent cup of coffee for me. This dishwater stuff is giving me heartburn."

"Will do, Norman," Jay said. "Will do."

# 18

Jay pinched his neck four times with his right hand, then left, left, then right. *Calm down. Breathe. There is too much at stake for you to come unmoored inside your skull.*

He checked his watch again. Fifteen minutes before Vargas would be back, but enough time to start looking. He found an empty stairwell and hunkered down with the CI file.

On the one hand, it was hard to imagine Sam with the Ghosts, largely because Jay couldn't think of his sister as being part of a terrorist cell that actively threatened the safety of the country; but on the other, her history of activism and dubious selection of friends didn't do much to ease his anxiety. To be completely honest with himself, he had no idea what she'd been through in the last seven years.

He split open the file.

Jay didn't remember much about Dumpy Felder, more impressions and sensations. Always smelled like Natty Boh and Kools and sweat. He used to stick one of the couch cushions under his shirt and pretend he was Rick Dempsey, which Jay figured was how his name had become Dumpy. Jay thought back to the living room of their childhood, thought that was why his mom always left the room when Dumpy came over—she didn't want to think about the guy's sweat all over her upholstery.

The beginning of the CI file was largely benign, mostly summaries of early meetings between Dumpy and his FBI handler.

Jay snorted at a reference to them discussing who shot JR in *Dallas,* but it had been the early eighties. The reports were otherwise largely devoid of personal details, laying out arrangements, parameters, expectations—the usual stuff. Jay paused at the handler's name, Todd Hart. The same as Vargas's ASAC in Pittsburgh. Jay paused for a moment, wondering where the line between coincidence and clue was, then moved on.

The first handful of papers confirmed Jay's suspicion that Dumpy had been involved in activism, mostly protesting the Iran-Contra scandal, among other hot-button political issues of the time. The range of groups this man had worked in meant he had been informing a pretty long time—into the early nineties— and seemingly successfully. The guy seemed to think he was just like Whitey Bulger. Not many people get through more than a couple years as a CI without cracking or getting caught. Jay flipped through the files, stopping to read every couple years, and he saw Dumpy's paranoia growing toward the end of 1985.

Several of the transcripts mentioned another informant in their group of activist friends in the neighborhood—annotated later by Hart with reference number CI-7—an informant that, to Dumpy's mind, did a piss-poor job of hiding it, asking questions they shouldn't be asking to people they shouldn't be talking to. On several occasions Dumpy told his handler he was sure the group was onto CI-7 and they were going to get both of them killed. The handler did his job, a combination of persuasion, praise, and outright threats. Each time Dumpy agreed to continue, but he began to imply that if his handler didn't deal with the other informant, Dumpy would. *I'm not getting killed for no one,* the transcript read. *To hell with that. You can't rein 'em in, I'll take care of 'em myself.*

His phone vibrated in his pocket.

*Send me that photo?*

*Photo?* Jay thought. *Who is this?* he responded.

*Vargas. Personal phone. The license plate from WV.*

*How'd you get my number?*

*Copied it from a bathroom stall. Photo please.*

He waffled a moment, trying to come up with a pithy response, but finally just sent the photo.

*You back?*

*No, I thought I'd see if anyone at Burger King recognized it.*

Jay waited a second, the next text coming as if on beat.

*Of course I'm back. Be there in a minute.*

Jay returned his phone to his pocket and moved on to the thin Felder file. As soon as he opened it, he stopped cold.

Dumpy—*the* Dumpy—stared at Jay in a mug shot. He pulled the photo out of his wallet, the one of him and his mother and Sam at the protest, and examined it again. There was a face behind his mother's right shoulder, checking her out. *No,* he thought, looking at it more closely, *glaring at her.* The same hair, same mustache. His bony jaw set, eyes narrowed, cheeks hollow. Fucking Dumpy Felder. Jay's eyes flicked back and forth between the mug shot and his photo, absorbing every detail until he had to physically make himself set it down. *Everything is connected,* he heard his mother say. *You are wrong,* Jay told her, making himself believe it. *You were wrong about so many things.*

He forced himself to turn the page. Personal details filled the sheet and filled Jay's stomach with sharp rocks. A Billytown address not far from theirs in Locust Point. Descriptions of cars, aliases, frequent locations, previous offenses.

Then Jay stopped again.

"Holy shit."

He had to read the lines aloud to make sure they were real, to confirm them for himself. *Known family: Alice, wife, 35; Eric Christopher, son, 10; Patrick, son, 8; Amelia, daughter, deceased.*

He couldn't help but smile. "Got you, assholes."

The next page gave a detailed account of Dumpy Felder's arrest. The undercover agent meeting him at Hammerjack's, a hair-metal club downtown that had since gone dark, to set up arrangements. Tracking the shipment of cocaine from the

Central American suppliers as it made its way to a wharf in Cherry Hill, where Dumpy and his partners in crime offloaded it before transporting to a local contact. By this point, they'd done it a dozen times, enough to fund their activism for more than a year.

Jay almost laughed aloud. He could envision them pissing and moaning about the US government meddling in Latin America by selling weapons and drugs, when these idiots were doing the same damn thing, hurting the same people they advocated for by propping up vicious cartels who had no problem murdering citizens who got in the way. Jay moved on to an account of the raid, the seizure, the arrests.

Then the pitch: become an informant or go to jail. Dumpy Felder took it.

His partner did not.

A partner named Jacob Brodsky, Senior.

Jay slammed the file closed. He held out his pinkie. Right, left, left, right, left, right, right, left, left, right, right, left—*stop it, Jay, breathe, be aware*—right, left, left, right. *You are in control.* The room pressed against him, every particle of air weighing more than physically possible, crushing him, filling his lungs with cement. They'd been right in cutting off that son of a bitch without even knowing it.

His father, partner of Dumpy Felder in trafficking narcotics.

Dumpy Felder, who was the father of Eric Felder and Patrick Felder, who were associates of Luke Jennings.

His father and Dumpy Felder, both one step removed from the Crimson Ghosts, also one step removed from his sister.

"Please don't be into this, Sam."

He wondered for a second if his mother knew, if that was actually why she would leave the room when Dumpy came over. If she knew but couldn't stand what they were doing. A second, briefer thought passed through: did this have anything to do with her suicide?

His phone buzzed again and he started, as if it answered his question. Vargas again.

*Get back here right now.*

Jay closed the files and slipped them under his arm, trying to conceal them as best as possible. *On my way.*

# 19

The cable news anchorman breathlessly reported one development after another, toggling between cameras and correspondents so quickly Oscar Forlán worried the young man would pass out from lack of oxygen.

On one half of the screen, a woman on a street corner sobbed uncontrollably, telling the field correspondent that she'd been rear-ended by an uninsured driver five years ago and had racked up more than twenty-thousand dollars in medical bills, compounded by fines because she couldn't afford the six-hundred-dollar monthly payment. But now, since her debt had been erased, she could use that money to take her son and daughter to Cuba to meet their grandparents for the first time.

Oscar smiled and felt his eyes mist a little. He ran his hand over the back of the couch, the same one his father had built for his mother as a wedding present nearly fifty years ago. She came from a poor family, as did he, and had never had a couch, as much because their two-room house was too cramped to fit one as they could never afford it.

He flipped to another news station and found two dour-looking men in expensive suits on either side of the split-screen, the anchorwoman asking how they were going to explain the loss to their stockholders, what kind of remuneration they could expect. The men paused a moment, the air pregnant with discomfort, before they both began speaking at the same time, talking over one another, throwing out industry jargon like *actionable items* and *forward-facing* and other phrases Oscar vowed to never let pass his lips during meetings. After a minute of their shouting at each other, the anchorwoman eventually cut them off, saying, "What you're telling me, what you're telling your stockholders, what you're telling America, is that you are completely defenseless against attacks such as these that could derail our entire way of living?" The men paused, then began yelling once more.

Oscar's smile broadened.

He flipped to another channel, where a man held his arms as wide as they would go, indicating the size of the TV he was going to buy now. He began counting on his fingers everything he would get to go with it, starting with a 3D Blu-Ray player, a PlayStation, two—

"I'll bet he has sweatpants money," his teniente said as she came in from smoking out on the deck.

Oscar muted the television, a shiny screen sitting flush with the wall, and turned to face her. "Sweatpants money?"

"Yeah." She slid the door closed. "He sets a couple bucks aside every time he gets paid so he can buy new sweatpants every month or two. His sweatpants money. Biggest challenge is to not spend it all on Doritos."

"Samantha, the wonders never cease with you."

She gave a joking curtsy, then went to the fridge for a glass of water, came back with a rice cake clenched between her teeth. Forlán watched the tiger tattoo on the side of her neck writhe as she chewed and swallowed. She pointed at the screen.

"This is good, but we need more."

"We're already planning for five additional states. What more do you want?"

"Fifty?"

Forlán smiled and nodded.

"And more than just health insurance. Student loans. Mortgages. Payday loans." She counted on her fingers while rattling off various ways people were beholden to corporate overlords.

"Oscar, this is just the beginning of a complete social liberation, a future where people aren't working themselves to death and rationing insulin and choosing to sacrifice themselves to the army just to afford college. A new day is rising, and we're on the front lines of it."

Forlán smiled. "*Hasta la lucha,* Teniente."

She bit down hard on the rice cake, as if for emphasis, and nodded her head while chewing. "What else are they saying?"

Forlán shrugged, flipped through additional talking heads. "Mostly the same reactionary talking points. Economic terrorism. Russia. The Red Scare. Conservative news turned up to eleven."

But as he flipped to the local news station, Samantha told him to stop. The headline at the bottom read *Tidewater Mutual CEO Stepping Down Amid Hack Controversy.*

The newscaster turned to her co-host and made what Forlán assumed was a banal comment but the words were lost under Samantha's yelling.

Forlán turned up the volume.

"...has announced he will officially resign his position as CEO during a press conference tomorrow in order to spend more time with his family. He has received vicious criticism in the wake of the widespread hack a few days ago that subsequently wiped out tens of millions of dollars of revenue for the company, one of the three largest in the state. However, because this is a resignation and not a termination, he will still receive a bonus payment of more than one-hundred-thirty-two-million dollars, plus additional stock. Police are still searching for the group behind the information hack."

Samantha hurled her glass at the brick wall, jagged little shards littering Forlán's hardwood floors.

"No. No. No no no. No. Fuck that," she said as she paced back and forth. "After all they've done, all the lives they've destroyed, they think they can just walk away for free—walk away *and* get paid? No. Fuck that."

Forlán sat back in the couch, massaging his jaw. "What do

you propose?"

Samantha paced another moment before coming to an abrupt stop. "Call everyone and tell them to be ready at six tomorrow morning."

"For what?" he said.

She smiled. "I have a plan."

# 20

Jay walked into the conference room to find Agent Vargas hunkered over a take-out container from Applebee's, the juice and barbeque sauce of her hamburger running down her forearms, a small spot of brown soaking into the cuff of her shirt.

Vargas pocketed the food in her cheek, mumbled around the cowboy burger. "What took you so long?"

"Had to take care of something."

She pushed a box of fried onion strips toward him. "You okay? Look like you've seen your own ghost."

"I'm fine." Jay sat across from her, nodded at the food. "Why are you eating that?"

"What, you think I only eat at Chicken Rico? Which is Peruvian, by the way."

"No." Jay smirked. "I meant because you're not a divorced father taking your daughter to dinner before bringing her back to her mother's."

Vargas winced slightly, then smiled, washed down her food with a long drink. "I'm starving, it was close and edible, and I despise McDonald's."

Jay tut-tutted. "I knew you weren't a real American."

In place of an answer, Vargas took another big bite, waiting for Jay to open up. When he didn't, she set the burger down and talked around the mouthful of food.

"Brodsky, look, we're supposed to be partners. All things

considered, you're a mostly competent partner." She smiled a bit, tried to take the edge off. "If something's going on, get it off your chest so we can move on, yeah?"

"I said there's nothing." He tried to keep his voice even but felt it strain. Dumpy Felder. The Ghosts. His father. Sam. They were pieces from different puzzles he was trying to fit together. They shouldn't fit together, should they?

She crumpled a napkin between her hands and wiped the barbecue sauce from her lips, set her eyes on Jay. "In the interest of fairness, I'm sorry I threatened to put my foot inside your ass at the jail, and not just because I really like these shoes. That phone call I got was from a friend who's a court clerk."

"Did they finally discover you're the Zodiac killer?"

"Not yet." She took a long breath, seemed slightly hesitant. Maybe resigned was more accurate.

"My brother Ramón died a couple years ago. He had a heart condition, and after he lost his job, he lost his insurance. With no insurance, he had to pay market price for his medication, so when that got to be too expensive...," she trailed off. "I went looking for him after he stopped answering my calls. Found him in his apartment three days later."

"Vargas, look, you don't—"

"We're partners, right?" She shook her head. "Anyway. Me and Ramón were really close growing up, and his death was so senseless, so avoidable, that it kind of...sent me off the rails."

"Of course it did."

"I, um, engaged in risky behaviors." She cleared her throat and straightened her back, looking Jay right in the eye, almost as if daring him to look away. "I drank too much. Stayed out too late. Cheated on my husband a couple times." She paused a second, gauging Jay's reaction, but not seeming like she'd back down if he balked. "I'm not proud of it. It was a reaction, and an ill-advised one, but it was all me. I just—I don't know, I needed to feel something."

"I can understand that." He felt like an asshole saying it,

something so sterile and canned, but he didn't know how else to respond.

"So Mark, my ex, he's a lawyer—he filed for divorce with a judge he knew after I told him everything. The judge took one look at my actions, then coupled that with the erratic work schedule of a federal agent, and—well, he gave custody of our daughter to Mark."

"You have a daughter?" Jay blinked a couple times, felt the room shift.

"Esmeralda, named after my mother." Vargas picked up her phone, showed him the home screen. "She's ten."

"Oh, I just..." Jay told himself to shut up and stop acting like an idiot. "She's beautiful, I just had no idea."

"Why would you?"

Jay had no response. He suddenly felt petty, wondering how his thirty-year-old betrayals could begin to compare to Vargas's anxiety about the future of her ten-year-old daughter.

"I had visitation rights, supervised, but only with a week's notice. How often do you know a week ahead of time what your days will look like? I didn't get to see my baby girl for two months." She looked at the photo, a smile bubbling to the surface before she turned off the screen. "You have no idea how long two months can be until someone is keeping this bright, beautiful, vibrant young life away from you."

Jay briefly considered telling her about Sam, or his mother. About the weeks after she died that he spent in his room, wedged beneath the bed. About how Sam was the only one who could get him out, and even that began with her bringing food up to his room and lying on the floor as they ate their dinner. They worked their way out from under the bed, then to the desk in his room, then the stairs, then finally the kitchen table. That was also the time—according to Sam—that his tics started. And once she left, how they redoubled, threatening to overtake him completely. But as quickly as that urge arose, he pushed it aside, not willing to let her in that far yet.

"And yes, I understand I didn't act in the most responsible way. Mark had every right to be angry, to want a divorce. That's fine. But I have never, *never* done anything to jeopardize Esme. I would die for that little girl a hundred times, then ask for a hundred more. I think that's what hurts most. Not that I torpedoed my marriage, but that they think I would ever do anything to hurt my baby.

"Anyway," she made a broad gesture with her hands, "the custody battle was months of constant hell, but it did wake me up and make me get my shit together. I filed for joint custody a year later, but it was denied. So I filed again last year. And my hearing was supposed to be next month, but it got pushed back again, due in some part to his influence and/or vendetta against me."

"Dads can be assholes." And in saying that, Jay felt a pang of something—guilt? jealousy? loneliness?—and wondered what his and Sam's lives would be like if they'd actually had parents. At their core, would they be the same? How much so?

"He's definitely that."

"But is your daughter safe with him?" Jay said. "Is he good to her? Does she—?"

"You have kids?" she said, her voice so sharp it should have sliced her tongue to ribbons. "Then shut your fucking mouth and eat your blooming onion."

Jay held his hand up. "I'm sorry, I didn't mean anything—"

She grabbed a few papers sitting on the edge of the table and slapped them down between her and Jay.

"Anyway," she said. End of conversation.

Four of the papers featured MVA photos; one was a printout of the license plate shot he'd taken.

"The resolution is crap and the techs couldn't get a better look at it. I think the numbers you gave them were wrong too," she said, then pointed at two spots on the photo. "Those could've been *B*s and fives, or eights and *S*s. Reason I called you back early is because I went and ran all the different combinations, and came up with four names."

She spread out the photos.

"One of these people can help us stop this before it torpedoes the country. Who do we like?"

An old woman with a jeweled brooch. A Hindu man with a red bindi on his forehead. A hard-looking dude who was meth-skinny.

Then a man with bad neck tattoos, who was chunky enough that a polite person might say he was big boned.

A more colorful way might be Texas Big.

# 21

Texas Big—Christian name, Zane Thurgood—lived on a quiet street in Parkville, just outside Baltimore's northern limits. Each house was nearly the same, squat Cape Cods with tiny back-yards ringed by rusted chain-link fences, lined up block after block. Despite the downtrodden vibe, many of the houses were nicely kept. Trim yards, colorful flowerbeds, orange and purple flamingos—Orioles and Ravens colors—in true Baltimore fashion.

Zane Thurgood's house had all of these, plus two large hy-drangeas on either side of the house, the petals so vibrant you could see them even at night. A midnineties Chevy Cavalier sat on the parking pad, a large chunk of the rear bumper missing. Jay couldn't determine the color in the dark, but he would have placed it somewhere between Bondo and rust.

"You think this is his grandmother's place?" Jay said as they approached the house, their own car parked a half block down.

"It's listed as his. I hope there's no granny home. I'd hate to bang on his door at"—she checked her phone—"ten-thirty and wake her up."

"Maybe she's watching *Golden Girls*."

"You're kind of a prick sometimes, aren't you." Vargas stepped onto the small front porch while Jay cupped his hand against the glass and peeked through the windows. He didn't see anything.

"It's been a day," Jay mumbled.

Vargas knocked on the door. Jay stood behind her.

A series of thumps inside coming toward the door, someone large and lumbering. Jay's hand went to his hip by instinct.

The door swung open, revealing Zane Thurgood standing shirtless with his stomach folding over paint-splattered basketball shorts.

As soon as their credentials came out, the door began to close. Jay stuck his foot in the jamb.

"We didn't wake you, did we?" Vargas said, stepping into the house. Thurgood shimmied back and forth, like he wasn't sure whether he should answer or throw them out or call a lawyer.

"My partner asked you a question," Jay said.

"Uh-uh," Thurgood said, finally stepping away from the door. His eyes darted from the agents to the living room to the steps.

Jay flicked the lock off his holster. "Is there anyone else in the house, Mister Thurgood?"

"I live by myself." He wiped a meaty hand across his forehead.

Jay stepped past him, scanned the living room quickly. Box TV in the corner on a flimsy entertainment stand. A black long-sleeve shirt and black work pants lying over the arm of a plaid couch. Faded green Berber carpet covering the floor. Someone might have sat in the same set-up and watched Reagan's second inauguration. Two long-leaf ferns hung in the corner, beaded ropes holding the plastic baskets. They bookended a wire rack holding half a dozen exotic plants, each more than a foot tall. A small dining room adjacent, with a circular table and two chairs amid an explosion of flowers, but no sign of people, photos, nothing. Jay felt a twinge of the man's loneliness.

"Did I do something?" Thurgood said.

"Good question." Vargas moved into the living room, keeping her eyes on Thurgood. "Did you?"

"No." He tried to declare it but it came out more as a question. His hands, adorned by splotchy sparrow tattoos, went from his waist to his forehead, then crossed over his chest. Fidgeting. Nervous. And they hadn't even said anything yet. He glanced over at the couch again, but Jay didn't see anything of note. He did find it interesting that Thurgood's hands and neck were tattooed but his chest remained bare, as if to give the appearance that he was more heavily tattooed when dressed.

"Where are you from, Mister Thurgood?" Vargas said.

"Dundalk. Why?"

"You have relatives around here?"

"Couple." His arms uncrossed, hands went back to his waist, then back to his bare chest, like the birds were chasing one another through the air. "Mom's in Catonsville. Gram's house is two blocks over."

"What about your dad?" Jay said. He came up to a shelf made of cinder blocks and stained two-by-eights holding a turntable and four rows of records.

"Dunno."

"Don't know where he is or don't know who he is?" Jay said.

"He's a dickhead, is who he is."

"I feel you on that. My dad was an asshole too. Turned into a drunk after my mom died."

"Heroin, coke. Basing, mostly," Thurgood said, something like relief coming into his voice. "Him and Mom both. I stayed with Gram."

Jay nodded. "We got a lot in common, Mister Thurgood."

"It's Zane," he said, his hands resting finally. "It's only Mister Thurgood in court."

"You go to court very often, Mister Thurgood?" Vargas said.

The fidgeting picked up again. He rubbed the back of his neck. "That was just a joke. Mister Thurgood sounds like my dad."

"Right," Jay said. "Mine abandoned me and my sister for a bunch of years, then came back saying he was all straight and sober. And he was, sober I mean. Still an asshole, though. It's tough growing up like that because you start to think, if he's an asshole, and I'm his kid, does that mean I'm going to become an asshole too?"

"Did something happen to Gram?" Thurgood said.

"No, but we were wondering if you had family in Pentress, West Virginia?"

Thurgood froze in place, his eyes wide. *This guy should not try to be a criminal,* Jay thought. Then, as if reading Jay's mind, he began moving again. He shrugged, shifted his weight from foot to foot.

"Nah. Not recently. I don't even know where that is. What'd you say it was, Penfold?" He craned his neck forward, conspicuously trying to remember something, then shook his head. "Nah, don't know."

"Why else would you go out there then, if you don't have family?"

He swallowed hard. "I didn't—don't. I don't know what you're talking about."

"What do you do for a living?" Vargas said. "You strike me as the hands-on type."

Jay flipped through the rows of records. He saw a lot of the same albums as the ones in Sam's collection, but he wondered how either of these philistines had gone their whole lives without understanding how to put things in alphabetical order. Jay came across what looked like an original press of Sham 69's *Tell Us the Truth,* a classic Oi! streetpunk record he'd had on cassette. Another from Cockney Rejects, though Jay thought it was a later reprint. Rancid's first seven-inch. He remembered when this came out; Sam played it nonstop for weeks. He looked inside, raised his eyebrows, and looked at Thurgood. "How'd you get a Rancid test-press?"

"Hey, be careful with those." Thurgood stepped toward Jay but stopped when Vargas stepped in his path. "Those are worth a lot of money," he said around her.

"I heard vinyl's getting popular again," Jay said. He flipped past Chain of Strength's first record, an essential southern California hardcore album, and felt a chill rush down his back as he saw The Savages first seven-inch.

"It's always been popular, if you know where to look," Thurgood said.

There was an abrupt vibration, Thurgood nearly jumping in place. Jay's eyes shot to Thurgood's phone, sitting on the turntable five feet from him. He saw *Ki* on the screen before Thurgood snatched it, shoving it in his pocket.

Kim. Kit. Kirk. Some stupid hipster name that was a Europeanized spelling of a household object. It could be anything, but Jay still felt his fingers tingling with electricity, as if confirmation Sam was part of the Ghosts could come at any moment. The tension between wanting resolution on the matter and not wanting his sister to be part of a fucking terrorist cell.

Jay returned to the records, picked up the Turning Point vinyl behind the Savages one and held it to avoid suspicion from either Thurgood or Vargas, but examined the Savages cover. His sister in a leather jacket and black jeans, wielding a guitar like an axe at a group of people at her feet, photoshopped smaller to look like *Attack of the 50 Foot Woman*. He'd always thought it was funny because, as magnetic as her voice could be, she couldn't play guitar for shit. He replaced Turning Point and continued flipping, and saw several copies of another record he recognized from years ago. The *Live from the Chop Shop* LP, a compilation of songs from a benefit show for the drummer of a local band who'd gotten into an accident and didn't have health insurance. Thurgood had four copies, each with a different color of vinyl inside. A collector's collector.

"Can you please put those down? Does it have anything to do with—"

"I asked what you did for a job, Mister Thurgood," Vargas said.

"Landscaping," he said, clearly frustrated with Jay. "Sometimes construction."

"You ever work with Patrick Felder or Luke Jennings?" Vargas said.

"What?" Thurgood's breath caught before he sputtered out, "Who?"

"Or was that Eric Felder? I forget."

Thurgood's lip curled. "I don't know who that is," he growled.

Vargas stared at him while Jay noted it, continued to flip through records.

"I dunno, man." Thurgood rubbed the back of his neck. "I work landscaping, okay? I don't know who I work with on any particular day."

"Day labor or contract?"

"Seriously," Thurgood said to Jay, "if those get fingerprints or creased corners, the value goes down."

Jay set the record back, turned to Vargas. "I think we're good here."

Her eyes said she didn't agree but was too tired to argue.

"Thank you for your time, Mister Thurgood." Jay walked toward the door without waiting for a response.

"We'll be in touch if we have further questions," Vargas said, then followed Jay.


They sat in the car without starting it, the thrum of summer insects and passing cars filling the night outside. A helicopter circled nearby, its searchlight tracing the neighborhood. Over all it was surprisingly quiet, the proverbial calm before the storm.

After a minute, Vargas finally spoke up. "Was there a particular reason you didn't push him about Felder or Jennings before you walked out on one of our two leads?"

Jay pointed at Thurgood's front window. As if on cue, the curtain fluttered, a thick hand parting the cloth before his face appeared, glancing up and down the street before disappearing once more.

"He's never going to outright give us an answer. He's dumb, but he's not stupid. Instead," Jay nodded at the house, "we rattle his cage, get him upset, then wait for him to screw up. Shit, you see how he reacted to Eric Felder's name compared to the others? We didn't know how Eric fit in, but given that reaction, I'm sure he's mixed up somehow. Thurgood doesn't just know the guy—he *hates* him."

"Okay, fine." Vargas sighed. "But next time, maybe do your trip down Memory Lane on your own watch? It's been a really long day."

When it became obvious that Thurgood wasn't leaving tonight, Jay started the engine and started back downtown.

The lights flashed by them as Perring Parkway turned into Hillen Road, the sodium-yellow streetlights turning into neon-red liquor stores, green takeouts offering lake trout, blue police boxes flashing from on high. A few people shambled up and down the sidewalk, a group of young boys riding wheelies on their bikes across the intersection.

"That story, about the parents," she said a couple minutes later. "You did a good job of making him comfortable so he'd let his guard down."

"Thanks."

"How much of it was a story?"

Before he could answer, Vargas yelped and grabbed Jay's hand. He stood on the brake pedal, screeching to a halt less than a foot from two kids who'd darted across the street. They turned their heads, revealing homemade Crimson Ghost masks, then took off again.

Jay and Vargas sat silently a moment, letting the sight sink in before he slowly let his foot off the pedal, heading downtown once more.

Vargas left her hand on Jay's. He didn't move it.

# 22

Jay walked Vargas to her rental in the garage, a small Korean car that probably handled like a lunch box on wheels.

"You should've at least gotten a standard size. It's only a couple bucks more than the compact."

"You think the Bureau will pay for a three-dollar upgrade?" She shook her head. "You should get some sleep," she said, stifling a yawn. "Tomorrow will probably be just as long a day."

"That's a good idea." He stood there for a minute, wavering slightly between his heels and his toes, his temples buzzing with anticipation.

But before he could open his mouth, Vargas smiled and said, "Good night, Agent Brodsky."

Jay sucked in his lips and nodded. "Night, Vargas."

Jay navigated his car through the city, back toward his apartment in south Baltimore. He found signs of support for the hack as he drove. Spray-painted messages on the doors of doctors' offices: *Healthcare is a right. Burn the suits.* Wheat-pasted posters of the Crimson Ghost face covering a full side of a row home. Picket signs with more anti-corporate rhetoric left against the wall of a drugstore. Small actions designed to make the people feel like they were actually making a dent in the behemoth of a megacorporation, as if they only needed to find that one chink in the armor so they could open it up and tear it all down.

It was horseshit, Jay thought. Nothing ever changed by not showering and stomping around in front of a building with some incendiary slogans on cardboard.

It hurt more, because it was what had finally driven Sam away.

Though Sam had voluntarily withdrawn from the Jesuseater tour, Jay knew it was because of him. And some part of him actually resented her for doing it. He knew it would be tough without her, but also hated being looked at like a broken toy, something to be fixed by his big sister. He thought that college would change things, help them be what they had been once again.

And things did get better for a while. Jay graduated with a double major in political science and computer science, snaring a position with the ACLU.

He was surprised to hear her laugh when he told her about the job, thinking she'd be proud of him, like he was finally joining the cause, albeit in his own way.

"Watch out for paper cuts," she said. "Nerds hate that shit."

As much as he loved his sister and admired her values at their core, he thought her approach was pretty shit, as was her attitude. How handing out flyers or teaching people to garden in vacant lots between houses effected more real change than the ACLU was beyond him.

Once she realized she was being a dick, she apologized, eventually wrapping her arm around his shoulders and pulling him in close. "I'm proud of you, kid. Not everyone needs to throw a brick through a window. We need people like you too."

It was a small consolation for Jay, one that seemed increasingly prescient as time passed and he became more disillusioned. Where he thought he'd be out in the field, he found himself instead filing law briefs, reviewing deposition transcripts, and doing the legwork of discovery research.

In short, he was goddamned bored.

If you wanted to make people's lives better, you had to actively go out, hunt down what was harming them, and destroy it. Class consciousness and courtroom litigation were great back in the seventies, he thought, but they wouldn't do a goddamned thing in the face of a terrorist group equipped with real weapons that could inflict real damage, real quick.

He hated to admit Sam was right about that, but unlike her, he could admit when his thinking had evolved.

Which was when he decided to join the FBI.

Jay had walked into the apartment he and Sam shared, a cardboard box in hand containing everything he'd had on his desk at the ACLU.

"Stealing office supplies?" Sam said, shaking her head.

Jay startled when he saw her. He'd thought she was hanging out at her girlfriend Emma's house.

"I thought you could use more three-ring binders." Jay dropped the box on the kitchen table, away from Sam.

"Did you get fired?" She snorted out a laugh, reaching into the fridge to get an apple. "Who gets fired from a nonprofit? They have to beg people to work there."

"It's actually pretty hard to get a job there," Jay said. "Lots of qualified applicants."

"So what'd you do?" Her teeth bit into the apple, a spray of juice landing on her cheeks. "Wait, did you really get fired?"

Jay shook his head.

"Did you leave?" Sam pushed.

Jay shrugged, moved to the cupboard and rummaged aimlessly through the little food he had. He wasn't hungry, just trying to avoid Sam's eyes, which was nigh-on impossible.

"Jacob." Sam loomed tall in the center of the room. "What's up, man?"

"Nothing. Just hungry."

"You haven't looked at me since you walked in."

Jay shrugged. "Thought you were over at Emma's. Been a

116

long week and I was just looking forward to some quiet."

Her feet tracked across the linoleum floor, coming to rest behind Jay.

"Seriously," she said. "Are you okay?"

Jay bit the inside of his cheek, turned to face her. "I got a new job."

Sam's worry evaporated instantly. "Why didn't you say that, dick?" She punched him in his shoulder as she'd done a thousand times before, in the exact place she knew would dead-arm him.

Jay shook his arm, rubbing it with his other hand. "It's not that big a deal."

"Course it is! ACLU is great, but I've been telling you for years there are better ways to make a change. 'Direct action leads to revolution, and no real social change has ever come without revolution.'"

Jay knew she was quoting someone, even if he didn't know who that someone was.

"So where's the new gig?"

He swallowed hard. "Better position. More hands-on work. It'll be good."

"That's awesome. I'm proud of you. Where is it?"

He scratched the left side of his neck, the right, the right, the left, unable to control himself even though he could see Sam watching him, analyzing his movements.

A cloud passed over her face. "Where is it?" Her voice dropped an octave.

Jay shrugged again. "The Bureau."

"You fucking stooge. A government job?" Her head drooped forward. "Bureau of what, Land Management? You gonna *kick the injuns off their land*?" Her tone mocked Jay.

"That's not what they do."

"Might as well. They don't do shit when all those shitbird libertarians take over government buildings, but we protest actual war crimes against indigenous peoples and we get the fire hose and teargas."

Jay screwed his face up, not knowing how to respond to that.

"And then when we—" Sam stopped short. Her eyes narrowed. "Wait, what do you mean, the Bureau? Not *a* bureau. *The* Bureau."

"I don't know how I'm supposed to respond to that. Can we just drop this? I'm tired."

"No." She grabbed his still-throbbing arm when he tried to walk around her. "Answer my question."

"You're overreacting."

"You're evading. Answer my question."

"There's nothing to answer."

"Then just answer it or—"

"The FBI, Sam." Jay immediately felt guilty for shouting. "I start in the academy on Monday."

Sam stood there, trembling with anger.

"They've been in contact since graduation. Think that my skill set could make me a valuable asset."

"Are you serious?" It was her turn to yell. "That can't be legal. That's fucking entrapment or..." She spit the words out, sputtered. "That has to be illegal. They're targeting students who are at their most impressionable."

"I'm not a student anymore—"

"It is. That's how they get people in. They feed them a bunch of shit about being superheroes and how they can be the one to stop the next 9/11—"

"No, they just—"

"Meanwhile they're indoctrinating them on all the ways to surveil their neighbors and—"

"You have to apply!"

Jay's voice echoed in the kitchen. Sam's face hung blank, a sight scarier than any of her multitude of anarchy screeds.

Silence stalked around the room, its claws grazing Jay's skin.

"You applied for this?" Her voice was barely more than a whisper.

"I just...," Jay started, then stopped, rearranging the words in his head. He'd known this moment would come at some point. For all the time he'd spent rehearsing it, he'd never figured out the right way to do it, the words to somehow bridge the distance that had grown over the last year without either of them resenting the other.

All he could manage was, "I just did it."

"You did it." The words hit the floor like a stack of weights. She laughed to herself, incredulous. "You did it."

"I can't go to shows and hand out vegan food the rest of my life. I have to grow up sometime."

"Grow up?" Her voice cracked, she screamed so loud. Which, given she screamed in a band four nights a week, was saying something. "You were grown up. You had a fucking job at a place that actually did good work."

"I just filed paperwork. I want to do actual work."

"Revolution isn't always fun. Sometimes the small things make the big ones possible."

Jay laughed aloud. "Says the woman who constantly complains about zoning restrictions and backlogged applications and people not being able to vote."

Sam's face tightened. "This isn't growing up. You're fucking brainwashed, man. You are a robot."

Jay felt his face flush, his chest contract. "I'm brainwashed? You see any logo on a shirt and want to cut it out because it's not punk."

"This isn't you. You're not one of them."

"How do you know?" He stepped toward her, the welling anger in him feeling good in some perverse way. "How do you know what I like when all I ever do is follow around in your shadow doing things you want to do?"

"Because anytime I left you alone, you had a fucking panic attack."

"That's not true."

"You called me every day your first year of college because

you were having a panic attack."

"I was checking in on you."

"This was not who you were raised to be. You were raised with morals, with a sense of justice. We all fought for the oppressed, the disenfranchised, people who couldn't fight for themselves because the system has been designed specifically to keep them down for generations. That's what Mom taught us and I sure as hell have done my best to do the same."

"And look how that went!" Jay reined himself in, trying to remain calm. "None of this shit is normal. How many kids spend their weekends at protests and wheat-pasting anarchist shit on the sides of abandoned buildings? You said they spent their entire lives fighting, yeah? What do they have to show for it?"

"They helped a lot of people."

Jay actually snorted when he laughed. "Yeah, helped a lot of people." The disdain in his voice canted the words. "Sure, they gave some people some food. Okay, that helped them for the six hours after. But what then? How did their lives get better after that?"

"Change is incremental. It doesn't happen immediately."

"That's a copout and you know it. They put everything they had into trying to change and nothing happened because you can't change society by handing out food. This"—Jay stabbed a finger in the air at her—"is how you change things. By making real moves. By getting into someplace where you have the power to make a difference with your voice. *That's* what I want to do, Sam. *That's* what will really make a difference. You don't change something by screaming stuff. You change it by doing stuff. And that's why, no matter how hard you try and how many casseroles you make, you won't have the impact I could while wearing a tie in some fucking building."

Sam flung the half-eaten apple at him. "What-the-fuck-ever. You go ahead and enlist then. Punch your card and let them brand you. See how it feels to be a number."

"You know what your problem is? Somewhere deep inside,

you know I'm right. But saying I'm right would mean admitting you're wrong and you've always been too damn stubborn and too married to your fucking ideology to do that. You'd rather burn alive than admit the house is on fire."

"Fuck you, narc."

"You are shapeless, Sam. You only know who you are by what you're against. If you didn't have anything to fight against, you wouldn't exist." The words scored Jay's tongue as he spit them out.

"And you by what's keeping you penned in. You're too scared to step outside and experience anything uncomfortable. You're not broke, JJ. You're just a bitch."

Jay flinched like her fist had kissed his face. He ground his teeth, anger pummeling through his veins, the last year bubbling up and spewing out, concentrated in one sentence he knew would cut her to her core. "And you're going to end up a fucking loser," he said, cold and even, "just like Dad."

When the words had been sitting in his mouth, they felt righteous, accurate, like they would force her to sit up and take notice that her little baby brother was becoming a man. But as soon as they landed, they felt like a cheap shot, meant only to show the other person how little he cared about them, how they meant less than nothing. It was something his father would say.

"Sam," Jay said, his mouth flapping open and closed and trying to reverse-engineer something that would deflect the blow.

Before he could get anything out, Sam spun on her heel and hurried out the back door, slamming it behind her, leaving him alone inside the echoes of the empty house. The last image he'd have of his sister, her storming out.

Even now as he parked a few blocks from his apartment, seven years removed from the incident, he could still feel the vibration of the door slamming on his skin.

He climbed out of the car, the air a mix of rank salt water from the harbor and static electricity from the approaching storm. *She saved my life back then and I drove her away,* he thought. *I have to do whatever I can to save hers now.*

Then a separate, darker thought popped up:

*But what if she doesn't want to be saved? What if she likes being with them?*

# 23

Zane Thurgood was freaking the fuck out.

He was going to get arrested. Not even arrested. Cops arrest you, so who knew what FBI agents would do to you. He had read on the internet what they did to those boys down in Gitmo. Hell, Zane didn't even like hummus in his mouth, much less up his asshole. And those boys had never even been convicted of anything. Running around with the people he was, doing what they'd been doing, who the hell knew what they'd do to him. The *federales* got a bead on Zane and his people, Jesus, he'd be begging for hummus instead of car batteries and nipple clamps.

Zane stopped a minute, told himself to relax, pull himself together, and think.

Two *federales* had shown up on his doorstep at ten thirty at night asking about the West Virginia job, which meant they knew something and they knew to come to him. How much they knew about the group or how far they saw into the operation, he couldn't tell. If they pinched him and threw his ass in jail, then Gram would have no one to come over and help her out. His mom sure as hell wouldn't bother driving the twenty minutes from Dundalk to help her own mother, the lazy skag. Gram would be all on her own and that, that was something Zane couldn't abide. His heart beat even harder just thinking about it.

This was the very thing Zane had worried about when he

joined up with the group. They promised him, they gave their assurances that they'd never get caught, that there was no way the cops or the Feds would get them because they wouldn't be around to get caught. Less than a week between the two jobs, then let the plan take care of itself. Besides, Mr. Forlán had it all figured out, explained all that hacker shit in a way that even Zane could understand.

Zane wasn't stupid, despite all the times Eric would say so, but Zane had a different kind of skill set. Eric, that midget asshole, he spent most of his day staring at a computer screen. What would happen when the power went out, when the old table finally broke, when someone caught a nail in their tire? Could Eric fix any of that? Hell, no. Zane could damn near build a new house, much less fix some piddly shit, but Eric always thought Zane was the stupid one. At least Patrick didn't talk to him like he was an asshole.

Aside from all the stuff Mr. Forlán said—because really, Zane *did* want to make a difference in the world and do something positive with his life—it was Kat who'd tipped him into throwing his lot in with the group. She was the kind of woman who could make a man do something he wasn't expecting and make it seem like it was his idea the whole time. No, that wasn't right, because that sounded manipulative. She didn't have to manipulate you into doing something: she *inspired* you to do it. There was a big difference between those two. When Eric went on about not being able to wipe out all debt because they were a small group, it was Kat who said small choices could have big impacts. And no matter how many times Eric told him he was barking up the wrong tree, Zane knew that if Kat could get to know him, to know the real him, she'd see that, together, they could make a big difference.

That thought, combined with the Feds and the possibility of Gram being in trouble, helped Zane realize what he had to do.

He snatched his phone and closed his eyes, saying the long string of numbers to himself both to refresh his memory and to psych himself up, then dialed and hit send.

The phone was silent a moment. Would the call go through? Were there roaming charges for this? Could you even do roaming with this phone?

He almost jumped when the ringing chirped in his ear, like a wake-up call. What was he doing? This was his chance. Why was he calling Forlán when he could call Kat, show her that he was reliable, that she could count on him and should give him a chance? He hung up before Forlán answered, called her instead. She answered on the third ring.

"Hey, it's—" Zane stopped himself short, started over. "Teniente, this is a comrade. The, um…" He tried to figure out how to describe himself in a way that would be vague enough so anyone listening couldn't figure out who he was—though they said over and over that there was no way anyone could listen in—but still let Kat know who was calling.

"Yes, comrade, I know who you are," she said.

Zane felt a flutter inside his chest.

"Okay, cool." *Cool? Jesus Christ, Zane.* He shook his head. "I know this is breaking rank, calling you, but it's important." And: to hell with Eric Felder.

"It's fine. What happened?"

"I just had two agents come to my house. It was—"

"Stop," she said. "I already know who it was."

"You do?" Goddamn, she really was good. And super hot. "What did they ask?"

"About my job, my Gram. They asked if I'd been…anywhere to visit relatives recently."

"And what did you tell them?"

"Jack shit," he said with a smile, then grimaced. "I told them nothing, Teniente."

"Great," she said. "You did a great job."

"Is there, like, something I should do next?"

"No, you hang tight and get ready for the morning. I'll take care of this."

"Uh, okay." He tried to think of a good signing-off line, something to make Kat know how capable he was, let him know she could count on Zane—really count on him. But before he could think of anything, the line went dead.

"You did a great job," he said to the empty space around him, smiling to himself. "Suck my dick, Eric."

# 24

Jay should have known better than to think he would sleep. Between the over-exhaustion of being awake nearly twenty-four hours and the fissures in the dam of this case that threatened to rupture and drown him—and the country, for that matter—in a current of shit, it was all he could do not to scream at the ceiling as he twitched and blinked and pinched the skin of his neck. He spent two hours alphabetizing records, working his way up to *T*, hoping that would calm his brain, but no such luck. He could have walked to one of the late nights on Fort Avenue and picked up a bottle of something that would knock him out, but having a hangover on top of an impending crisis wouldn't do much to help. Plus, it'd probably piss off Paloma.

*Paloma, now,* he thought. *Not Vargas?*

Jay rolled out of bed and got a glass of water, then padded across the carpet to the turntable and pulled the chain of the floor lamp beside it. He kneeled in front of the bookcase and pulled out two inches of records, sifting through them until he found the *Live from the Chop Shop* LP. He set the record on the turntable and plugged in Sam's headphones—*because records deserved real headphones,* she always said—and dropped the needle. A squeal of feedback beneath the singer shouting that he wanted to see everyone on the stage and jumping off the speakers, then the band kicked in.

Jay had gone to Emma's apartment a few days after Sam

127

walked out to see if Emma had any idea where she'd gone, but Emma was even more confused and angry than Jay. Apparently, while Emma was at work that afternoon, Sam had taken the few things she had at Emma's place and disappeared without a word.

Jay spent the next few months exhausting every lead he could think of. Emma gave him a name or two but generally saw him as the reason her girlfriend left and, coupled with the fact that he was now their antithesis—a federal agent—wanted nothing to do with him. The only act of kindness she showed Jay was to give him Sam's records.

"I can't have these in my place, but I can't throw them away. All of it makes me think of her, and thinking of her hurts too much," she said, letting her Chelsea cut—long bangs and side-burns, shaved everywhere else—hang over her eyes to keep the narc from seeing her tear up. "But it's not for your benefit. You can rot in hell for all I care."

Jay sighed and pulled out the album art to study it.

The cover was a black-and-white photo of the club, shot from a low angle to catch the neighboring fire escapes and the silhouetted rat-drinking-a-martini logo of the Aught-O Bar next-door—the zero and O symbol of the bar's name meaning Aught-O Bar to those who knew, Zero Zero to everyone else— where bands congregated before and after a show. Jay flipped it over to the back, which had a photo of the crew who hung out around the club, shot from overhead. In the center of the crew was Sam, her arm hung around Emma's neck. He noticed Zane Thurgood standing two people behind them, his arms crossed over his chest as he stared straight ahead while everyone else looked up. Jay scanned the crowd, looking for familiar, albeit younger, faces. Then, on the edge of the photo, he saw Patrick Felder standing next to a black girl with thick dreads. Jay stared at the photo a moment, sifting through faces and connections and long-lost punk shows.

"How did this Felder fit in?" he said to the empty room. He

had a sinking feeling, like it was so obvious in retrospect.

Comrade Pat. The club's promoter and de facto boss. He should've seen that coming. Patrick Felder—née Comrade Pat—had been a big Marxist at that point and had incurred several black eyes because of his incessant lecturing and badgering people who just wanted a coffee from Starbucks. Jay knew that name was familiar.

"Got you, asshole."

*Slow it down a second, because proximity does not equal conspiracy. It sure as hell suggests it, but suggestion isn't prosecutable.*

Jay continued to scan the crowd. When the first side of the record ended, he got his phone before starting the B-side. He flicked the camera on and zoomed in, looking at shirts, hands, patches, anything that might be something.

The record ended with a scratch. Jay put on a Quicksand record and resumed the search.

Halfway through *Slip*'s B side, he saw a face, standing near the back of the crowd—Luke Jennings, standing next to someone who could've been Comrade Pat's twin.

Eric Felder.

Patrick was arrested for brawling for a labor union protest, while his brother worked IT for IBM, and likely would know how to program. Such divergent paths for two siblings raised under the same roof that it gave Jay a twinge of nostalgia. Patrick and Eric were also sons of an activist, who was also a snitch. Jay wondered how much the brothers knew about their father, how much more there was to know about his own parents.

Jay snapped a photo, then yanked off the headphones and went to his home rig, a laptop running Linux with custom-coded security measures. He got online and ran an image search with the photo but got nothing. Then he ran a normal search for Eric Felder, clicked on images.

Forty pages of results. He began to sort through faces. The name didn't seem that common to Jay, and he was surprised at the array of faces on his screen, including a woman with long red hair and an Adam's apple.

Jay clicked through the third page. Near the bottom, he found a small photo. It wasn't very clear, but he blew it up and held the album cover beside it.

"Found you." He took a photo to show Vargas.

He tapped his fingers on the desk, rapid-fire. The clock broadcasted one twenty-one in accusatory red numbers. Calling Vargas this late, or early, would be rude, but she should know about this. He stared at the album photo while considering it.

*Screw it,* he thought. *A text.* If it didn't wake her up, they'd talk in the morning. If it did, they'd talk now.

*You awake?*

He tried a few more search terms, looking up various combinations of their names. He found one photo with both Thurgood and Jennings in it on a woman's Twitter feed. The woman stood in the middle with her arms draped around both, the caption reading *#TBT me n my boyz Eighty-Five and Luke, pit kingz.* Eighty-five because Thurgood was born in, wait for it, 1985. Jay wondered if all their nicknames were that derivative, then laughed to himself, hearing Paloma say the same thing to him. A five-minute search showed the woman was now a kindergarten teacher with three kids of her own and a penchant for half-triathlons. Jay reminded himself that the fact Thurgood and Jennings were in the same photo didn't prove they knew each other, since a lawyer could easily posit that they merely had a common friend.

He wondered if Zane Thurgood knew about Dumpy Felder, that part of his crew came from a line of snitches. Not that informants weren't an important part of work in the Bureau, but Jay had expected more from these people. If Jay couldn't figure out their operation, what did that say about his abilities as an agent? Still, showing up in photos together was something to file away, one more possible piece of an increasingly disparate puzzle.

His phone buzzed.

*I'm not sending you photos of my tits. You can jerk off to Twitter like every normal adult who doesn't want porn in their browser history.*

He typed out a response. *Who says I'm not right now?*

He'd barely set his phone down when it rang.

Her voice was thick with sleep. "For as straightlaced as you look, you're pretty fucked up."

"That's actually not the first time I've heard that."

"I'd imagine not." She yawned on the other end. "What's so important?"

He took her through the night, explaining the record he found in Thurgood's house and his face-by-face investigation of it.

"So you weren't just record shopping."

"A little bit of ogling, but no, not shopping."

He explained the Comrade Pat connection, then Eric Felder, Zane Thurgood, and Luke Jennings, but veered far wide of his sister and Dumpy Felder.

There was a long silence at the end of it. He wondered if she'd fallen asleep.

Finally, her sleepy voice came through. "We have secondary connections"—she paused long enough for effect—"but nothing explicitly connecting them to each other or to the break-ins."

"Not yet. But I bet we run those names through NCIC, Accurint, LexisNexis, and we'll come up with something. Especially with Comrade Pat."

"I bet we will," she said. "In the morning."

"Sounds good. Soooo," he said, "no nudes, then?"

She breathed out a laugh. "Good night, Agent Brodsky."

They lingered for a moment in silence.

"You're still on the line."

She sighed, then ended the call without a word. It was the nicest hang-up Jay had ever had.

If there had been little hope of sleep before, there was no way in hell Jay's brain would stop its whirring now. He went to the kitchen, the sky over south Baltimore softly shifting from deep blue to burnt pink while a pot of coffee brewed.

Jay switched to his work laptop and logged into the Bureau's server through a secured portal, entered his authentication information, and navigated around to open the IP address logs related to the case. Even if he had been working on his custom-built home machine with its superior memory and processing power, he'd half-expect to see steam puff from the keyboard and a cartoon RIP tombstone pop onto the monitor after opening all of these files. He hoped to god his work laptop would hold up. He began searching the logs, first for *comrade*, *Chop Shop*, then *Marx*, *punk*, *savage*, anything he could think of that might link the groups. Most of them were stupid—he hoped that someone he was chasing so hard wouldn't so baldly use *Punk Rock Pat* as a handle—but few produced any real results.

As he searched, he saw a handle pop up a few times. *Tupac the Second*. He'd been joking with Vargas about the digital incarnation of Tupac Shakur, but now it got him thinking.

He set the work laptop on the carpet and went back to his home rig, dove into some hacker forums and message boards, scanning for anything related to Tupac—his actual name; his name with the number two; or Makaveli, one of his other stage names—but found little outside of quoted lyrics or conspiracy theories regarding his death.

Frustrated, Jay pushed the laptop aside and went to get another cup of coffee. He stood by the bay window, the steam from the coffee wafting up into a small oval of condensation on the cool glass. The sun had broken the night and was steadily climbing up the horizon, likely the last nice day they'd have until the storm passed. He'd have to head into work soon, and he could probably do with a shower. But something kept pulling at him, like the connection, the key to everything, was sitting right in front of him if only he could figure out which switch turned the light on.

Four stories below him, two girls in sequined going-out clothes wobbled down the street, the cobblestones exacerbating the battle between gravity and blood-alcohol level, their arms slung around each other's neck to keep them upright. Their shoulders heaved up and down, convulsively, like they were crying, maybe a result of beer-goggle judgment or a liquor-sharpened tongue. Then one of the girl's head flew backwards and they stopped in place, bracing against each other. Even from up here, Jay could see that they weren't crying, they were cracking up. The taller girl stomped her foot on the street, it was so funny, which threw them both off-balance. They toppled over, sprawled out across the dirty asphalt, still howling with laughter. Jay wondered what exactly they were feeling, and how that felt.

His phone dinged. His alarm. He rested his forehead against the window. Barely six in the morning and it was shaping up to be another long day.

Then Jay thought, *it's not crying, it's laughing. It's not what it looks like.*

He hurried over to his home rig and brought up a search engine, plugging in Tupac and the Roman numeral II. Like Tupac the Second.

The first hit was not for Tupac Shakur, but for José Gabriel Túpac Amaru—known as Túpac the Second—the leader of an indigenous uprising against the Spanish in Peru and the inspiration behind one Lesane Parish Crooks taking the handle Tupac Amaru Shakur.

*Goddamn,* Jay thought. *That's more like it.*

# 25

The butter was still cold and solid when Ron Kuzak shoved the toast in his mouth. He washed it down with a swig of hot coffee, turning the food into a viscous slurry as he swallowed. A chunk of crust stuck in his throat, making him cough. He pounded his fist against his chest, feeling his eyes water.

"You can't even make toast right?" his daughter said as she slung her backpack off her shoulder, landing on the marble floor next to the chair at the breakfast bar.

Ron tried to respond but by the time he cleared his throat, she'd already put her earbuds in, those white stems protruding from her ears like radio antennae. Ron mumbled something incoherent and poured more coffee down his throat. He saw the bottle of Suntory Hibiki thirty-year sitting on the counter, resting against the backsplash. It was supposed to be a birthday gift from his wife, Karen, but she gave it to him early in the days after the breach happened. The stone in the backsplash had been imported from Thailand after she saw it on vacation with the kids two years ago and insisted on using it in the remodel. Ron was grateful his bonus covered it all so he could just buy it and not have to argue with her.

"Michael," he called out, getting no response from upstairs. "Emily, is your brother dressed yet?"

She bobbed her head to whatever music she was listening to, repeating the lyrics under her breath. When he was young,

Ron's father used to tear the headphones off his ears when he was studying if he didn't answer quick enough. While the urge to pluck those buds from her ears rose at times, Ron had sworn never to be like his father. So instead, he tapped Emily on the shoulder to get her attention.

"Your brother. Is he dressed?"

Emily's face screwed up as if he just told her he started following her on Snapchat. "How would I know? I'm not his mom."

Ron reconsidered the bottle, thought a splash or two might make the day go better. He quickly reconsidered: having to step down as CEO of Tidewater Mutual because of this damn security breach was bad enough. Doing it while publicly drunk would make things that much worse.

Karen whisked into the room, adjusting the pin in her hair. "Emily, please be nice to your father. This is a bad day for him."

Emily muttered, "I'm not the one who fucked up."

Karen snapped at her. "Don't use language like that in my house. All I'm asking is that you try to be pleasant this morning. Is that too much to ask?"

Emily stared at her. Karen stared back harder. "No, Mom," she said, drawing out all the vowels.

"Thank you." Karen gave Ron a peck on the cheek before smoothing down the lapels of his suit and plucking a piece of fuzz from his sleeve. "You're going to kill it today."

Ron grunted.

"Say it with me."

Ron sighed, then gave his best version of a smile. "I'm going to kill it today."

"You're goddamned right you are."

"Hey, language," Emily said.

Karen took his hands in hers. "The breach wasn't your fault. We'll be in Koh Samui in two days, and by the time we get back, you'll already have something else lined up."

Ron brought her hands to his lips and kissed them. His phone vibrated, the message saying his driver was outside.

"Is the generator ready, in case we lose power?" Karen said.

"Storm's not coming till late tonight or tomorrow. I'll get it together after work."

Karen flashed a disapproving look.

"It'll be fine, hon. Tell your brother I said bye," he said to Emily before turning back to Karen and nodding. "Time to take care of this."

Ron slid into the back seat of the Land Rover and told the driver to hurry up. The driver responded with something but Ron ignored him, immediately turning to his phone to get the public's pulse on the whole deal. Most was run-of-the-mill outrage, concerns about personal security and whatever. Nothing to make him change tack for his press conference. He felt a bead of sweat roll down his chin and reached for the rear climate control but found it wasn't there.

*Goddamn piece of shit*, he thought. He usually had the driver bring the Maybach or Rolls but thought that would come off as insensitive today. The job didn't really matter too much, but he didn't want public opinion to turn any further, which would delay whatever new appointment he would get. Maybe some sort of cabinet position if he played this right.

After twenty minutes of flipping through Twitter and various news sites, he was sufficiently satisfied with the coverage. It wasn't positive by any means, but whoever had hacked into their systems wasn't really concerned with exposing things. They went straight for billing and stayed there. If they'd poked further, looked deeper—Ron didn't want to think about it. Didn't need to, anyway. He'd be out of there soon enough, on to other projects. *That is,* he thought, *if this damn driver ever got there.*

"Hey, I'm on a schedule here," he yelled up to the driver.

"You want to hurry the hell up?"

Then he looked around, saw the row homes with plywood across the windows, the dirty little kids running around through the streets, opening up fire hydrants and spraying each other. He didn't know which neighborhood this was, wasn't even sure this was Baltimore.

"Asshole! What the hell?"

"GPS rerouted me."

"To where, Compton?" Ron laughed to himself.

"Not sure, sir. I just follow the directions."

Ron craned forward to get a look at the driver, just now realizing this wasn't his normal one. He couldn't remember what the guy's name was. Clark or John or Tyrone. But it wasn't this lardass. And now that he took a better look at him—the tattoos peeking out from under his uniform collar, the scraggly gang tattoos barely covered by his driving gloves—he wasn't sure he wanted this son of a bitch to continue driving him.

The Land Rover slowed down, turned right into a warehouse parking lot. Chain-link fence surrounded the area, and another person dressed in a chauffeur uniform wheeled open the large gate.

Ron began to sweat, to panic.

"Wait—wait—hold on. What's going on?"

The driver raised two fingers as the Land Rover passed through the gate, the other chauffeur wheeling it closed behind them.

"Who are you? Where are you taking me?" Ron's voice betrayed him, cracking as he yelled. He tried to fling the door open, but the lock wouldn't budge.

"Just following GPS, boss," the lardass said, pausing for a moment while the warehouse's metal bay door raised, revealing what looked like an abandoned auto parts distribution center. "Sorry about the child locks."

They pulled to a stop in the middle of the cement floor. Skeletons of storage racks lined the sides, pocked by broken-down industrial equipment, forklifts and such. In the far corner stood a floodlight, shining down on a large swath of black cloth hung between several poles, creating a black backdrop.

Standing in the center of it all were two suited men, both of whom he immediately recognized from the golf course. Wade Roane, who ran Bay State, and Dan Moore, head of Exemplar.

What scared him wasn't so much that they were in an abandoned warehouse in god-knows-where Baltimore, but that neither Wade nor Dan wore blindfolds. These fuckers weren't worried about them seeing their faces.

His door opened, a tall, tattooed woman standing in front of him.

"Welcome to the revolution, Mister Kuzak," she said. "We've been waiting for you."

# 26

Jay's phone was buzzing as he got out of the shower. He figured it was Vargas and pulled on a pair of track pants first, as if she'd be able to see him.

When he got to his phone, he found it wasn't Vargas calling, but Yemin texting—*u c this?*, followed by a link.

If this was more blueprints for *Star Wars* furniture, he was going to scream. But instead of galactic paramilitary beds, it was a press release from Bayside Bank, one of the largest banks in the region that wasn't a national chain. Jay skimmed it.

*We cannot overstate how important it is for everyone to remain calm.*

*We are well aware of the security breaches that have occurred in various local health insurance providers, but we want to reinforce to all of our loyal customers that their money is absolutely, 100 percent safe.*

*We are one, united company, and no branch in any of the twenty-six states where we operate will be affected any more than they would be at our main branch in Maryland.*

Then the closing sentence:

*It is important to note, for the safety of our customers as well as every other bank in the country, that withdrawing large amounts of money quickly will only serve to encourage these types of terrorist attacks.*

Jay's stomach sank at that last bit. He could read between the lines: they didn't give a shit about additional terrorist attacks; they were worried about the stability of the national banking system were there to be a huge outflow of cash. He'd been concerned the hack would spread across the country and tank the economy, but he hadn't considered the secondary effects like this. And data integrity was small potatoes compared to the all-consuming wave of public panic that was about to wash over the eastern seaboard.

You tell people they got hacked, they'll get annoyed and change their password. You make them think their money isn't safe? They will lose their collective minds.

Jay texted back, only needing one word.

*Wonderful.*

He flicked on the television. A map showed the projected path of Hurricane Donovan, headed right up the Chesapeake and making landfall within the next day. He changed the channel. A field correspondent stood before a group on the street, asking for their reactions to the hacks, a scene Jay had been seeing more and more in the past few days.

A younger bearded man crossed his arms and leaned back. "I think it's cool, you know, seeing that people still care about stuff, but where's that line, you know? How do I know they're not going to hack me next?"

The woman beside him said, "I think it's terribly illegal, just going in and deleting things like they are. Who gave them permission to do that? Who do they think they are?"

The correspondent leaned down to bring a small girl into the frame, ponytails arcing off either side of her head. As the camera panned, Jay caught at least four people in the crowd with Crimson Ghost masks on. One held a poster-board sign with a Xeroxed image of the Harper twins. *They have their martyr and they have their look*, he thought. *This is going to spread like crazy.*

"I think they're mean," the little girl said. "They took my dad's job with all their stuff."

An older man pushed his yellow-tinted sunglasses back up his nose, leaned into the reporter. "Let me tell you something. This is all the government's doing. Sure, they're gussying it up like terrorists, but it's all them. They're just trying to get us angry and scared so we sign over more of our lives to them. Been happening the last fifty years but everyone's too damn busy texting and phone-watching to see it."

His wife beside him coughed into her fist, a deep, rattling smoker's cough. "Those pig fuckers can burn in hell for all I care."

The correspondent jumped in front of the old woman before she could trigger more fines from the FCC and sent it back to the studio, where they were covering the imminent press conference of the Tidewater Mutual CEO announcing his resignation.

Jay turned off the TV and downed the rest of his coffee. They had a hell of a lot of work ahead of them and time was running out.

Jay was sitting at the conference room table, staring a hole through the wipe-board, when Vargas walked in. He'd closed the door to keep out the constant murmur of people on the phone with other departments, secretaries diverting calls for comment. A heavy tension had spread throughout the office.

"I figured you wouldn't sleep last night so I made a stop on my way in," she said, setting a Dunkin' Donuts bag and two coffees on the table.

"I don't do doughnuts," he said with an apologetic smile. "Too much sugar."

"And you said I'm not a real American?" She shook her head. "Did Agent Yemin show you that press release?"

"Yeah, texted me the link this morning." Jay paused a second. "Wait, he texted it to you too?"

Vargas glanced over her shoulder and gave him a look he couldn't decipher. Jay changed his mind, grabbed a doughnut, and took a bite. "You think people will listen?"

"Hell no. Shit, I saw two protests outside the bank on my way in."

Vargas closed her eyes and exhaled hard before gesturing toward the board. Written on it were a number of nicknames— Eighty-Five, Comrade Pat—with their legal equivalents listed beneath. Jay's laptop hummed on the desk beside him.

"These are our guys?"

Jay grabbed a coffee and walked over to the board. "These are our guys."

He smacked his marker on the names, harder than he meant. Knowing they were just out of his reach was getting to him. "To recap, in case you were groggy last night, Zane Thurgood used to go to shows at the Chop Shop, which was booked by Comrade Pat, whose brother is Eric Felder. Luke Jennings also went to shows there and presumably knew Patrick and Zane because they were in a photo together."

"Not necessarily."

"I know that. It might not hold up in court, but the punk scene was incredibly incestuous, especially in Smalltimore, Maryland, so for our purposes we can run with it right now. If they didn't actually know each other, they knew about each other."

"'Comrade Pat,' 'Eighty-five,' 'Kat Savage,'" Vargas said. Jay winced at hearing her name—which he'd left off the board—but he kept it internal. "Why can't you just have normal names?"

"Because that would be conformist," he said, the sarcasm clear in his voice. "Though you have no idea how many Jim Joneses or Crusty Petes you'll meet at a crust-punk show."

"I don't understand anything you're saying."

"Doesn't matter. These are the players we know, so we need to figure out how we find them."

"Let's take a step back," Vargas said. "Their first target was straight medical billing. Large conglomerate. The second was likely the same but had an extra element of social consciousness—in my opinion—but the furrier was completely personal.

No message beyond that, maybe like ADB. All of which is consistent with your, what, punk ethos?"

"It's more...nuanced than that. But ADB attacked animal-cruelty sites specifically. This is bigger. These Ghosts have a real purpose and a dangerous vendetta." Jay could feel the pieces of this case floating around inside his head, but each was too slippery to hold on to. He blinked, right, left, left, right. Left, right, right, left. *Don't start this. Not now.* "And to top it off, they have enough technological prowess to know which phones to use so that we can't access any of their data."

Vargas inhaled deeply, stopped partway. "What if they're not all smart enough to use them?"

They looked at each other, said, "Thurgood," at the same time.

Vargas snatched Jay's laptop and started typing. A few seconds later, she smiled and ran her tongue along the edge of her teeth. "Pay-as-you-go."

Jay pulled up a chair beside her. "Let's see who young Zane likes to talk to."

It took some cross-referencing between LexisNexis and NCIC, but after a while they had a full record of Thurgood's call log. Scores to Comrade Pat. A few to Eric Felder. A bunch to his grandmother and the occasional incoming from his mother. A dozen to a burner phone.

Then one to a number flagged as unlisted. Not just unlisted to the general public, but completely unavailable.

"What the hell?" Vargas said. She put the unlisted number into the database, hoping to triangulate it. They both sipped at their coffees, no longer hot, while the computer searched. "How are you still functioning without sleep?"

"Had a lot on my mind. Need to keep moving."

She shook her head. "I need at least three hours, a little recharge."

"I also had a pot of coffee before I came in."

The search ended, displaying only one call from the unlisted number to an eight-digit number starting with country code 5-9-8.

"What the hell is the Palacio Legislativo?" Jay said, completely butchering the pronunciation.

"Legislative palace. It's where congresses meet."

"Where's five-nine-eight?"

Vargas keyed in the country code and came back with Montevideo, Uruguay. She leaned back in her seat and let out a long breath while Jay walked over to the wipe-board, staring at it.

"Why is this number," Vargas said toward the ceiling, "who gets calls from Zane Thurgood, calling an MP in Uruguay?"

Jay tapped the marker in his palm. "Wait, I saw something in the IP address logs last night. Remember *Tupac the Second*? It was actually a warrior not a rapper. He led an uprising in Peru in the 1700s."

"Seriously, Brodsky. Not all brown people are the same. Peru and Colombia are totally different countries."

He wrote the name with roman numerals in the center of the wipe-board, then came next to her. "I'm saying, google Túpac the Second and Uruguay and see what you get."

The first listing that popped up was for the Tupamaros, also known as Movimiento de Liberación Nacional-Tupamaros, who were a left-wing urban guerilla group in Uruguay during the sixties and seventies.

"I can see why Tupac Shakur picked the name," he said a little too chirpy, while he was thinking, *What the hell, Sam? Please don't be doing what I'm terrified you're doing.*

Jeanie burst into the room, startling Jay. She held a laptop in her hand and a terrified expression on her face.

"What?" Jay said, feeling his entire body tense up.

"You," she sputtered. "You need to see this."

# 27

Jeanie set the laptop on the table. On the screen were four figures, all dressed in black jumpsuits, a red armband wrapped around their left biceps, their faces obscured by masks painted like the Crimson Ghost. They made a semicircle around three men in suits, positioned in a triangle, each pointing a pistol at the next. Each had a piece of paper taped to his suit jacket with a name scrawled on it: Bay State, Tidewater Mutual, and Exemplar. Just so it was abundantly clear.

Jeanie cleared her throat, gestured toward the screen. "We've been monitoring social media and the web since the first videos surfaced. This just came online. We followed up and none of the CEOs reported to work today, not even the one with the press conference." She pointed at the counter beneath the video. Already millions of views. "We're tracing the account, but I'm sure it'll come up as a puppet of a puppet like the others."

"Is it live?" Jay said.

"Came online ten minutes ago," Jeanie repeated.

"That doesn't mean it just happened. Could've happened hours ago and they just posted it."

"Darragh is working with forensics to analyze it, see what kind of metadata we can pull from it."

Jay grunted approval, then pressed play.

The Ghost in the middle—a woman—stalked back and forth, a hyena surveying its prey.

"These ghouls have ruined the lives of hundreds of thousands of people with their companies. Yet they believe they can simply resign and wash their hands of their crimes against the public—and not just walk away, but walk away with hundreds of millions of dollars? That is their reward for perpetrating financial and social violence? They are in charge of companies that should help the people, but instead they suck the life from them. Cursed is the soldier who turns arms against their people."

Jay's ears lit up as the Ghost spoke those words, his childhood crashing down on him in a rush of violent confirmation. *Maldito sea* whatever, whatever. The phrase their mother always used to say, that Sam started saying because of her. This woman, the Ghosts' mouthpiece, was definitely his sister. The performer of the group, as always. The sister who had disappeared from his life seven years almost to the day was currently standing in front of three terrified men pointing guns at each other. His palms went slick, temples pounding. Bile crept up his throat, an acrid, metallic taste filling his mouth. He inhaled hard through his nose, feeling beads of sweat on his forehead. *Don't lose it now.*

Jay swallowed hard as Exemplar choked out a plea.

"Please, please don't do this. We said we'd give you all the money we have." He sniffled and snuffed between words. The pistol wavered in the air.

"He is correct," Sam continued. "They offered to give all their money to help people affected by the fascistic policies their companies employ. But these men here, if they were stripped of all their wealth, how many people would that really help? Four hundred? Six? Maybe a thousand? While that would alleviate stress for some, what about the rest? Those who would still be suffocating under crippling debt, those who have sold their houses to afford medical treatment, those who have had to ration insulin—the one thing that keeps them alive—until their coverage period restarts. What about them?"

Tidewater sputtered, "We'll—we'll give them anything they—"

He was cut short when one of the Ghosts stepped forward and smashed a pistol on the back of his head, yelling at him to stop groveling. In the background, Jay saw another Ghost—a fat one—cringe.

Zane Thurgood. Jay was sure of it. His jaw clamped down hard, feeling the pain radiate through his muscles, absorb into his bones. He had his chance with Thurgood and let it ago. He wouldn't do that again.

"What about the ones who died for lack of coverage? Sarah Harper, who had to choose which one of her sons to let die? What are her sons' lives worth? There's not enough money in the world to make this right, so you will not pay with money. You will pay with your blood."

Sam stepped forward, behind Tidewater. "To ensure that everyone understands we are not spiting the face, know that we will in fact seize those bonuses you offered. We will distribute that money to those who have been traumatized by these companies. And to show mercy, we will allow one of these ghouls to go free and let the people decide what his fate should be. If no one touches him once he is roaming the streets, so be it. I will not argue. But if the people decide to seek justice, retribution, then it is the people's will."

The man from Tidewater began sputtering again, then quickly quieted and lowered his head when the Ghost stepped forward.

"The rule is simple. Whoever lives, leaves." She looked down at them, and even though her face was covered, Jay could feel disgust radiating from her. "Now, choose."

She stepped back.

The CEOs glanced back and forth between the others, their faces wrought with terror, the pistol muzzles jerking and bobbing. Bay State swallowed hard as he looked at Tidewater. Tidewater shook his head.

"We can't just," Tidewater stammered, "we can't just kill someone. We're not animals. We're not—not murderers."

"These people," Sam said, "they have no problem dealing

out death to the masses, but they are afraid to get their own hands dirty. They will make a mother choose which of her sons to let die, but refuse to disappoint stockholders. They step on us, down here in the gutter, to protect their shoes that cost more than we make in a month." Sam crouched down, put her face close to Tidewater but spoke loud enough so the camera would pick it up. "You are murderers. Your companies, your policies, they kill thousands and thousands of people every year. You do not cure disease; you *are* the disease. Now you choose. Will it be him?" She pointed at Bay State, then moved to Exemplar, who shook his head violently. "Or will you let him shoot you first?"

"They won't shoot. They're better than that." He swallowed hard, as if steeled. "Better than you."

Jay could feel Sam smiling behind her mask. "You sure about that? You're sure he won't kill you to save himself?"

"Yes, I'm sure."

"Do you think Emily, Michael, and Karen would agree? Would they trust him?" Her voice dropped, low and menacing. "Or would they tell you to pull the fucking trigger so all four of you can be in Thailand next week?"

Tidewater's eyes were wide with shock, his mouth opening to ask how the hell she knew who his family was, when a blast rang out. Bay State blinked as if just waking, staring at the muzzle of his pistol, the thread of smoke twisting from the hole, the mess of gore that sat where Exemplar's head had been three seconds ago.

"Wade," Tidewater said, his mouth moving but no words following.

"They know everything. Our families. Our addresses. I can't...," he trailed off.

Then something passed over both of their faces, the curtain of realization lowering. They both pointed their pistol at the other and tried to squeeze the trigger first.

Two bangs, nearly simultaneous. Blood splashed across Sam's

mask. The two carcasses fell over, landing on the floor with a sigh of finality.

Jeanie coughed out a sob, then hurried from the room.

Sam moved around the bodies, positioning her face in the center of the frame, her eyes glittering behind that mask.

"This is the beginning."

The video ended, silence hanging heavy in the conference room. Jay's brain vibrated as if a hundred angry hornets were trapped inside his skull. His sister, the one who took him to shows, who coaxed him from beneath the bed after his mother died, the only family he had left, had just coerced three people into murder.

Something boiled inside Jay's stomach, roiling in his gut. Sam had gone too far. It was bad when they launched the attack, but they had murdered three people. This was the beginning of a new, more violent, deadlier phase with their group.

He had to end this now, before more people got hurt.

Jay stalked out of the room, Vargas calling out behind him, "Brodsky, where the fuck are you going?" Instead of turning and answering, he fled faster, doing all he could to not sprint out of the building, getting away before they could catch up with him.

He didn't know where to find Sam, didn't know whether this was live or taped in the last twelve hours, but he knew one place he could get answers: Thurgood.

# 28

Jay's hand hung in the air, two inches from Thurgood's front door. His knuckles and palm throbbed from pounding on it, knowing that Thurgood was in there hiding, that Thurgood *had* to be in there, because Thurgood was the one weak link in the chain that connected to Sam. He had searched for her for years and couldn't bear the thought of her slipping away again now that she was so close.

Jay was ready to start pounding again when he heard a distinctive click from next door.

He froze in place, called out, "I'm an FBI agent."

"I don't give a good goddamn what you are," a woman said, her voice covered with thousands of spent cigarette butts. "Waking my ass up after the overnight is what you are to me. Zane there wanted you to come in, he'd let you in. But apparently he don't."

"I'm going to lower my hands slowly," Jay said, turning to face her, "and show you my identification."

"I said I don't—"

"You might want to make sure your safety isn't on before you start threatening people," Jay said.

Her eyebrows made a *V*, and she glanced down to check the pistol. When she looked back up, Jay had already drawn and was locked on the middle of her forehead. She pursed her lips. "Made me think I'd left it on a second."

Jay shrugged. "As I was saying, Miss…"

"I don't have to tell you shit."

He glanced at the mailbox, squinted, and almost laughed to himself. "As I was saying, Miss Samson, I'm an FBI agent and I'm looking for Zane."

"Course you are." Miss Samson shook her head. "That boy's always in trouble. Only good things he ever done was care for Mamie and redo my flower beds."

"They are very beautiful," Jay said, trying to defuse her. "He been here today?"

"Like I said, I *was* asleep," she said, "so I didn't see anything."

Jay looked closer at the pistol in her hand, examining the shape and design. "Miss Samson, you know what kind of gun that is?"

"Yeah," she said, clearing her throat with a rattling cough, "the kind that puts holes in people who bang on doors too loud."

"Looks to me like a Smith and Wesson. Is that right?"

"Sure."

It wasn't. It was a run-of-the-mill Colt.

"Then I'm sure you also have a license for it."

"Course I do."

She didn't.

"Semiautomatics are illegal in Maryland, Miss Samson." It also wasn't a semiautomatic. Jay loosened his grip, lowered his pistol to show he wasn't all bad. "I'm going to be frank. I don't have time to argue with a hardworking woman who is obviously trying to get some sleep, much less write up a report for an illegal firearm. How about you go back inside, I keep it down out here, and we forget this whole thing ever happened?"

She looked at him a minute, then arced spit over the porch railing. "Y'all can be real pricks sometimes, you know that?"

"I've heard, Miss Samson."

He waited a moment for her to retreat back inside, then for the lock to slide across her door, then to make sure she wasn't peering through the blinds. When the street was as quiet as it would ever get, Jay took a deep breath to calm himself, then reared back and smashed his foot against the door.

The wood gave with little hesitation, the doorknob smacking back against the wall. Jay stepped into the house. Where before it had vibrated with loneliness, with age, now it just felt like a nonentity, a non-space. Jay pushed that all aside and began scouring the house for anything useful, anything that could lead him to Sam.

He started in the entertainment stand, rifling through the papers stacked on either side of the box television. Past-due notices. Solicitations from retirement communities, addressed to Mamie Thurgood two blocks over. Coupon clippers. Nothing useful. He moved to the cabinet beneath the TV, found only VHS copies of *Black Belt Theater* and bootleg copies of punk shows. One caught his eye: The Savages logo, drawn in Sharpie. A piece of paper stuck out from the case. He pulled it out, found it wasn't paper, but a Polaroid. In it, the group posed together as a crew. Sam's head was canted slightly back, her expression somewhere between stoic and ballsy, as if daring the photographer to tell her to smile. She was still young, though it was post-Savages—and, apparently, pre-terrorist. Standing next to her was Thurgood, his forearm resting on her shoulder. Something about his posture, his composure, made Jay think he was achieving a lifelong goal in that moment. On either side were the rest of them: Comrade Pat, Luke Jennings, other assorted punks.

Jay felt something bordering on nostalgia looking at the photo, seeing anew the woman he'd looked up to for so many years, so strong in her convictions—even if Jay didn't always agree with them—and determined to let nothing stand in her way. Left, right, right, left. Right, left, left, right. Right, left, left right. Left, right—*stop, just stop*. The nostalgia ebbed into a sensation closer to disgust, but a warm disgust, where he wanted to hug her and scream at her at the same time, then take a brick to the face of these people she'd chosen over him.

Jay slid the photo back into the tape case and tossed it in the cabinet, continued searching.

The kitchen revealed nothing except a surprising amount of soy products and protein bars. Off the kitchen sat a small room, a sitting nook Thurgood had repurposed as a greenhouse. Several orchids lined a shelf by the window, their scent thick and musty. In front of those were carnivorous plants, some Venus flytraps and pitcher plants. Thurgood was nothing if not a study in contrasts. There was no basement, which meant the only remaining room was Thurgood's bedroom.

He came back into the living room, frustrated at the lack of something, anything, that would help him track down Sam, help him stop them before they did something even worse than pushing three men to murder each other. Furious that all of this had gone so far, that he hadn't seen something earlier in Sam to tip him off. Livid—and crushed—that she'd chosen this group of assholes over her own brother. That she'd cast him aside.

His eyes fell on Thurgood's prized record collection, the one the fat fucker almost had an aneurysm over because Jay kept touching them. A thought began to form in the back of his skull. A small smile formed on his lips.

Jay pulled out a dozen records—the Savages one, of course, plus the Rancid test-press and more that had made Thurgood clench up—and set them on top. He pulled the Rancid one from the sleeve and bent the cover in half, then replaced it before moving on to the others. For the last one, the Savages record, he took his keys and dragged his key across the vinyl, so Thurgood would never again be able to listen to it.

After putting away the records, Jay was starting down the steps when he got a text.

The screen read *Paloma Vargas*.

*I found something you're going to want to see. Meet me at Aught-O.*

The bar next door to the Chop Shop, where he shared so

many memories with Sam. Frequented by the rest of the Ghosts and managed by Comrade Pat.

A chill passed through Jay. She said *meet*, so Jay didn't think she was actually there yet or else she would've said *come*. But it meant Paloma was getting close to Sam.

Jay needed to get there first.

# 29

Jay jumped on the brakes, his tires chirping as the car stopped halfway into a parking spot on the side of the street, the hood hanging over the sidewalk while the trunk stuck out into traffic. He glanced in the side mirror, waiting for two cars to pass before tumbling out of the car. Head on a swivel, scanning all the parked traffic on the block. No sign of Vargas anywhere. The knot of nerves in his stomach loosened slightly, his chest opening up. Whatever was inside the bar that had to do with the Ghosts—with Sam—he had a chance to find it first, control how the scene played out. Jay was sickened to his core by what he'd witnessed on that video. He hadn't always agreed with her methods when they were younger, but those were philosophical differences. Varied ways of addressing a problem. This? This was murder. This was terrorism. This was a real and direct threat to the country. How could he stand aside and let this go unpunished, let any radical do whatever they wanted in the name of *progress* or *equality* or whatever the fuck they shouted at a protest?

But in the same breath, he felt a strong pull, down to a molecular level, to protect Sam, to do the same thing she'd done for him for years. He'd already found out his father was a scumbag drug dealer and narc; he wasn't ready to have his sister sent to Guantanamo.

The Chop Shop loomed across the street. Just seeing that brick façade, painted the same shade of reptilian green it had been years ago, sent a needle of electricity through his body.

One night, a few months after he'd started coming to shows regularly here, he caught a local band called This City Is a Grave whose members were friends with Sam's friends. It could have been the hollowed-out feeling of being left behind by his mother, or the leftover white-hot anger at watching his father surface from his blackout only to open another bottle of bourbon, or just that he wanted to destroy everything. But something about their music, the way the drums undercut the bass or the otherworldly sounds the guitar player summoned through his bank of pedals, the way the crowd of freaks and misfits sang along as one voice, the way people threw themselves off the stage only to have someone catch them, it touched something inside Jay. And then, in between sets, he caught a glimpse of the guitar player. During the set, he'd seemed completely normal, fluid and continuous and caught inside the moment. But when the music stopped, when the trance was broken, he'd blink his right eye a few times, then his left, stick out his right pinkie, then his left, take three quick breaths, then pause, then take three more. That was when Jay knew these people were his kind of freaks. He might not belong anywhere special, but he did belong somewhere.

Now, years later, standing in front of this building that looked nearly the same when everything else had changed so much, Jay could feel the earth move beneath his feet.

He shook away the feeling and crossed the street, headed for the bar next door. Red-brick front. Canopy with the silhouette of a rat drinking a martini. A zero and an O. Such a stupid name—and typically punk, as the community that was meant for everyone could also be incredibly exclusionary, even for something as petty as not knowing the right name of the bar.

But as he stepped onto the sidewalk, he paused a second. How did Vargas know this was called Aught-O? Had he mentioned it before? He remembered talking about the Chop Shop while looking at mug shots, but couldn't recall mentioning the bar. That knot of nerves threaded itself tighter.

As if the universe was answering, his phone vibrated in his pocket.

*Vargas.*

"Hey, I just got here," he said.

"Where the hell is *here?* I just spent twenty minutes pulling Dalworth out of my ass so you've got some explaining to do, prick. Where are you?"

"I'm at Aught-O Bar." He paused a second. "Zero zero. Next door to the Chop Shop?"

"Why." She didn't ask it like a question, but that wasn't what sent a chill through Jay. It was his phone vibrating, a text message from *Paloma Vargas*—not *Vargas.*

*You should've backed off.*

"Oh shit," Jay said.

"What?" she shouted into the phone. "Brodsky, what?"

Jay didn't have time to respond before he heard a crack, then a boom, then everything went supernova.

# 30

Dust stuck to the inside of Jay's mouth, bits of brick and mortar crunching between his teeth. He blinked open his eyes and saw enveloping darkness, blades of light slicing through. He reached out against that darkness, felt a coolness on his bloody palms and realized it was a piece of metal sheeting. Pushed it and felt scrap and debris scrabbling on the top, tumbling off the side. Jay rolled away and was dragging himself to his knees when a white-hot knife drew a line up his calf. Time seemed to slow, as if he could feel his muscle parting like water behind a swan. He stumbled, caught himself an inch before taking a face-full of charcoal. He pushed himself to his feet again and grimaced when he put weight on the leg, a thin line of warmth ebbing down his skin. Must've happened during the blast.

His pants already ruined, Jay ripped off the bottom half of the leg and tied it around the gash. Stung like a banshee, but that probably meant it was fairly superficial, no need for stitches. He hoped. He wouldn't know until he could sit and get a good look at it.

The smell of singed concrete and burnt insulation and the acrid tang of scorched electronics hung heavy in the air. What used to be the Aught-O Bar, the left-most side of a three-building fire, sat there smoldering. On the right, there was now only a blackened moonscape of debris in the space where the Chop Shop and a Salvadoran bodega had been.

Jay had the urge to scream, to run up and down the street and bash out car windows, to find someone who looked vaguely suspicious and beat the living shit out of them, to walk every sidewalk in the city avoiding stepping on the lines that sprang from corners and telephone poles and doorways, and to step right then left then left then right then left then right then right then left, then let the patterns take him over until he'd gone so far from shore that his mind would never recover. He knew none of that would change anything, but damn would it offer some relief.

It wasn't just that they'd tried to kill him—it was no coincidence he got a text from what he now knew was Vargas's stolen bureau phone telling him to come here only for the building to explode on his arrival. It was a deeper, more personal slight. Jay had little in the way of family and so he carried no nostalgia for virtually anything outside of Sam. But this club was the first place she'd taken him to see a show. The first place he got to scream himself hoarse alongside two hundred other people who identified with the same things he did. The first place—nearly the *only* place—where his tendencies didn't define him. The place he'd come out sweaty and bruised and with his ears ringing so loud he couldn't hear the echo of the detective saying *We need to talk to you about your mother.*

And now it was gone. Obliterated.

Not to mention that, on top of destroying one of the few places that carried any emotional weight for Jay, the Ghosts had escalated this again. Killing a citizen was bad enough but trying to assassinate an agent was a whole new step, one with grave consequences.

The Ghosts had tried to kill him. Sam was part of the Ghosts. Had his sister tried to kill him? Had she been part of planning it? Was she the one who'd texted him? Had she fought against the leader when they floated the idea of assassinating a federal agent? Had Sam told them Jay was her brother or did she hide it, say *fuck the pigs*? The possibility was too much for Jay to comprehend, threatened to overload his circuit board and shut the whole thing down.

Jay traced the perimeter, trying to dislodge the thought that his sister might have been involved in a plot to blow him up as he clomped across the charred wood and twisted, blackened shelving units. He heard sirens in the distance, drawing closer.

A small lump near the edge of the debris caught his eye, distracting him. He squinted first, then pivoted on his right leg, sending an electric current through his calf, and trekked over the wreckage, surveying the street to look for any passersby, any witnesses.

He came up to the mound and smiled when he saw he'd been correct. He leaned down on his good leg and grabbed it with his index finger and thumb, kept walking like it was the most natural action. From the corner of his eye, he scanned for anyone watching him.

The sirens drew closer still, just a few blocks away. Beneath them, there was the squeal of tires losing grip on the pavement, skipping and chirping. Jay hurried to his car, popped the trunk, and set the melted plastic inside.

When he closed the trunk, he saw Vargas's car parked in the middle of the street. She was already out and running toward him.

"Jesus Christ, Brodsky," she said as she came closer, drawing him in for a tight hug. He felt her body form against his, wondered why he noticed that at a time like this. He could smell her perfume under the tang of debris.

After a moment she pulled back, then reared back and punched him right where his arm and shoulder met. "Are you okay? What the hell?"

"I got a text from you—well, I thought it was you, but it was from your bureau phone—that said to come here. I was following up on the lead when…" He gestured toward the wreckage, flames now licking at the upper windows. Fire trucks came around the corner and began posting up, firefighters pouring off the side, grappling with hoses and wielding steel tools.

"It was them, wasn't it," she said, following it with a stream of whispered Spanish Jay assumed was cursing. Both of their eyes drifted over to the firefighters, the arcs of water spurting out and drenching the husk of buildings, the sizzle of fire as it was extinguished. With so little sleep and so much adrenaline coursing through his veins, the whole thing was hypnotic. Jay wasn't sure how long had passed while they watched.

"This changes things," Jay finally said.

When she didn't answer, Jay glanced over but Vargas was looking off at the crowd gathered on the other side, to the left of the fire truck. "What?" Jay said.

Vargas nudged him with her elbow. "Two o'clock. Black bomber, red shirt, purple bruises under his eyes. It's Felder."

Jay turned, looked without looking, and scanned the crowd. "I don't see—"

"He's moving!" Vargas took off in the direction she'd been looking, sprinting after the man.

Jay saw a big man hurrying away. He jumped to back up Vargas, but felt the flesh of his calf spread and came up lame. Vargas disappeared around the corner after Comrade Pat. Part of him was angry they'd been watching and Jay hadn't noticed. Mostly he was relieved it hadn't been Sam watching them, checking in on her handiwork. He did his best to walk the perimeter, as much for crowd control as to see if any other clues were lying in the rubble, but didn't get very far before his phone rang again.

*Paloma Vargas.*

First, Comrade Pat had tried to blow him to hell. Now the Crimson Ghosts were trolling him.

"You've got some balls on you, coming after an agent like that," Jay said into the phone.

"'What matters in life is not what happens to you but what you remember and how you remember it.'" It was a man's voice, but masked.

"That sounds like a cop-out to me," Jay said, scanning the area. "Wishful and naïve. Like a child."

"And that sounds like the words of a cynic, someone who long ago lost sight of what they once cared so deeply for."

Jay looked in windows, alcoves, shadowed areas, anywhere that someone could hide and watch and talk. "I know some people you would've gotten along with pretty well."

"I get along with most people."

"They're dead now, so you just might."

The man let out a breathless laugh. "You are standing in the way of history, Agent Brodsky. Of progress the world has never known. Let us work. You'll soon thank us for it."

"Murdering innocent people is progress? That's work?"

"You know very well they were far from innocent. What they said with their mouths did not match what they did with their hands. Words divide us, and actions unite us," the man said. Jay's blood thrummed at the phrase: that was the slogan of the Tupamaros. This was the leader, the architect. Which meant Comrade Pat was a foot soldier, along with Sam. "Those insurance vampires were only the beginning. First, we helped our community. Next we help our country."

"You go national, you'll have every law enforcement agency in the country gunning for you."

"I imagine we will, but they'll have to find us first. And once the people are freed of their health care shackles, we will liberate their minds, their homes."

*Minds and homes?* Jay thought. "Wait, student loans and mortgages? That will decimate the global economy. The crash was bad enough. You'll spark wars around the globe."

"There will be no reason to fight when everyone is equal. It would be brother fighting brother."

"That's horseshit and you know it."

"You've not always thought that way, Agent Brodsky."

"What do you know about—?"

"You cannot outrun your past. Remember that 'time does not pass, it merely turns in a circle,' and the next time, you will not be so lucky."

"What is that supposed to mean?" Jay said, but the line had already gone dead.

Vargas came back around the corner, her face flushed, her chest rising and falling. "Who was that?"

Jay didn't have to answer. She could tell from his expression. She shook her head. "Thanks for the backup, partner."

Jay grimaced again, displayed his leg.

"Holy shit. You fight with Freddy Krueger?" She knelt and went to touch it but stopped short. "You should see a doctor."

"It's fine. I've got some stuff at home."

"Seriously," she said. "When gangrene and MRSA bump uglies, this place is where they dump the baby."

"I said it's fine." He went to his car. "There's stuff at the office, too. I'll see you over there."

He had to get back and file these reports—both to cover himself for the bombing and unwarranted search of Thurgood's house, and to keep people off his back while he worked on the server—and file them before anyone caught up with him. He climbed in the car without looking back, afraid of what he might see.


Jay sat at an intersection, waiting for the light to change, when the college radio station cut away for a breaking news story. The president of Bayside Bank had just given a press conference announcing all branches were closing until further notice to avoid extreme financial stress on its system caused by an unprecedented number of withdrawals.

Jay banged his head against the headrest and clenched his eyes. This was not going to help anything.

The light turned green. His phone rang.

He knew who it was without looking and, for a second, imagined chucking it out the window, letting it hurtle across the street to be crushed beneath a garbage truck. Instead, he answered.

"What were you doing when I walked up?" Vargas said.

Jay saw a group of people gathering on the sidewalk a block up on the right. "Hobbling."

Vargas inhaled hard, exhaled through her nose. "What's in your trunk?"

As he pulled closer to the group, he saw placards held up on sticks, slogans spray-painted across them. *Our money, our lives, our choice. Turn your necktie into a noose.*

"Jesus Christ."

"Don't get an attitude with me, Brodsky."

"Not you. More protests outside the bank."

Two security guards tried to clear the sidewalk, shoving the protestors away with their batons. One protestor stumbled and fell backward, hitting the concrete hard. Another took that as an escalation and swung their backpack at the security guard, hitting him square in the face and knocking him into the sheer glass façade. Two more jumped in for support, piling on the guards. A delivery truck pulled up beside Jay, blocking his view as he continued down the street.

"There's nothing."

"If there was nothing in the trunk, you wouldn't say 'nothing.' Because there'd be nothing to say."

Jay held his pinkie finger parallel to the delivery truck's cab, so that there were two translucent images of his finger. *Breathe,* he told himself. *Please be aware, and count.* He blinked with his right eye anyway, then left, left, right. The driver pulled over into an open spot, turning on the hazards. Jay tried to blink left, right, right, left but the truck had left his field of vision, and Jay found himself growing irritated at not being able to complete the pattern, something grinding against the interior of his chest, his jaw throbbing.

Vargas exhaled hard. "If there's evidence, you need to bag it and tag it. You find anything out of bounds and it'll be inadmissible."

He blinked right, left, left, right, but it wasn't correct, didn't sate the need because there was no pinkie overlapping over a straight line. "Vargas, this, these two hacks, it's just their first stage. They said they're planning to take this national."

"Even more reason we need to keep it buttoned."

"Jesus, I've seen three protests just this morning."

As soon as the words left Jay's mouth, he heard a bang followed by a crash. He ducked down out of instinct and scanned the area. On his left, the wrong way down a one-way street, Jay saw four people running toward an alley, two with bottles in hand, all of them wearing Crimson Ghost masks. Flames engulfed the fronts of a row of luxury stores, ones that had been affordable apartments two years ago.

Jay started to turn in the direction they ran, but hit more traffic, people trying to leave the city before the hurricane swept through, people stuck because these protests were spilling into the streets. He hoped city police would catch them before they could lob the other two Molotov cocktails at more stores.

"People are losing it, Vargas." Her breathing ebbed and flowed on the phone. "The Ghosts' next step is to 'liberate the people's minds and homes.'"

"What the fuck does that mean?"

"Student loans. Mortgages."

"Jesus Christ. That's," she stammered, "that's a huge portion of the economy. If they do that—"

"I know. I get that there should be a fairer economy, but this is not the way to do it. I don't know if they understand what it'll do. So given all that, do you think I'd steal something from a crime scene that could help us find something?"

"Maybe. Does it have anything to do with your sister disappearing seven years ago?"

Something white hot flared inside Jay. "I don't know what you're talking about."

"I'd be a pretty shitty agent if I couldn't do a little digging."

"That's private. You don't have any right to go searching through my personal life." As angry as Jay was, he also wanted to push her, find out how much she knew. But that would mean conceding information he might not be ready to give up.

"If you're putting my job in jeopardy, which would directly affect my personal life, then yeah, I do." He could almost hear her grinding her teeth. "I showed you mine, about my daughter. Now you show me yours."

"Look, I never made you tell me anything. That was your choice." He heard himself spit out the words, badly wanting to take them back. But whatever was inside this server—which had been housed in the one place that connected all their suspects— could be the evidence they needed to stop the Crimson Ghosts before they crashed the country, the clues that would help him get Sam out first. Vargas could not be a part of this. "Maybe you just felt the need to unburden yourself."

"Fuck you, Brodsky." Her breath caught. "Look, you can file whatever you have, you can keep it and throw your career away. But you pull me into anything that might put my job at risk, put my daughter at risk of not seeing her mom, I'll burn you and never think twice."

The phone went dead. Jay banged the back of his head against the headrest four times, then another four. Glass shattered somewhere in the vicinity. Rain began to speckle his windshield. He let go a long breath and watched the dark clouds swirl above the city, the impending storm settling in.

# 31

Jay left the server in the trunk and started hobbling toward the stairs. It would be a more painful route, but he hoped to skirt as many people as possible.

He opened the door at the top of the steps and paused, checking both ways. Two agents in gray suits hurried past, thick files tucked beneath their arms. Jay stepped out of the stairwell and limped his way down the hall and over to his desk. Agents scurried around the office.

Twenty minutes later, he had a handful of incredibly sloppy, terse reports, but they would be enough to cover his ass and alert the team that the Ghosts had larger plans, while he got back to his apartment and got to work. The last thing he needed was an angry call to come back to the office and justify his actions when he was levels-deep into hacking a server he'd pilfered from a crime scene.

He shoved a couple case files he might need into his bag next to the Dumpy Felder files and a bottle for Norman in archives. But when he stood up to leave, Dalworth was standing behind him.

"Christ on a crutch, Jay." Dalworth bent his knees to come closer to Jay's level, his eyes surveying Jay's face. "I heard the reports. Have you been seen by a doctor yet?"

"I'm fine. Wasn't as bad as it sounded."

"They tried to blow up a federal agent. It's exactly as bad as it seems."

"Well," Jay said, feeling the heat of the plastic box in his trunk four floors below, "rumors of my demise have been greatly exaggerated."

"I'm glad you're okay, but you really should get checked out. Just to be safe."

"Sure. I'll go by the clinic on my way home. I'm just...really tired."

Jay started to tell him about the phone call when Dalworth said, "Where's Vargas?"

"I told her I had to take care of these reports but we'd catch up tomorrow." Jay swallowed hard, put on a good face. "Why did she come down here anyway? To Baltimore."

Dalworth's face changed slightly. "Because I asked for help. Why, is she not working out? You two have been inseparable."

"No, she's fine. She's a great agent." Jay shifted on his feet and felt electricity spread through his leg. He bit the inside of his lip to stifle it. "Just wondering why she was chosen."

"I asked her boss for his best agent. He sent her."

"Kind of him to do," Jay said. "How do you know him?"

"Who, Todd?"

"Yeah," he said as he cleared his throat. "Todd Hart."

Dalworth shrugged. "We were partners here when we came out of Quantico. Back then you actually had partners, not squads like we do now but..."

Jay saw Dalworth's lips move but couldn't hear any of the words he was saying. His body had turned cold. Todd Hart was Dumpy Felder's handler. Brett Dalworth—Jay's stand-in father figure for the last seven years—had been Todd Hart's partner.

Jay reached out and braced himself against the back of his chair. *Everything and every person are connected*, he heard his mother say.

"You okay?" Dalworth grabbed his arm, making sure he stayed upright. He glanced down and saw Jay's leg. "Jesus Christ, Jay. Forget the clinic, just go to the hospital. Get yourself cleaned up."

Jay nodded. "Yeah," he said. "I need to clean up."

Jay walked away from Dalworth, keeping his back straight, not allowing the man to see him wince or wobble. That prick could read about the call in Jay's reports. And anyway, Jay needed all the head start he could get, to find something that led him to Sam, to get her away from the Ghosts before it got too far. As soon as he got to the elevator, he cut hard to the right and took the steps down to the archives, his chest heaving the whole way.

At the bottom of the stairwell, Jay ducked into a bathroom, checking for shoes beneath the stall doors. All empty. He hid inside the largest one, then pulled out Dumpy Felder's CI file and skimmed the back half of it.

After hearing the Dalworth-Hart-Felder connection confirmed, Jay expected to find something revelatory in this file. But with every page he turned, he grew increasingly frustrated.

More names and dates and times. More mention of drugs smuggled through the wharf. More protests. More bitching and complaining about the CI who was going to get Felder killed.

Jay flipped to the summer of 1986. Dumpy sounded different, less harried. In some of the transcripts, he almost sounded relaxed. Hart asked about Dumpy's drinking, whether he'd been laying off it as he was supposed to. Dumpy just laughed at him, said he could handle anything that got thrown at him. FBI? No problem. Piss-poor CIs? He'd dealt with them. Alcohol? His blood type was National with a side of steamed jimmies.

Dumpy's arrogance made Jay want to tear the damn file in half. But that would piss off Norman.

He paused a moment, backtracked, and looked at the interview dates. Dumpy's tone began to change at the end of July, just a few weeks after Jay's mother died. Some half-formed thought niggled at the inside of Jay's skull. In reality, it probably meant nothing and was just a coincidence. At the same time, Jay had been trained to see coincidence as clues that had yet to be connected.

Jay stood and felt the throb in his leg but continued to flip through the file. The reports became more and more routine, and Jay found himself skipping six months at a time.

Throughout the rest of the pages, there wasn't a single mention of CI-7.

Then, on the last page, Dumpy told Hart he was ending his arrangement with the FBI. He'd had to go to the ER the week before on account of his skin being discolored. According to the doctor, he might have been able to handle the booze, or the hepatitis, but not both. They gave him two months, and he was going to spend it with his kids.

Jay slammed the folder shut and crammed it in his bag.

Dumpy Felder, that piece of shit, got to spend his final days surrounded by his family.

Wasn't that just fucking perfect.

Norman was in the same position as before. Face down, head sweating, ignoring the world as it passed by.

Jay slid the files beneath the gate, gave the old man a big smile. It had taken Jay a few minutes to compose himself in the bathroom, then another few to fix the stall door after he'd kicked it off its hinges. Norman took the files without looking and moved them aside. Jay then slid the paper bag underneath. Norman didn't look at this either, but did pause long enough for his hand to get the overall shape.

"This isn't rum, is it?" he said to Jay.

"Would Bobby Mitchum drink rum?" Jay had no idea, but figured Jameson was a fair bet.

Norman raised his eyes from his book—a different one this time, *Pronto*. "You're a good kid, know that?"

Jay nodded.

"What do you need now?"

Jay brought up the case file number on his phone and showed it to Norman, who glanced at the screen, then at Jay's face.

"Next time, you're going to need a much bigger bottle."

Norman hefted himself off his stool and disappeared into the depths of archives. A warm trickle slipped down the back of Jay's calf.

Norman returned a minute later with another CI file, just as old and yellowed as Dumpy Felder's, but significantly thinner. This CI apparently didn't take as well to snitching as Felder had. Jay knocked on the counter, saying his thanks, and headed out with the file in hand.

"Agent Brodsky," Norman called out. Jay paused, the file slipping open in his hands. "For future reference, I prefer things from the island of Islay."

"Duly noted, Norman," Jay said, and as he turned his eyes fell on the top sheet of the file and his skin went cold.

CONFIDENTIAL
FEDERAL BUREAU OF INVESTIGATION
BALTIMORE FIELD OFFICE
INFORMANT WORKING AGREEMENT

*I, Catherine Marie Brodsky, hereby agree to assist the Baltimore Federal Bureau of Investigation in the investigation of criminal violations.*

# 32

Jay dropped into a chair at his kitchen table. Rain tapped against the window behind him like tiny fingers begging to be let in. On the right sat the melted plastic box pulled from the embers that had once been the Chop Shop, a six-inch mess of smooth black contours riding along jagged spikes of pitted, reformed polymer, the faint scent of acrid smoke still lingering. On the left, a tan accordion folder, half-an-inch of reports and files, detailing his mother's involvement as a confidential informant. Again, running in the same circle as Dumpy Felder. His own mother. Patron saint in the Church of Sam.

Who was she really? Any story these papers told would contradict the mother he knew: a tough woman who was dealt a shit hand and played it as best she could. Did she play it wrong? Probably. Did Jay wish she'd played if differently? Ab-so-fucking-lutely, but Jay had never faced what she did, so he had no idea how he'd react in her situation.

His bigger concern was how this file would affect the way he saw her now. Five minutes ago, his feelings toward her were complicated, to put it lightly. Saddened. Heartbroken. Missing her. Angry at her. But now, with her cast in the same light as Dumpy fucking Felder, with so much unknown about her bubbling within that single folder, he didn't know how to feel. Confused was a start, but it didn't have the magnitude necessary to even scratch the surface.

More important, he now had to make a choice between the file and the server. Was it more urgent to know the information about his mother, or where to find his sister?

He saw his phone on the table, within arm's reach. The CI report was only what his mother had reported to her handler. Whatever was recorded had been filtered not only through her perspective, but her mood that day. How crazy he and Sam had been that morning. Whether she got stuck in traffic or spilled coffee all over herself and was in a bad mood. How receptive she felt her handler was being and whether she felt like he was taking her seriously. Jay knew how subjective informant reports could be—you had to know the CI's personality and dig through what they were saying to get to what they knew. It was a static document, revealing only what was recorded. But Jay could easily get more information. Ask questions and follow up on points and clarify answers, interrogate the scenes to expand on secondary characters.

Phone in his hand, finger hovering over the home button, Jay considered calling his father. Considered what he could learn and what it would mean.

They hadn't spoken since he'd reached out to Sam and Jay, around Jay's sixteenth birthday. He'd gotten sober and was trying to make up for lost time. And he was honestly sober, Jay could hear it in his voice, but it also seemed to sharpen his tongue where the booze had dulled it. Regardless, too much had happened in the past, and too many things had *not* happened, for either of them to let him back in. So why was Jay sitting here, thinking about calling him? Sure, he wanted to question him about what had happened, but was some part of him also looking to prove something?

Fuck it. Jay tossed the phone aside. Some people were better left behind. What more could he learn about his mother—given his father had been drunk more than he was sober—that this report wouldn't show him?

None of that mattered right now. This case was his job, and

his job took priority. The case would lead to Sam. He could do nothing about his parents, but Sam was still out there and he could help her.

Jay hobbled into his room and went to the closet, set the folder on a low shelf. It could wait.

He grabbed the small toolkit in his closet and went back to the kitchen. He spread the tools out on the table, shifting the melted box in the center of them before picking up a small screwdriver. He had to use enough force to get in without damaging the contents inside. Still, there was no guarantee that the protective shell had done its job during the building's collapse, or that the heat hadn't fried the circuits or fused the silicone. But, he thought, there was only one way to find out.

He closed his eyes, then took a deep breath and got to work.

Fifteen agonizing minutes later, he peeled back the last sheath of melted plastic and set it beside the rest of the scraps and pieces and shavings covering his table. He nestled his fingers beneath the metal casing and pulled it out into the light, held it up. No dents, no real evidence of warping on the exterior.

The server, it appeared, had made it.

Jay swiped his forearm across the table and pushed the debris to the side. He hopped out of his seat to get his home rig and nearly fell down when he put weight on the injured leg. He bit his lip and squinted the pain away. He needed to get this server open and see what was inside. He'd tend to the leg soon. Anyway, leaving it was just another way of strengthening his immune system.

He brewed some coffee while his machine booted up, splashed some cold water on his face and the back of his neck.

This was a gamble. He didn't need Vargas mean-mugging or lecturing him on chain of custody to let him know this wasn't a good idea. If there were something in here that backed up their theories of the Crimson Ghosts and conclusively tied Sam to the group, he'd be forced to decide whether to turn in his sister and have her sent to some black-water site in Siberia or risk his career to cover for her. Would he be able to make the right call? Would he even know what the right choice was? She'd given up so much to help him when he was younger. Would he do the same for her now, knowing she was the mouthpiece of a terrorist cell?

If a soldier turning his arms against his people was the lowest form of human, did she think *people* held the same value as *family?* Had she turned her weapon on him, or had she fought against the attempted bombing? And how exactly was he going to get her out? Kidnap her? Offer immunity he knew she would never take? Appeal to her sense of nostalgia? Help her flee the state, the country? Hide her in his closet?

Jay sat at the table, a cup of coffee beside him, and tossed his head back and forth to crack his neck. He took a deep breath, then plugged in the server.

He launched a few programs and started sifting through IP address pings, tracing the path back as far as it could go. The usual names popped up—Iran, North Korea, a couple in Africa, several from Syria. He kept expecting something to ping in Uruguay, but nothing did.

His stomach growled as he poured another cup of coffee, but he ignored it. It was time to go deeper.

He went down a level, running decryption software on folders upon folders filled with text files. He found a few variations of *Your time is over. Our time is now* anarchic rhetoric, variations on the video he'd seen on YouTube. READMEs and DAT files and a couple filled with bad poetry or song lyrics. Two where someone attempted to illustrate a psychotic-looking face using ones and zeros and some backslashes. Beneath the graphic, in all caps, it read FIRST WE EAT, THEN WE FIGHT. Jay had no idea what it meant but it sounded cool.

Further down, he opened a folder and found what looked like a rootkit file.

Now that was interesting.

Rootkits were designed to hack into a computer and run in

the background without the user knowing, but Jay found it odd to see something this rudimentary in the set-up. He began to wonder whether these people were script kiddies or competent black-hat hackers. If he were to shift his thinking to this being a rootkit instead of a virus, it had succeeded in infecting a number of computers. But the kit had done nothing to hide itself, and in fact called attention to itself, which seemed counterintuitive and just plain amateurish. It was like a spy confessing to a beautiful woman that he was a spy just to get her up to his hotel room. It defeated the whole purpose. This rootkit did not jibe with the sophistication necessary to construct whatever was tearing through computers up and down the mid-Atlantic.

Jay stood up, winced again, and got another cup of coffee. His vision went gauzy at the edges when he turned too quickly, so he grabbed a portion-sized bag of almonds from the cabinet and one of the orange juice bottles from the fridge before sitting back down. Passing out with his face on the keyboard would be less than helpful in figuring out what was hiding deep inside this server.

He pressed his palms against his eyes, then hunched over, drilled down further into the root directory. A number of empty folders gave way to labyrinthine directories that looped back on one another, a digital ouroboros of misdirection and deception. Jay thought that maybe he'd misjudged Eric Felder; maybe he was sandbagging some of the top-level stuff to lower expectations to deter anyone from navigating further into the files. IBM might be a stable job meant to fund his extracurricular activities.

In the sixth repetition of one directory, Jay came across a folder. Had he seen this before? He was pretty sure he hadn't. A sudden thought washed over him that the directories weren't set up like an ouroboros, but a hall of mirrors—so that the seventh level of the directory mirrored the first—with the intention of disorienting anyone who tried to hack into the server. The idea thrilled Jay as much as it made him sit back in admiration.

But not for too long, because he clicked on the folder and

found a single file inside: h3rbsn2s.exe.

*This is it,* he thought. *This is what's spreading from building to building, state to state. I don't know exactly what it is or how it works, but this is what I've been looking for.*

He constructed several layers of firewalls around the folder to protect his rig from contagion.

What did the name mean? Harbor Season was his first thought, though that made little sense. The previous targets had a purpose, the locusts in the medical centers. They had a message. But this name? It looked like an auto-generated password, symbolizing nothing.

He rocked back and forth in his chair. What if it had to do with Túpac the Second or the Tupamaros?

He toggled screens and began searching through message boards and forums across the web, dipping in and out of IRC channels to see if anyone was talking about them, even diving down into the dark net for hints.

And, Jesus Christ, he found stuff. Left-wing groups in France, Colombia, China, and Iran. Far-right cells co-opting the message and distorting it from the economic targets to racial ones. Basque, Catalan, and Spanish nationalist groups, all claiming the Ghosts' message as their own. The Crimson Ghost mask overlaid with a dozen different flags of nations and semi-autonomous regions.

None of which would help lead him to the Ghosts. All of which showed the global powder keg that the Ghosts could spark.

*Focus. Back up. Reboot.* He searched for *Túpac Amaru the Second, Tupamaros, Uruguay, revolution,* all in different combinations, but found the same things over and over: historical recounts and the occasional think-piece from some white kid in Brooklyn who fancied himself a revolutionary because he could grow a beard.

*Reboot,* he thought. *The simplest programs are always the best.* He typed in *Amaru.*

The first hit showed a mythical creature from Andean civilizations, a double-headed serpent that dwelled underground and generally featured the heads of a bird and puma. Interesting drawing and it would make a cool tattoo maybe, but not quite what he was looking for.

Halfway down the page, though, he found a listing for Amaru Cyber Storage, headquartered in east Baltimore, near Fell's Point.

*Get the fuck out of here,* Jay thought. *That's a peculiar—and very specific—name for a cyber company.* And one headquartered not more than a few miles from where the first hack occurred. Jay felt an electric charge thrumming beneath his skin.

Thunder boomed outside. He glanced out the window, saw dark clouds in the sky, but no rain or lightning. For a second, he wondered if it wasn't thunder, but a bomb.

He searched through the Amaru Cyber site, and located the name of the founder and CEO, Oscar Forlán. That name sounded familiar but his fingers were moving too fast for his brain to linger. The screen already displayed background information and several tabs worth of articles on Forlán.

Bingo again.

Forlán was born and raised in Montevideo, Uruguay—"Country code five-nine-eight," he said to himself—and founded Amaru Cyber Storage when he was only twenty-nine. A midsize company, Amaru provided secure data storage and cloud backup for more than thirty businesses, five of which were listed on the Fortune 500. Jay half-expected to find Community Health or one of the other affected companies on the client list, but knew it couldn't be quite so easy. On the whole, the guy seemed like any other tech savant.

Until Jay got to the fourth article, detailing South American guerilla movements on a revolutionary-thought website.

*Fucking bingo.*

According to the piece, Forlán's father, Héctor Forlán Huidobo, had fought alongside Raúl Sendic and José Mujica in none other than the Tupamaros. Jay's forearms tingled with the visceral click of disparate pieces of a large and vaguely related puzzle finally coming together.

Héctor and his comrades were captured and jailed by the right-wing president Gregorio Conrado Álvarez Armelino. After two years inside, Héctor went on a hunger strike to protest the group's incarceration. But the president didn't care, and Héctor died one day shy of the three-month mark, causing great public outcry.

Fearing retribution from the government or paramilitary groups, Oscar's mother took him and his brother Mauricio north, finally landing in the States. Álvarez was eventually overthrown, but it would be two decades before Oscar's mother returned to Montevideo, joined by Mauricio. By that point, Oscar was already working in IT and on his way to founding Amaru Cyber Storage.

Besides having a good job stateside, Oscar didn't have the incentive to return that Mauricio did, namely, a position as a cabinet minister under recently elected President José Mujica. Jay heard another mental *ting* as more threads began to wind around one another. True to his anti-capitalist upbringing, Oscar began donating large amounts of money to social equality organizations once Amaru Cyber became a highly profitable firm.

Jay had to shut the laptop a minute, his head swirling with all of these revelations. So much of it now made sense, but still so much was oblique. Though it would be convenient, the unlisted number that Thurgood had called—and the one that had also called the Palacio Legislativo in Uruguay—could still belong to anyone, and Jay was going to need a hell of a lot more evidence than Google searches for anything to hold up in court. But a couple nothings meant something, and he couldn't help but feel like they were finally getting closer to what they'd been searching for.

Why would Zane Thurgood be calling Oscar Forlán? Did Eric and Patrick Felder also know Forlán? There were too many intersecting points for this to all be circumstantial. And Forlán being the head of a cyber security firm would be perfect optics for showing themselves as philanthropic and nonviolent—which would be perfect camouflage for him funding activist groups.

Which still didn't explain how Sam ended up cavorting with these people, but he'd get that answer once he got her clear.

He heard a pounding somewhere. It dawned on Jay that after years of worrying about it, his head was finally about to explode.

Another one. He realized it was heavy knocking on the door.

Jay stood from his chair, the blood raining needles through his legs as he walked to the door. He passed the window and saw it was pitch black outside. Last he'd remembered it was early afternoon. Jesus, and now it was past midnight.

More knocking.

Maybe Vargas had come to apologize. If she'd already found out about Sam's disappearance, he bet she knew where he lived. And as soon as the thought hit, Jay laughed: he didn't know her that well, but well enough to know she wasn't going to apologize. More likely, she'd come to tell him again that he was a prick and she'd kill him if he jeopardized her badge, with coming over to begrudgingly help a close second.

On the ceramic-tiled vestibule in his apartment, he combed his hair back with his fingers, then pulled the door open.

It was not Paloma Vargas.

Jay saw Texas Big, looming in the doorway.

"You bent my records," he said.

"You stole my sister," Jay said back.

Thurgood lunged forward, Jay ducking just in time for a heavy fist to fly over him. He struck out with a quick right, sinking into Thurgood's thick gut. The big man grunted, then slapped Jay's arm down. Jay spun around with the force of the strike, feeling the gash in his leg tear again, weeping blood. He bent low on his knee, went with the momentum, and raised up his back leg, catching Thurgood square in the knee.

Thurgood stumbled backward, thumping against the wall beside the door, his head thrown back in a howl. Jay sprang to his feet and swung hard at Thurgood's ear, knuckles connecting with cartilage. The big man lashed out in pain, the back of his massive fist catching Jay in the face. Jay spun around, catching himself before falling. Thurgood shifted from one foot to the other, testing out his knee. When he was midstride, Jay sprang forward, swinging at his face. Thurgood ducked back, dodging it, but Jay jabbed his other elbow back and up, catching the underside of Thurgood's jaw. The big man's head snapped back. He swung his thick arm out to keep balance. That arm caught Jay right in the chest, stealing his wind. Jay stumbled forward, gasping, and grabbed the wall to hold him upright. His hands landed inches from a wooden-handled broom.

Jay grabbed it, swung it.

"What the fu—" Thurgood yelled, his words cut short by the broom handle smashing against his face. Jay reared back and laid two more cracks against the big man before he could grab it and yank forward, pulling Jay in. Thurgood threw his head forward, smashing it against Jay's. Jay hurtled backward, slamming into the wall. He felt it crease behind him.

Jay retreated two steps, putting space between them while he cleared the white dots from his eyes.

Heavy breath rolled out of Thurgood's nostrils as he balled his fists. Something caught Jay's eye—the phone in his pocket. *I have to know who was texting him. I have to get that phone,* Jay thought as he set his feet.

Thurgood charged, fist cocked back, ready to crush Jay's temple.

Jay feinted right. Thurgood bit, shifted course, and uncorked his fist. Jay jumped back, throwing Thurgood off-balance when his blow didn't find Jay's skull as expected. Jay seized the opportunity and threw his hand out, snatching the phone from Thurgood's pocket.

But getting that close to Thurgood also put him just inches away from the big man. Jay saw something flash out of the corner of his eye, saw a black box in Thurgood's paw, heard a crackle in the air, then felt an electric bite radiate through his chest.

Static cascaded over Jay's eyes. Sound morphed and wavered, disappearing with a deep *whoomp*, and he felt himself slipping away. Jay caught a glimpse of Thurgood's phone on the floor. He moved his body to land on it, protect it, just as the darkness overtook him. Again.

# 33

The smoke detector loomed above Jay, winking at him, he thought. Unless it was Morse code, saying *get up, get the hell up*. Or maybe *dude, just stay down*.

His mouth tasted of dirty cotton and electric sparks, his head ringing so hard he could nearly see the sound waves. He ran a hand over his chest, felt the twin marks just below his collarbone. He couldn't believe he'd missed Thurgood carrying a taser, but figured it could've been worse. Especially after watching that video.

After a few minutes, when it felt like his brain had resumed functioning, he rolled over onto his stomach and pushed himself up. He walked into the kitchen. The server was gone, along with his laptop. He thought about all that he'd uncovered last night—the search results, browser history, downloaded unencrypted text, connections between urban guerillas and the Crimson Ghosts they were chasing—and felt his whole body deflate.

The rest of the room seemed untouched. He shuffled back to his bedroom, the static electricity between his feet and the carpet making his head throb anew. He'd never liked carpet in apartments anyway, but goddamn if he didn't despise it right now.

He flipped on the light in his closet, shoved aside the hamper of dirty clothes and pushed two boxes out of the way, then crouched down and exhaled hard. His backup server hummed along as if nothing had happened. He bent over and kissed the plastic protective case, saw the accordion folder glaring at him but looked away. Of all times, not right now. He had another machine back here somewhere, set aside after he'd picked up his new rig. It would only take fifteen minutes to restore the files from everything that auto-saved to the server.

Then he walked out into the living room and saw Sam's records.

He knelt down before the cabinet. Jagged half-moons of black vinyl peppered the floor around him. He scooped some up in his palm, tipped his hand, let them tumble back to the carpet. Easily thirty records, if not more. Sure, it had been a dick move for Jay to crease Thurgood's records. He could admit that. But other than scratching The Savages, those were just creases, a collector's transgression. This was deeply personal. This was knowingly destroying not just the records, but all the memories that went along with them. This was a gigantic *fuck you* from Thurgood.

A Minor Threat seven-inch someone had tried to buy from Sam for a hundred bucks. The Gorilla Biscuits LP Jay had bought Sam for her seventeenth birthday. A UK import of the Simpsons' "Do the Bartman" single she'd found at Jet Black Records on Thames in Fell's Point. The American Nightmare cassette tape demo that they sold on their first tour, one of a hundred fifty.

It wasn't about what the records were worth; it was Jay's last tactile connection to his sister, his childhood, lying there. Crushed, smashed, obliterated. He hadn't even had the chance to finish putting them in order.

Something struck cold within Jay. He sifted through the ripped center labels on the floor, tossed them aside, but didn't see it. He'd left it on top of the other records two nights ago. He searched through the shelves of records, at first flipping through quickly and, when he couldn't find it, going through one by one.

The Savages record was nowhere. Neither was the *Chop Shop* LP. Thurgood stole them, and only them. Which meant he knew

Jay was closing in on them.

The room pinched in. *Breathe, be aware, count. Breathe, breathe.*

The phone. Jay had forgotten about it. He went back to the front door, found the broom handle snapped in half, dents in the walls that would eat into his security deposit, not to mention massively fuck with his sense of organization and order. What he didn't find was the phone.

He searched around frantically, sure that he'd landed on top of it before the taser had pushed him underwater. He'd woken up in what he thought was the same spot, meaning Thurgood hadn't moved him while he was busy destroying his records, but didn't see anything. Jay scoured the floor in the entryway, the area leading into the living room, even into the kitchen. Nothing.

Jay dropped to his hands and knees, crawling around his floor. The friction between his clothes and the carpet built up enough static electricity that it almost made him cry, but he pushed on. Until there, under the small shelf where he arranged his shoes, he saw the prepaid phone. He snatched it out from beneath the shelf, hit the home button. It didn't dawn on him until after the home screen lit up, icons filling the panel, how lucky he was Thurgood didn't have a password. Jay went for recent calls.

Some numbers he recognized from the scan the other day; others were family, pizza shops, a sub place Jay had heard a lot about. Nothing from the evening he and Vargas had interrogated Thurgood. He closed the screen, moved to texts. More of the same.

Jay groaned aloud, frustrated. He briefly saw himself hurling the phone out the window, letting it skip along the street until it ricocheted into the harbor and sunk down in the mud with the crabs. But that wouldn't help him track down Sam.

He scrolled through the icons. Most were innocuous—some stupid games, sports score updates, a Bloomberg News app that he didn't really understand.

Then he saw it on the third screen: Signal. An end-to-end encrypted app. One that wouldn't show up on the Bureau's records. Jay launched it.

The first entry: Kiki Laughton. His mother's maiden name.

A cold finger traced Jay's spine. This was the closest he'd been to Sam in seven years, and it was through some mouth breather's phone. He thumbed through their texts, blessedly short and superficial. Jay wasn't sure what he would do if he found deep conversation between these two, much less mention of him. But he did see a phone button in the top right corner.

His thumb hovered over the button for several long seconds as breath rolled in and out of his lungs. Why was he scared? Was scared what he was actually feeling? Anger? Betrayal? All of those mixed into some malignant amalgamation? He would never find out why she left, where she went, by dancing around the fact. He'd have to confront her sometime.

He hit the button before he had a second chance to think.

The ring was a drill bit in his ear, through his heart.

After three rings, the phone went quiet, a hushed static taking its place.

"Sam?" he said.

Jay heard a catch in her breath. The static took on a different quality. Somewhere in the background, he heard what sounded like seagulls.

Jay's mouth opened and closed, words struggling to make their way past his lips. After what felt like hours but what was really several of the longest minutes of his life, he finally eked out, "Where did you go?"

Nothing.

The phone vibrated. A text from someone. Though it was mere centimeters from his head, the idea of other people was miles away. Still, Sam sat quiet on the other side, wherever she was, her terrible silence filling that gap.

"I just want to know why you left me. That's it."

More breathing.

"I know about your plans. Mortgages. Loans. This is fucking *dangerous*, Sam. Please, talk to me."

"Fuck, JJ, you shouldn't be anywhere near this—"

"Anywhere near this?" he yelled. "This is my job. All I want to know is why you disappeared. Jesus, you want to know how bad this is bugging me out? I almost called Dad tonight."

"That would've been stupid."

"My point exactly. So the least you can do is tell me, since I'm risking my job and my life to try to keep you safe."

"Then stop trying."

In the background, there was a blast of music that abruptly shut off, then someone shouted, "Fell's Point, one minute."

Before he could respond, the line went dead. His hand went slack, the phone tumbling from his palm. Three sentences. That had been the most he'd heard from his sister in seven years. How could something so inconsequential crush him so deeply? It was fifteen words that translated as rejection.

*No*, he thought. *You didn't do this. This isn't on you. It was her choice to leave, her choice to join the Ghosts. There was nothing wrong with you two having a different point of view, but she chose to pull a Mom and leave when things didn't go her way.*

He dialed the number again but got no answer. He wasn't going to let her have the last word. Not after so much time, not on this. Jay opened up the text box and sent her a message: *You're not getting away with this. I'm going to find you.*

He tossed the phone on his table. He needed to take a long, hot shower and finally clean his wounded leg. He needed to clear his head, wash away the emotional static that had been building for the last seven years. Then he would get to the bottom of this. And this, like most things Sam did, he thought, began and ended with their mother.

He waited until the bathroom was jungle-thick with steam, then stepped in.

It was nearly five a.m. when the water began to run cold. He dried off and dressed for work. Bailing the day after there had been an attempt on his life wasn't a look he was willing to put out there.

He poured himself a cup of coffee and watched the sun crest above the horizon, the bars of pink punching through midnight blue. It was reassuring to watch the sun rise, to observe the inevitability of the world. No matter how hard he fought, life would be what it would be. That gave him a feeling of relief, like none of this was his fault.

That same inevitability meant he couldn't run away from the folder in his closet. The facts were there. Ignoring them wouldn't change them any more than closing his eyes would prevent the sun from rising.

He took a slug of coffee, then shuffled to the closet to fetch the folder.

August 23, 1980
11:35 AM
Interview of Catherine Brodsky
Brett Dalworth, Field Agent, FBI

*Brett Dalworth: Thank you for coming in today, Mrs. Brodsky.*
Catherine Brodsky: You didn't really give me a choice.
*BD: You don't have to be here. Everything you say and do from this point on is completely voluntary.*
CB: Can we just get this done? My meter's going to run out.
*BD: I need to make sure that you understand that.*
CB: Yeah, you made that real fucking clear when you said Social Services would take my kids if I didn't talk to you.
*BD: I did not say that, Mrs. Brodsky. I merely reminded you what would happen to your children if you were deemed an accessory to your husband's drug trafficking activities and both of you went to prison. How is Jay doing? Five months, right? Is he sleeping through the night yet?*

CB: His name is Jacob. He's wonderful. And he'll stay that way. Always.

BD: *I remember those days. My wife and I would do anything to stay awake—*

CB: I don't need a friend here.

BD: *Of course, right. Per our agreement, and under the threat of perjury or imprisonment, you, Catherine Marie Brodsky, agree to assist the Federal Bureau of Investigation in our attempts to stop radical communist attacks before they occur and injure citizens.*

CB: Yeah.

BD: *And you are also aware that all information hereafter revealed will remain confidential and protected until an appropriate time to be determined in the future, thereby allowing you to speak freely and truthfully.*

CB: Right.

BD: *Okay then. [clears throat.] Mrs. Brodsky, were you aware your husband, Jake Brodsky, had conspired with [CI-6] to import and distribute cocaine trafficked into the United States by the Medellín Cartel?*

January 15, 1981
2:54 PM
Interview of Catherine Brodsky
Brett Dalworth, Field Agent, FBI

BD: *You feeling okay?*

CB: No. Yeah. I'm sorry. I haven't slept. Jacob was up all night with the croup and Samantha is going through one of her bed-wetting phases again.

BD: *That happens sometimes. My oldest started doing it when she would get jealous of her brother. They don't know how to respond, so they do anything to get a reaction. Good or bad. [shuffling] Do you need more cream?*

CB: This is fine. Thanks.

*BD: Last week, you said most of the activist groups you associate with had gone quiet?*

CB: Well, it is winter. It sucks standing out in the square when it's pissing rain and thirty-four degrees.

*BD: Of course. But...looking at planning. What's in the works for spring? Anything important? Anything we should be worried about?*

CB: Not that I know of.

*BD: You remember that providing information is part of our agreement. This wasn't a one-time thing. You need to keep helping me if you and Jake want to stay out of jail.*

CB: I get that, Agent Dalworth. But I haven't heard anything. I'm not really in a place to go out and pound frozen sidewalks while I've got a nursing kid strapped under my jacket, okay? I told you about those clowns who hit the research facility, like two weeks ago.

[papers shuffling]

*BD: That was November, Catherine.*

CB: Time flies, apparently.

*BD: Just so you know.*

CB: I know, okay? I know.


April 1, 1984
10:14 AM
Interview of Catherine Brodsky
Brett Dalworth, Special Agent, FBI


*BD: Jesus, he's four already? Didn't you just have him?*

CB: With those lanky elbows? [laughs] He'd tear me open.

*BD: Can I see the photo again?*

CB: You should see him on that bike, though. Boy's not afraid of anything. Half the time I can't watch because I'm sure he's going to break his neck. The other half I can't look away because I'm sure he'll fly out into traffic and get himself hit. All you hear is little kids parroting me. "JJ, wait! JJ, stop!"

BD: *I saw a coffee mug once, said, "Insanity is hereditary. You get it from your children."*

CB: That's about the size of it.

BD: *How are things with Jake? Any better?*

CB: Not really. Falls asleep on the couch watching Letterman most nights. Not that I'd let him in the bed anyway. You know what that son of a bitch said to me? "I can't believe you're working with the pigs." Those two pricks get picked up for dealing and threaten our entire group, and what does Jacob do? Get all high and mighty. At least Dumpy, piece of shit he may be, took his lumps like a man and did what needed to be done to make things right. My pussy-ass husband suddenly gets some morals and lets his wife handle things for him. Guess I shouldn't really be surprised, though. He's always been like this.

BD: *I guess he's dealing with things his own way.*

CB: Dealing with them? He isn't dealing with shit. If it weren't for me, he'd be coming up on four years inside. I should've let him go in the pokey. Would've if it weren't for JJ and Samantha. Ha, dealing with things.

BD: *He drinking again?*

CB: Do empty mouthwash bottles count?

BD: *He need help?*

CB: He can get it himself if he wants some. I'm the one who needs help. A maid, a washerwoman. Hell, even just someone to watch the kids for an hour so I can get my hair cut without spending five dollars in gumball machine prizes. Jake doesn't do a goddamn thing. It'd be easier if he weren't even there because I wouldn't have to clean around him.

BD: *What about [REDACTED]? Wasn't she helping out some?*

CB: We had kind of a falling out.

BD: *Over what?*

CB: I told her about [CI-6], what he was doing.

BD: *That's still happening? I thought he'd stopped.*

CB: There's not really that much to start, much less stop. It's not—there's nothing outright that he's doing. It's just...I don't know. He makes me nervous.

BD: *Has he been hanging outside the house again? You said [shuffling paper] back last October that you thought you saw him in his car, watching your house.*

CB: I don't know. I usually leave the room when he comes over to see Jake.

BD: *Kiki, has he threatened you or the kids?*

CB: Not per se. And I don't know that he's watching the house, or watching me. It's Baltimore. Neighborhoods are neighborhoods. He's not far away. Maybe he was at The Hole drinking. Maybe it wasn't even him.

BD: *You seemed pretty sure last time that it was him. Concerned, even.*

CB: I don't know. Maybe I'm going crazy.


September 19, 1985
4:12 PM
Interview of Catherine Brodsky
Brett Dalworth, Special Agent, FBI


BD: *You look tired.*

CB: I am tired. I don't know how much longer I can do this.

BD: *Do what?*

CB: This! [loud noise] Everything.

BD: *Deep breath, Kiki. You're okay. It's just you and me here.*

CB: I'm just—I feel like I'm going insane. Like there are two different people inside me and, for right now, it's okay because they don't know the other is there. But once they look, and realize what the other one is? They're going to start tearing each other to shreds.

BD: *Kiki, do you need to take some medication? It might help you relax.*

CB: I can't relax. If I relax, then something slips out and if something slips out...

BD: *Is this about [CI-6]? Is that going on again?*

CB: It would have to stop in order to start again. I'm scared, Brett. What's going to happen to JJ and Samantha if he hurts me?

BD: *I'll have a word with my colleague. I'll take care of it.*

[shuffling papers]

BD: *What have you heard about [REDACTED] recently?*

CB: Jesus Christ. [coughing] Nothing.

BD: *That's not what we're getting from other sources.*

CB: Then why don't you ask the other sources about him.

BD: *I did. Now I'm asking you. We're hearing he's renewed his friendship with D'Andre Bell, an associate of Melvin Williams. Seeing as how Mr. Williams has taken up a twenty-five-year lease in Lewisburg, Mr. Bell needs some help maintaining the business.*

CB: Can I have a cigarette?

BD: *You don't smoke.*

CB: Yes or no? [shuffling, matches striking] Look, I don't know anything about Williams or Bell or [REDACTED]. But [REDACTED] is an asshole. A scumbag. You know he pays male prostitutes at The Eagle to blow him in the bathroom, then beats the shit out of them and calls them a faggot? Leaves them on the floor bleeding, piss all over the tile.

BD: *How do you know that?*

CB: Heard it around.

BD: *Exactly. That's the kind of ears you need to have. Go see [REDACTED]. Hang out with him. Get a drink, loosen his lips. See what he's talking about.*

CB: Who's going to watch the kids? Jake Junior is hell on wheels now.

BD: *I...I could watch them if it helped.*

CB: Yeah, that'll be the day. I think the Bureau would look down on consorting like that.

BD: *Just—just find something for me. Soon.*

June 25, 1986
6:57 PM
Interview of Catherine Brodsky
Brett Dalworth, Special Agent, FBI

CB: No. Absolutely not.

*BD: Excuse me?*

CB: No, fuck you.

*BD: Kiki, you need to calm down.*

CB: Calm down? Are you serious?

*BD: Dead serious. This is incredibly important and a very, very high priority for our people. Do you understand?*

CB: Do you understand my family is a high-fucking-priority for me, you piece of shit?

*BD: Listen, Lieutenant Colonel North is scheduled to testify to the House Commission soon, and we've heard rumors that [REDACTED] and his group of communists are planning to sneak in a bomb. Onto the House floor, North's office, a hallway, we're not sure yet. But this is serious, and it sounds right up their alley.*

CB: Oh, to hell with Ollie North. He's trying to get Noriega to wipe out the Sandinistas for him, keep his hands clean.

*BD: We are trying to get rid of them. You included. Communism is a threat to our country. They are a threat to our country.*

CB: No, they're not. They freed the people from the Somozas.

*BD: I don't know who that is.*

CB: The family regime that has destroyed Nicaragua since, I don't know, the thirties? Did you know they'd go into villages and—*

*BD: Samantha. Jake Junior. That's what you should be focusing on. Not the junta. So I will ask you again—*

CB: I can't just go in and start asking about that. I barely know those people. It'll throw flags immediately. I already feel like everyone's watching me.

BD: *You're fine. This is your job. Find things, tell me, go home, and kiss your kids good night.*

CB: It's too risky.

BD: *It's not. I'll help you. It's a protest like any other. Down with Reagan. Ban the Bomb. Let the Ayatollah Rule. Whatever you want to say. Hell, maybe the more incendiary, the more they'll take a shine to you.*

CB: I really don't know about this, Brett.

BD: *It'll be fine, Kiki. I promise, okay? Remember: you're doing this to keep your kids safe.*

CB: Not much I can do to keep them safe if someone kills me.

BD: *I won't let that happen.*

CB: [laughing]

BD: *Whatever. Let's run through it one more time, then.*

# 34

The phone startled Jay. He glanced at the screen. Vargas. He looked back to the clutch of papers, to the jagged top edge where someone had ripped out the last few pages of transcripts and reports at the back, processing everything. Dumpy Felder was CI-6, the one who had stalked outside their house, who'd been a constant threat to their family. The one who'd bragged about taking care of CI-7—his mother—just weeks after her death. The missing pages at the end of the file would've detailed how she met her untimely end. No one had access outside of agents. Felder had killed his mother, and the Bureau had helped him cover it up.

Jay felt the room spin, punctuated by the sound of his phone ringing.

He set the papers down and accepted the call.

"Where the hell are you?" she said before he could get a word out.

"My apartment." He didn't have the energy to come up with something witty.

"Why aren't you here?"

Jay glanced outside and the rain had darkened the sky. "What time is it?"

"Half-past get your ass in here."

"Shit."

"The Ghosts have their sights set on destroying the global

economy and the best you have to say is *shit?*" Vargas said. "You better think of something a lot better if you don't want Dalworth to wear you like a coat."

*To hell with Dalworth,* he thought. That lying, manipulative, scheming son of a bitch. All of these years he'd known the truth about Jay's mom—the truth about Jay—and not once had he ever let on, given any indication. Not even so much that he knew, but that he was the one who had precipitated it. If he hadn't forced Jay's mother into narcing, she would still be alive today. Right, left, left, right. Left, right, right, left. *Breathe, Jay. Close your eyes and breathe. Do not let him win.*

He cleared his throat. "I got tased."

Vargas laughed. Left, right, right, Left. *Stop it and breathe.* Right, left, left, right. "Wait, are you serious?"

Jay let out a long sigh, then started with the server, the h3r file, Amaru, Oscar Forlán, the call from Thurgood to who-might-be Forlán, and the connection to Palacio Legislativo, the possibility of a resurgence of the Tupamaros. For ten minutes, he recounted the evening in excruciating detail, keeping his mouth moving and head far away from the folder, and she said not one word.

"And then someone knocked on my door."

"After midnight?"

"I thought it might be you."

"You seriously thought I'd booty-call you after the way we left it yesterday afternoon? You must've got hit in the head."

"I was hoping you were coming to help. And it was tased in the chest, not hit in the head."

"Is the evidence okay?"

"It's gone."

"I suppose it was inadmissible anyway, after your little stunt." She sighed. "Are you okay?"

"I'm doing better now."

"Jesus Christ." She exhaled hard. "Did you see who it was?"

"Yep."

"It was Zane Thurgood, wasn't it."

Jay didn't have to answer.

Vargas muttered some curse in Spanish. "Well, run a dryer sheet over you and get your ass in here for debriefing."

Jay glanced at the burner phone on his table, the stack of papers that had decimated the memory of his family, the laptop humming in front of him.

"I'll be in as soon as I can," he said, then hung up before she could answer. He went back to the closet and rooted through drawers, tossing aside old hard drives and soldering irons and coils. Buried under an old laptop, he finally found what he was looking for, then returned to the table.

He didn't know where Sam was, but he had an idea of how to find her. He'd already searched through the rest of Thurgood's phone, not finding much of value: more photos of plants than expected, some bookmarked YouTube videos of old punk shows, a Twitter account that followed several internet celebrities. But most important: call information for one Kiki Laughton. He pried the back off Thurgood's phone and extracted the SIM card, the small, thin piece of circuits and silicon that contained all of the information stored on the phone. Jay plugged the reader into his laptop, then inserted the SIM card and launched a custom tracing program, which he'd modified from the Bureau-issued Stingrays.

Normally to trace a phone, he'd get a warrant and bring it to the phone company so that they could track the phone to within a couple of feet. But that would require actually getting a warrant—which Jay couldn't do—and time, which Jay didn't have. He had to find Sam before they did.

The dialogue box filled with numbers, letters, and other systems information scrolling past. Jay's eyes glazed over as he watched its hypnotic movement, like a snake made of data. Information filtered through his skull, wondering how his mother managed to keep it together and never let the stress show to him and Sam, how Dalworth had looked at him for the last seven years without betraying anything despite knowing what he knew, whether Jay even got his job because Dalworth felt sorry for him and made a pity-hire.

When the card was fully loaded, Jay entered a few commands and isolated all the information associated with Kiki Laughton's number. He flipped through a complete call log with time and date and duration, then moved into the scrolling scripts of text messages until he found what he was looking for.

GPS location points.

He scribbled down the coordinates on the back of a Chinese take-out menu, then toggled screens to open an interactive map.

His phone vibrated on the table. Vargas. *Dalworth is on the hunt. I can't stall forever.* Jay was surprised to see an hour had passed. He felt the urgency building, knowing that he had a short window of time to track Sam before Dalworth completely lost his shit. Jay wouldn't be able to use the Bureau's equipment to stop his sister from terrorizing the country if he didn't have a job. Still...

He texted back. *Don't do anything that gets you in trouble. This is on me.*

Within seconds he received another text in all caps. *I FUCK-ING KNOW THAT.* Jay couldn't help but smile a second. Back to work.

Jay entered the coordinates into the map, then took a breath and hit enter. The machine computed, analyzed, narrowed down the towers the signal pinged off. A swath of color filled a section of the map, one block in the southeast corner of Fell's Point. Ironically, it was edged in by high-rises on two sides, a boat dock on the third. *Nice place for a revolutionary to lay their head.* But in between were scores of small row homes, built in the 1800s when Baltimore was the major shipping hub of the east coast. The map wasn't as accurate as Jay would've liked, but as good as he was going to get. He zoomed in and examined the area. A yoga studio. A French-inspired café. An art gallery Jay remembered being a source of controversy a couple years earlier. A nouveau-riche dive bar. Two water taxi stops on opposite sides of the pier.

And then he remembered the burst of music. The one that cut off as if someone had just closed the door.

Bars were as common in Fell's Point as morning-after regret.

But *Fell's Point, one minute* sounded like a water taxi announcement. One stop was to the east across a portion of the harbor, but blocked by a building. The other was to the west, not as far but also blocked by buildings.

So if Jay was able to clearly hear the announcement, that meant there was nothing standing in the way. Like, say, the end of Fell Street, which looked out over the harbor.

Sam had to have been outside, on a deck or rooftop porch. Though she was a woman of the people, he doubted she would be walking around the streets on the slight chance someone would recognize her.

Jay zoomed in as far as he could, some stupid part of him hoping the satellites that captured this footage had passed over while she was outside smoking.

He jotted down the range of house numbers and toggled screens, logged into the Bureau's database, and began pulling property records. Two deeds were under Eddie Aymar, whose name Jay recognized from a couple articles in the *Sun* about shady renting practices and frequent complaints from tenants. In other words, a slumlord. With all the development and gentrification Baltimore had experienced in the last ten years, it was bound to start happening in the nicer neighborhoods.

"Hold on, hold on," he said to himself. He was starting to sound like Sam now. "Focus."

He continued scanning through the names, expecting to see Felder's name pop up. Either of them.

So he was a little surprised—and excited—to open the fifth deed and see a name he vaguely recognized radiating on the page.

Mauricio Huidobo.

"Mauricio? Mauricio?" Jay stood and began pacing in front of his laptop. Rain lashed against the bay window that overlooked the harbor. The hurricane was becoming more powerful.

*Mauricio.* He knew that name. Where had he seen it? No one with the Ghosts. No one from the Chop Shop. No one—

Mauricio. Uruguay. Cabinet Minister.

Oscar Forlán's brother.

Oscar Forlán, founder of Amaru Cyber Storage and son of a Tupamaro guerilla.

"Got you."

He was a little surprised that Forlán would put a house in his brother's name, given that he owned a reputable company in the city, but if he had a hand in the revolution business, he could see Forlán wanting to stay off the radar as much as possible. Jay cross-referenced the address on the deed with the map, saw it was the one on the northeast corner, right where Wolfe Street formed a *V* with Fell Street. Nice view of the harbor. Back porch from which you could clearly hear the water taxi announcement. Maybe it was the perfect place to plan a revolution.

He snatched his phone and dialed Vargas's number, Thurgood's contact list open before him.

"Seriously, Brodsky. What the—"

"Get a pencil."

"What?"

"Get a pencil and write these numbers down."

She muttered under her breath, but Jay could hear scrabbling, meaning she was actually listening. "Go," she said a minute later.

Jay read off three phone numbers. "The first two are Eric Felder and Comrade Pat. The third is Thurgood's grandmother."

"Why do I need them?"

"Because with the hurricane, he's probably helping take care of her, and I don't know her address—or if she's even at her house."

"What's up, Brodsky?" Her voice had taken a softer, more-concerned tone. "What happened?"

"Get Yemin and team and scoop up the Ghosts."

Her breath rolled over the phone.

Jay felt his throat swell before he could say anything. He swallowed hard.

"I found the ringleaders."

# 35

Rain hit the roof of Jay's car like bags of nickels shot from a fire hose. A squall tore through the street, amplified by the tall buildings on either side that acted as a funnel, intensifying the wind. The car rocked on its axles, Jay keeping a tight grip on the wheel. Still, despite the terrible weather and impending flooding, a handful of protestors remained. They stood before a branch of Bayside Bank, arms linked together beneath their yellow rain ponchos, chanting some sort of anti-capitalist slogan at the business, which was closed because of the storm. Meanwhile, two city cops tried to force the protestors to vacate. Jay drove past.

Though the storm caused anxiety to well inside Jay, it was his destination that fueled the tics that threatened to overtake him. As he wobbled his way around the harbor up Light Street, dodging groups of twentysomethings running across the street with cases of beer tucked under their arms, Jay tried to visualize his next act. Could he really arrest Sam? What would it take for him to do that? She was, after all, part of a terrorist cell. Conversely, would she pull a gun on him? How far would he have to push her to do that? If he tried to arrest Forlán, who it seemed was funding their revolution, what would she do?

And perhaps the most important: why did Jay think she would have any kind of loyalty to him when she'd chosen to extract herself from his life for seven years?

He could see, objectively, that she wouldn't want to be too close to her federal-agent brother while planning something as large and dangerous as this, but completely disappearing from his life was a step beyond. Where did she go during those years? What else was she doing other than planning a revolution? Was she still doing music? What did she do with friends? Did she have friends? Jay had more questions than answers, more vague gestures of inquiry than actual ways to express it, a mountain of detail that only made him feel increasingly disconnected from his sister. The only thing he could say for sure was that she had completely crushed him.

A bolt of lightning cleaved the sky, blinding Jay for a second, followed by a concussive rumble of thunder. When Jay's eyes cleared, he saw the leaves of a tree burning, flames licking the trunk, a short distance in front of him. Jay sped up, pulling past the tree a few seconds before it fell over. He told himself to take a deep breath, told himself that *no, that was not a sign.* Told himself that again.

Jay rounded the top of the Inner Harbor. Normally this place was filled with tourists, pickpockets, people hawking crap that no one actually wanted to buy. Now, rain hit the green water so hard it looked like the harbor was boiling. Water lapped over the edge of the broad brick pedestrian walkway ringing the area, covering nearly half of it, the water level a good six feet higher than normal, and the storm wasn't even halfway done.

Jay hadn't seen flooding like this in almost fifteen years, back when he was in college. He remembered seeing two kids from his sociology class on the news, paddling a kayak through Fell's Point the day after the storm passed. This current storm was following the same path, those hundred-mile-per-hour winds pushing water from the ocean nearly two hundred miles up the Chesapeake Bay, dead-ending here at the harbor. This whole area would be underwater by tomorrow morning, along with a good portion of downtown—and most important, Sam's place in Fell's, not more than a hundred feet from the water.

But that didn't stop all the idiots with Ghost masks. Jay passed a mass of easily seventy protestors, linking arms to form a circle and protect those in the center, standing defiant before a line of riot police gradually moving them backward. Whether it was to arrest them or get them out of danger, Jay didn't know. It didn't seem to matter, though, because one of the protestors in the center winged a road flare at the line of police, followed by another with a smoke bomb. The police retreated, protestors disappearing behind the wall of purple smoke. Being obscured boosted their confidence, and someone launched a brick or heavy bottle at the gigantic glass windows of Bank of America's flagship location. The huge panes splintered, barely holding on until a gust of wind hit them, raining glass down on the sidewalk.

*This is the legacy of your people, Sam,* Jay thought. *Mindless destruction under the guise of equality.*

He stepped on the gas, ready to get this over with.

Jay made it as far into Fell's as he could but had to ditch his car on Lancaster Street, less than a block from where the water had overtaken the street and five blocks or more from where Sam was. He was scared to think of how high the water had gotten down there. He gripped the wheel tight, squeezing until his knuckles turned white, then took three deep breaths. Relaxed his grip, then checked and double-checked his pistol before kicking the door open.

The rain stung his face as he ran down the sidewalk, water quickly filling his shoes. Even in the middle of summer, the water still made his skin turn gooseflesh. At least, he told himself it was the water. He sunk past his ankles in the storm runoff flooding the streets, iridescent with oil. Rivers of garbage streamed down the gutters, headed toward the storm drains. Jay banked right at South Ann.

There was no reason to check the intersection before running across, with no traffic able to pass. As he headed south, water sloshed across his calves, creeping up his shins as he approached the house. He slowed as he approached the end of Ann, where it split into Fell on the left and opened into the harbor on the right.

Standing here, with his sister down one side of the intersection and the harbor sloshing over the street on the other, he felt like the universe's metaphor was a little on the nose. He couldn't tell where the street ended and harbor began, and if he took a single step too far, he'd sink down into thirty feet of polluted water and be swept under the shelf downtown was built on, his body lost until the storm receded and the tide pulled it out, if it ever did.

Jay took extra caution and stayed far to the left, going so far as to press his shoulder against the row homes' walls to stay anchored to the land.

He made his way to the last house on the block, the rain stinging his face, and stood at the base of the marble steps. He laughed to himself, which felt absurd given the situation: standing in front of the house where his long-lost sister was hiding with the son of a guerilla while he reminisced about how much he loved the stereotypical Baltimore marble stoop. The current broke around his knees, threatening to knock him off-balance.

Jay unlatched his holster as he sloshed up the steps. Full-length glass windows stood on either side. Jay peered in but couldn't see anything past the hallway.

He took one last deep breath, then slammed his foot against the door.


Jay held his pistol at the ready, let it lead him down the hallway. Cream tile floors with azure accents, exposed beams in the ceiling, postmodern art on the walls, air cool and dry as a cave despite the storm raging outside. No one in sight. Rain lashed against the house, so loud it covered the sound of Jay's ragged breathing.

The hallway emptied into a large space, modestly furnished.

Plaster walls ran parallel with the beams on either side, two steps on the right leading to a recessed living room, only an old couch and small end table and a large glimmering television mounted flush in the wall. Three large windows opened up the wall. If he squinted, he would've been able to see across the harbor, nearly to his own apartment, if it wasn't for the rain streaking down, nearly two feet of floodwater sloshing at the base. Jay wondered how bad it would get down here before it was all over.

And on the left, standing behind a rustic wooden kitchen island, was Oscar Forlán. He looked up at Jay and gestured with the espresso cup in his hands. "I could pick you and your sister out of a lineup."

The man smiled. His face appeared slightly more creased, his eyes a little more tired than in the photos. Jay supposed the revolution business could be a drag.

"Where is she?"

"Who?"

Jay pointed the pistol at the ceiling, squeezed off a round. Forlán jumped as a cloud of plaster dust snowed down on him.

"Don't fucking push me," Jay said, "or the next one goes in your knee."

"I told you—you can never trust cops."

A woman's voice came from the other room, as if cutting across years and dimensions, alternate lifetimes where none of this had transpired, where Jay hadn't been so scarred by the dissolution of his family that he hadn't poured himself into work, that he had made time for a social life, that he had met someone and had shitty little cookouts in his shitty little yard with Sam and his imaginary wife and kids. Still, her voice rang as clear in real life as it did in Jay's memory.

Sam walked into the kitchen, something like a sheepish smile playing across her face. Jay exhaled, didn't realize he'd been holding his breath.

"You look great," Sam said.

Jay just nodded, unsure of what to say, as if there was anything *to* say. Jet-black hair, tiger and chrysanthemum tattoos on the sides of her neck, clipper ship on her chest and geisha and warrior sleeves on her arms, she looked almost the same to him. Seven years had barely made an impression on her. He knew she dyed her hair, and the tattoos were a little more faded, but it was as if everything she'd done between now and the time she left had given her life. Which caused Jay to think for a second: *what, was I sucking the life from you?*

"Are you going to say anything?" Sam said.

"Jesus Christ," Jay said. "What would you like me to say, Sam? Where the fuck have you been? What the fuck are you doing? What the fuck is wrong with you? Are you still vegan and is that juice bar around the corner any good, because I could really go for a fucking cleanse?"

His throat burned. Forlán leaned back. Jay caught himself, realized he'd been screaming. He took a deep breath and exhaled through his nose.

"What, Sam. What should I say?"

And Sam, for once, seemed to be at a loss, staring at Jay with the saddest eyes he'd ever seen. Thunder clapped outside, shaking the walls of the house.

After a long minute that stretched and crackled over years, Sam finally sighed hard, cocked her hip out. "We might not be on the same side, but we both know we've always done what we've done—trying to find justice, trying to make the world a better place—because of Mom."

"That's what you want to start on right now? Mom? Fuck, Sam, I joined the FBI because her way was useless. It never worked," Jay yelled. "How does her taking us to protests end up with you executing CEOs on the internet?"

"No," she barked. "That was their choice. And they have done things a hundred-times worse to a thousand-times more people. Look at the Harper twins. Those companies forced a mother to choose which of her children should die because they had to look out for stock prices. Those twins are just one of a million examples. *That* is their legacy, and those economic terrorists deserved a hell of a lot more than what they got."

"It doesn't matter what they deserve, Sam. You"—Jay pointed at her and Forlán—"are not the ones to make that call. You don't right wrongs with murder. Jesus Christ, I can't believe I'm even saying that."

Forlán sneered at Jay. "You and I both know the government funds terrorist activity every day. Through its police force, through subprime mortgages, through deregulating trade, in developing nation-states all around the world."

Sam laughed to herself and shook her head. "You never did have the heart, Jay. Never could commit to the cause."

"Commit to the cause?" Jay found himself screaming again but didn't care. "What cause? The one that got Mom to bring her six-year-old son to a protest where we all got hit with a fire hose and I ended up with a scar on my head? Or the one that ended up with her and Dad in lockup and you lying to people so no one would know we were in the house for three days together with no parents?"

"That's police tyranny—"

"Shut the fuck up, Sam. I don't want to hear another goddamned word about it. You're doing this for Mom? You want to be the savior, want to keep her memory alive by rescuing all the poor people? You know something—Mom was a fucking narc."

The words reverberated through the room. Sam's jaw pulsed beneath her skin.

"You don't know what you're talking about." She pushed the words through her teeth, her fists pulsing, clenching and loosening, but Jay could see something like doubt crossing her expression, like clouds across the sun.

"I don't? Because I have the FBI files at home. Dad got caught buying heroin with Dumpy Felder, so Mom flipped. She started narcing to keep his worthless ass out of jail."

"That's bullshit." She jabbed her finger at Jay. "Complete bullshit."

"No, what's bullshit is that Dad continued to fuck up, which put Mom under more pressure to come up with intel. You remember that community center they were trying to build? Over in Poplar Heights?"

"Of course I do."

"Yeah, of course you do. No one was doing shit with that until Mom started working with the cops. Then it got the fast track. And you know why? So they could get information on the neighborhood. Who was coming in and out, who was moving what. Fuck, Sam, you think I'm shit because I'm The Man? Mom didn't even get to wear a badge. She did the same thing the CIA did to the Panthers back in the Seventies. The same shit you three used to complain about."

"Shut the fuck up, JJ."

But Jay couldn't hear her. The wave of repressed anger and abandonment and isolation that had been welling up for the last seven years had broken through and enveloped him. His mouth moved without any conscious thought.

"You remember what you told me about Mom's head the day she died? How the bruise on her head looked like a rotten plum and you couldn't eat them after that?"

Sam made a noise Jay assumed meant *yes*.

"Are you absolutely sure you saw it?"

"Why the hell would I make that up?"

Jay glanced over at Forlán, then looked away.

"Tell me about it."

"What the fuck, JJ?" She barked out a sigh. "It was swollen like, two inches from her skin. All yellow and purple and goop running into her ear. Almost on her left temple."

"You're positive it was her left one?"

"I will never forget that image as long as I live," she said.

"Because I've been carrying a picture of the three of us in my wallet for the last seven years and have memorized every damn detail. There's no bruise. There's nothing at all."

Sam breathed out a laugh. "And?"

"You were right, Sam. It wasn't suicide. Dumpy Felder killed her. The cops covered it up because he was an informant for my boss's partner, Todd Hart."

"I know I was right, asshole. I don't need you to tell me that. And it's convenient you suddenly come up with these supposed files two days before you find me."

"You'll believe she was murdered—by Dumpy Felder, by her own people, *by your fucking people*—but not that she betrayed the cause? *That* is convenient."

"Those are two totally different—"

"That's who she was, Sam! She was one of them, and she was a narc. I just—I don't know what else you need to hear to understand that she wasn't who you think she was."

"*¡Ya basta!*" Forlán yelled. "Enough. What you think of your mother, Agent Brodsky, does not matter in the least here. We are bringing about a new age in this country. We are freeing people from the indentured servitude forced upon them by these bloodsucking corporations. If a few people must die in order to bring about that revolution, then so be it."

"I know your family story, Oscar. Your father, the men he fought with, the family who moved back while you stayed here. I know you understand loss. I know you understand loneliness." Forlán gave a small nod. "Then you understand why I'm so angry at my sister. The only person I had left, who abandoned me for some half-cocked revolution that was horseshit to start with."

Forlán stood there, swaying slightly from foot to foot. Though his face seemed more worn down, his arms and chest did not, the shirt taut at the edges. This was a man whose mind stayed as fit as his body, who would outthink an opponent as easily as outmuscle him. Jay had the feeling he'd been ready for a fight since he could walk, and with a family background such as the Forláns, he wasn't surprised.

Still, his countenance softened on hearing Jay's plea.

"I understand how you feel, Agent Brodsky. Family is everything. I've operated my entire life with that thinking. To honor my family and what they believed." He stepped forward. Jay tensed by instinct. "But I respect her enough to not meddle in her affairs. She made her choice, the same as you must make yours."

"You want us to go back to how we were, Jay? You want the little family you remember?" Sam paused a beat and something cold spread through Jay's gut. He felt the sword hanging above his head. He knew what she would say before she said it. "You tank this case. Destroy the evidence. Get rid of whatever you've got. Then I'll come home."

Jay snuffed out a laugh. "You know I won't do that."

"Not even for your own sister?" Sam cocked her head. "*Maldito sea el soldado que vuelva las armas contra su hermana.*"

"Fuck you. And your fake-ass fucking Spanish." Jay ran his tongue along the back of his teeth, felt his jaw tense.

"What will it be, soldier?" She crossed her hands in front of her waist. *Everything is connected.* "Which is more important for you to have, Agent Brodsky: your sister, or your case?"

A career case. One that would raise his standing as well as give Vargas a much-needed boost. One that would be the crowning achievement for the Baltimore office, taking down a terrorist cell that affected the entire mid-Atlantic and threatened the global economy.

Or he could have his sister back. If this was even the same sister who'd left. Maybe she was never the person he thought she was. Maybe everything he'd built in his mind was a construct, a warped representation of what he needed her to be to continue functioning, to not let his stupid fucking brain malfunction swallow him whole. Maybe the Sam he knew never really existed outside his misfiring synapses.

Or maybe she was exactly who he thought she was. Smart.

Principled. Stubborn as all hell and completely to her own detriment. Unable to admit fault in her thinking even when it would benefit her cause. But above all: misguided. Jay wasn't sure which would be worse.

She shifted on her feet, held out her hand. "Choose, Jay."

Jay's mind sparked and fizzed. So many things rode on a simple handshake. Wars began and ended. Empires built and felled. Families created and destroyed. All with one simple word. A name.

"The Sam I knew would never ask something like that. Choosing between family and the cause."

Forlán barked out a laugh. "Typical cop answer. You're so insulated. You have no idea what real sacrifice, real dedication looks like. You have no constitution, only convenience."

Jay felt something snap inside him. He lunged forward, swinging his fist, catching Forlán on the jaw. Forlán stumbled backward and Jay drove his shoulder into Forlán's stomach. They crashed into the wall, plaster chunks crumbling and falling on them. Forlán swung but Jay threw his head to the side. Forlán's fist narrowly missed, landing hard against the wall and breaking more plaster. Jay kicked his leg out, catching Forlán on the side of the knee. He howled in pain. Jay rolled over, away from Forlán. Sam screamed at them to stop their macho bullshit. Jay brought himself up to a crouch as Forlán flung his body forward, Jay swinging his feet up and planting them on Forlán's chest, flipping him over, landing flat on his back on the tile floor. Forlán gasped for breath and Jay seized the opportunity, jumping on his chest. Forlán's eyes broadcast horror, realizing Jay was going to strangle him, to pounce on him at his most vulnerable and end him like a feral animal.

"JJ," Sam screamed. "Leave him alone!"

But Jay barely heard her, focusing all his strength on his hands, as if by squeezing Forlán's neck until his breath no longer flowed, he could stem whatever had been roiling inside him, could stop the tidal wave of shit that had washed over him in the last few weeks.

It wasn't until he felt someone's hands on his shoulders, felt himself flying backward that it really registered. Jay tumbled across the floor, his back slamming against the glass storm door. He felt a crack. He jumped to his feet, hands up and already saying *What the fuck?* when he saw a wooden bar stool hurtling through the air. Jay ducked just as it sailed over his head, crashing against the glass and shattering it completely. Water rushed in around Jay's calves.

"What the fuck is wrong with you, Sam?"

"You. You are what's wrong."

"Me?" Jay flinched despite himself. "What, you left because of me?"

"No. This has nothing to do with you." She waved her hands around, indicating the apartment, the Ghosts, everything about her. "I spent twelve years of my life taking care of you, feeding you, getting you to school, missing the chance to tour with one of my favorite fucking bands of all time because I knew what it would do to you. I gave up everything, just for you."

"And you think I don't appreciate it?"

"You can appreciate it but you'll never understand it. All you can see is laws and restrictions, and if people don't follow those arbitrary guidelines, then they're fucked." She took several steps forward, her legs splashing through the water that was rapidly filling the house. "Who says that's how things are? Who says those are the rules?"

"Sam, this is not—"

"Who, Jay?" She swung a hand at him, not so much to slap him but more because she didn't know how better to move. "Cops? Politicians? The Founding fucking Fathers who were slave owners? As if any of them gave a shit about us, the ones who are getting ground to dust as they're helping this entire planet function? Who watches out for us?"

Jay started to answer but Sam cut him off.

"We do. And you, your agency, your fucking bootlickers are trying to keep us down." She came within inches of Jay's face. "We won't fucking let you."

"Sam, you are in way over your head. I know you. You are not a murderer."

"You know me?" Her hands slammed against Jay's chest, pushing him back against the metal frame of the door, a piece of glass jabbing his shoulder blade. "If you *knew me*," she said, practically spitting at him, "you'd know I don't get in over my head."

Jay held his hands up, palms out, not willing to get into a fistfight with his sister. Water sloshed against his shins, lapping against his knees. Sam didn't notice, or didn't care. "That's not what I meant."

"Then what did you mean? You never believed in what we were doing? You think I wasted my life? You're better than me because you have a steady job and a badge? The end of your necktie is a fucking noose, JJ."

"*I* am not the one who fucked up here." Jay stepped in close to her. "*You* abandoned *me* and I'm tired of trying to shoulder that blame."

Sam pushed him again, Jay's hands coming up into a defense stance out of instinct before he lowered them. Sam smirked, as if she relished breaking him down. "You might think you had it bad, JJ, but I was the one who had to raise my little brother when I was ten because if I didn't, he'd end up curled fetal under the bed like a puppy during a thunderstorm."

Jay's teeth ground against each other. In a flash, he imagined lashing out, striking her, then pushed the thought away as soon as it formed. Something tugged at the edges of Sam's mouth, the slight wrinkles that had formed there, the ones that made her, inexplicably, look more like their mother. But it was more of a pained expression than a resigned one, as if she was trying to find whatever way possible to make him leave, so she wouldn't have to make the decision neither of them wanted to be responsible for making.

"No," Jay said, shaking his head. "Fuck you. Fuck you, Sam." He holstered his pistol and brought out his handcuffs. Decision made. "This is over. You're done."

She barked out a laugh despite herself. "You're going to handcuff me?" Her tone was incredulous but her voice still strung tight as a garrote wire. "Your brain must really be broken if you think that's happening."

Jay winced but he hid it by gesturing around the room. "All this? This is all done. I radioed in. Agents are scooping up Thurgood, the Felders, everyone. I came down here so I could—"

"Bring me in yourself? Get the big collar and be Johnny fucking Utah?"

Jay swallowed hard, shook his head. "I came down here so I could see you again. Just one more time without it being through Plexiglass." Tears welled as he watched Sam's anger deflate, and he bit down on the edge of his tongue to stave them off. "I just wanted to see you."

"Jesus, JJ, I never meant to—"

Her words were cut short as Forlán yelled and sprang forward, tackling Jay by the waist. They tumbled out onto the patio, splashing into the water. Dirty harbor water rushed into Jay's nostrils, viscous with oil and gasoline runoff. It filled his ears, and would have filled his mouth if he hadn't clamped it tight. Forlán's grip tightened on Jay's neck, pushing him farther under the water until his back scraped against the concrete floor, and he suddenly remembered Yemin once saying that the drunk idiots who dared each other to jump in the harbor had to get tetanus shots afterward because the water was so polluted. He wondered which was worse, all this garbage water or the burning in his lungs from a lack of air.

Forlán's grip loosened as he readjusted his position and Jay took advantage of the seconds of relief, slid his hands under Forlán's and broke free. He rolled away, bursting through the water with a great, gulping breath. Forlán lunged at him again but Jay slipped away, the man's hands sliding across Jay's torso, slick with old car oil. Water seeped into Jay's mouth. He swallowed instinctively and it burned his throat. He doubled over, gagging, and felt something hard break across his back, dropping him face-first back into the water.

"You won't destroy my work," Forlán shouted.

Jay kicked out his leg blindly, clipping the side of Forlán's shin. It wasn't enough to knock him down, but threw him off-balance. Jay pushed himself up, and saw the broken barstool floating in the water.

He grabbed the wooden leg and swung. Forlán's head flung back, a thread of blood flinging from his cheek. Jay reared back to swing again but was cut short as Sam tackled him by the waist, hurtling him toward the railing around the ground-level deck. His forehead careened off the metal, the reverberation echoing through his head. He was about to yell at Sam but when he looked up, he saw Forlán pointing a handgun in the space where Jay had been. He reached out, grabbed Forlán's foot and yanked it, dropping the man down into the water with a splash. Jay clambered up on the man's chest, started swinging. Once, twice, three times he slammed his fist on Forlán's face, ignoring Sam clawing at his back.

He probably would've continued to pound, so blind with rage—at Forlán, at the Ghosts, at his mother, at Dalworth, at Sam—until the Uruguayan's face was a gelatinous mess, but Forlán brought up his knee, right between Jay's legs. Jay toppled over, groaning, and Forlán pushed himself up and over, his knee on the agent's left arm, his hands reaching toward the agent's throat. Sam threw herself at Jay, slid off because of the viscous water. The three of them writhed in the water, flinging each other over, thrashing and clawing and swinging.

Then there was the click of cold metal.

Forlán looked down and saw a handcuff on his left wrist, the other end clamped tight to the metal railing.

"What are you—?"

Jay grunted as he slammed his forehead into the bridge of Forlán's nose, the man's head snapping back, blood pouring from his splattered face. Jay grimaced against the pain and stood up, his head swaying and eyes losing focus. Head butts always looked badass in movies, but they really hurt in real life.

By the time his eyes came back into focus, he saw Sam across the room, hunched in the doorway, the right side of her shirt torn and tattered and black with her blood, her hands training the handgun on Jay.

"Sam." Jay started to tell her not to shoot, to ask if she had really meant to hurt him or if she was trying to save him— again—but fell quiet when she pointed the gun just over his head and fired twice. Jay didn't even flinch, he was too shocked.

The rain lashed Jay's skin as his sister slowly receded back into the house, her posture coiled and pained but the muzzle never leaving Jay's center mass.

"I'm not going to jail," she repeated.

"Sam," he said, as she shuffled backward into the kitchen with a trail of blood before her, just two feet from the hallway, the long tunnel she would step into and disappear from Jay's life once again, maybe for the last time.

He called her name again as she slouched into the hallway, only her face and hands visible beyond the wall.

"Sam—don't leave," he yelled, but it was lost under a crack of thunder, the torrents of rain on metal and broken glass, the water roiling under the downpour.

# 36

Yemin grabbed Jay by the arm before he walked up to the podium.

"You can't go up there like this. You looked like you dressed in the dark." He yanked Jay's tie to the side, then tightened it, the knot dimpling around his thumb. "You get laid last night or something?"

Jay flinched. "No. Why? Who said that?"

"Bruh. Because you're glowing after all that rancid-ass harbor water. It's a joke."

Jay loosened the tie slightly. *The end is a noose* echoed in his head. "You have any idea how many showers I've taken in the last ten days?"

"Never know. This might be your origin story. Come out the other end with some crazy superpower."

"Or a super drug-resistant disease," Jay said. "You done yet?"

Yemin brushed off Jay's lapels and gave a quick appraising glance. "Yeah. Now you look right."

Jay nodded his thanks, then stepped up next to the Deputy Director, who was already giving his victory lap speech. Jay noticed that one of the American flags displayed on either side of the podium had a small yellow stain in a white stripe and wondered how that happened. He thought of the hamburger juice on Vargas's cuff.

Jay smiled at the right times and nodded when he thought it

appropriate, all of the man's words washing over him like a wave across an oyster shell. He bent his head to let the Deputy Director drape the Medal of Meritorious Achievement, one of the highest honors the FBI granted, around his neck. They smiled and shook hands and Jay hoped the flashing cameras erased the dark half-circles under his eyes instead of exaggerating them. He liked the Misfits, but didn't want to look like them. And that singular thought made his eyes mist.

The Deputy Director thanked him again for his service, then made the rounds, glad-handing and joking with reporters and people Jay assumed were important judging by their girth and the boisterousness of their laughs.

Jay stepped down from the small stage, his eyes still adjusting after the flashes.

"Since you're all healed up now," Yemin said, shaking Jay's hand, "I expect I'll see you in my garage tomorrow morning?"

"I'll have to check with my secretary," Jay said. "I'm a national hero now."

"Right." Yemin clapped Jay on the shoulder. "Don't forget doughnuts for the kids."

Jay smiled and glanced over Yemin's shoulder, saw Vargas standing behind him, her hands crossed behind her back and a slight smile cocked on one side.

She lifted the medal with her finger, examined it, then let it drop. "Next time I'm in town, am I going to have to make an appointment to see you?"

"It's not that big a deal. Wait a week for the next school shooting and everyone will forget about this."

"Jesus, Brodsky." She shook her head. "You really know how to kill a mood."

Jay shrugged. "This tie is awful. I feel like someone's choking me as I'm walking around."

"I think you look nice."

"Really?" Jay straightened his back.

She smiled. "No, you look incredibly uncomfortable. You're

handsomer in the polos."

A silence fell between them, an odd tension humming at the corners.

"So," Jay finally said, "when's your flight?"

After the Forlán case, she'd called in a favor and had her custody hearing moved up, which wasn't hard, seeing as how she'd helped take down a terrorist cell that threatened to derail the nation. Dalworth wrote a letter of recommendation on her behalf and as of the last time they'd spoken, she was pretty confident she would be able to get weekends with Esmeralda. It wasn't perfect, but it was a start.

"Four fifteen. So, I have three hours." She glanced at her watch. "You know, we never got that dinner we talked about."

She bit her bottom lip and arched her eyebrow, sizing up Jay. She was saying Applebee's, but Jay heard the menu clearly: sex, likely with animal noises, likely at a hotel by the airport so she wouldn't miss her flight home.

It wasn't like he hadn't thought about it. Christ, he'd had a hard time *not* thinking about it.

"Soooo," Vargas said, "are you hungry, Jay?"

"Paloma?" Jay let out a breath so long he wondered if it would ever stop. "I am fucking starving. I *really* am."

"But?"

"But I can't."

She laughed to herself, shaking her head.

"Next time," he said. "I promise."

"You're promising me? That's not how it works, love."

"Doesn't hurt to try." Jay breathed out a laugh.

A long moment passed between them. Agents and officials bustled around, smiled before cameras.

"Why didn't you tell me your sister was Kat Savage?"

Jay flinched. "What are you talking about?"

Paloma looked at him out of the top of her eyes, her mouth straight. The look of a mother who clearly was not buying the shit you were selling. It looked good on her.

Jay took a deep breath and held it. "If it was Esmeralda, would you have told me?"

The smile she gave Jay was the saddest he'd ever seen.

She leaned forward and pressed her lips against his cheek, close enough that, if he were to twitch, his lips would touch hers. He breathed her in, a mixture of cigarettes and espresso—cortado, maybe—and stored it away for later. She patted his jaw before leaving, and he wondered about what she'd said. If she'd be back down, if there'd be a next time. He could only hope so.

With the FBI brass busy advancing their careers, Jay slipped away before anyone noticed. All the attention made him uncomfortable.

He ran into Dalworth on his way to the door.

"Isn't it rude to leave your own party?"

Jay gestured at the Deputy Director laughing too hard with another older man he didn't recognize. "I'm not so sure it's for me."

Dalworth nodded. "Yeah. It's the game we play."

"Suppose so." Jay started to walk away but Dalworth grabbed his arm.

"Where are you going?"

"Why do you give a shit?"

"Excuse me?" He pulled his head back as if offended. "Because people have questions that need answers."

"Like what?"

"Like why you evaded an all-agent call, why you chose to pursue the subjects without waiting for backup, why there was blood from three people at Forlán's house but we only found you and Forlán."

"I don't know, Brett, but I'm sure you'll figure out some way to cover it up."

Dalworth drew close to Jay, narrowing his eyes, and Jay couldn't help but think of the first time he'd come in after Quantico, the way Dalworth looked at him like a long-lost son or an animal that'd been hit by a car, equal parts pity and defensiveness.

"You better watch your mouth, Agent."

Jay clenched his teeth hard, blinked left right right left.

"I found the files."

Dalworth pulled back slightly, though his expression remained. "What files."

Not a question.

"Fuck you, Brett. You forced my mother to narc and Dumpy Felder killed her for it. You lied to me about it for all these years."

"I don't know what you're talking about."

But now, Jay thought, the creases on Dalworth's cheeks, the shape of his mouth, said that though some of this might be genuine concern, more of it was covering his own ass and outright suspicion.

Because between the look in Dalworth's eyes and the room quieting slightly, Jay felt pressure collecting in his temples. "Dumpy bitching to Hart about CI-7. My mother telling you she thought CI-6 was going to hurt her. The gigantic bruise on the side of her head that wasn't there in a photo I have from a couple hours earlier. I know everything, Brett, except what's on those last pages in my mother's file that were ripped out. I'm guessing they explain how the cops covered it up with the pills and slashing her wrists and getting rid of whatever Dumpy hit her with. What was it? A hammer? Baseball bat?"

"How the fuck did you get those files?"

"I used my charm."

"You think I haven't been carrying this inside me for the last thirty years? That I don't think about how I failed her, what I should've done to keep her safe?" Dalworth said. "Jesus Christ, I've lost CIs before. Things happens sometimes. It's bad luck. But your mother—despite what you might think, she was a good woman. Tough, smart, ballsy. She was in a bad situation and she played the ever-loving hell out of it. And you know why? To keep you and Samantha safe, out of foster care."

"You forced her. I read the transcripts."

"No." He paused a moment, giving a fake smile to some asshole with a bunch of distinction pins on his breast pocket. His face slid down as he turned back to Jay. "No, I encouraged her. Your father forced her when he decided to start trafficking with Dumpy Felder. You can be angry at me if you want—"

"Angry?" Jay shouted.

Dalworth pulled Jay so close he could smell the coffee on his breath. "—but you need to remember who put her in that spot in the first place. Your father. You three deserved better than him. I was only playing the cards I was dealt."

"My father can go to hell along with you," Jay said. "You let Dumpy Felder get away with murdering my mother."

"It wasn't as simple as you think," Dalworth said. "There were other agents involved, other CIs, other operations to consider."

"Other operations," Jay spit. "You asshole."

Dalworth let out a sigh that threatened to never end.

"Sometimes you have to make a decision, Jay. And the outcome of that decision will affect all future decisions, because you'll always question whether you made the right choice or if you're making the same mistake again. And you'll have to live with that for the rest of your life."

"Yeah. I guess I'm learning that." Jay had the sudden urge to laugh, like this was the funniest damn thing he'd ever seen. The whole pomp and circumstance, everything they were celebrating, everything that had brought them to this point—it was all so ridiculous that Jay was afraid to laugh because he was afraid he'd never stop.

He shook his head and breathed out a small laugh, like bleeding the pressure. "You killed my mother, Brett. You played me like a pawn. You destroyed my life." Jay fought to keep his voice reined in but couldn't help it. "You turned me into a lie, making me no better than you."

Dalworth's lips didn't even part when he spoke. "Lower your goddamned voice."

"So you think I did something? You come at me straight. No more hiding like a coward." People around them whispered and Jay knew that he should just shut the hell up before he really hung himself out, but there was nothing he could do to stop the words. "I put my goddamned life into this job and you turned it into one big lie. But that is not me. I am not you. I'm not going out like that. You want my badge? Then take it yourself." Jay stepped toward Dalworth, knowing full well that everyone could hear every last syllable. "You said make a decision and I did. I'm not going anywhere."

Dalworth's mouth finally moved, arcing up into a thin smile, the creases at the edges cracking like the crow's feet beside his eyes. "You have a meeting with Internal Affairs tomorrow morning at nine. If you're late?" He shook his head, answering the question.

Jay spun on his heel to leave, the dignitaries and agents parting as he passed, doing all he could to not sprint out of the room. When he reached the door, Dalworth called out.

"Agent Brodsky."

Jay considered ignoring him and just walking, but knew that would give Dalworth the upper hand. He stopped, turned, and faced his boss. The man who'd been his mentor, his guide, his friend, for the last seven years. Jay raised his eyebrows, saying, *Yes?*

"You going to watch the walk this afternoon?"

Jay's jaw set tight, his eyes narrowing.

"Fuck you," he said, "ASAC Dalworth."

# 37

Jay glanced up at the TV playing local news above the bar. He couldn't remember the last time he'd had a beer in the middle of the day, but today seemed as good as ever. The broadcast moved from another terrorist bombing in the Middle East to the exterior of a courthouse. Throngs of people piled against the protective barriers, many holding signs. He paused the music and unmuted the feed.

"And in Baltimore this afternoon, all four defendants will be formally charged for their role in the largest insurance hack and financial crime in recent history, as well as the murder of three prominent businessmen…"

The talking head droned on as police led four people in orange jumpsuits into the courthouse. A small man, a muscular man, and a man who might be described as Texas Big. Jay felt his stomach tighten as the final person entered the screen— Oscar Forlán, sporting a slight limp and huge dark crescents beneath his eyes.

"…dubbed 'The Crimson Ghosts' by law enforcement, the group was involved in a terrorist conspiracy that aimed to destabilize the national economy, causing shock waves around…"

A series of images scrolled as the news anchor ran through the details of the case. The first ones were full of smoke and broken windows, people in Crimson Ghost masks hurling bricks at businesses and a now-famous photo of a mother scolding her child.

"The purported leader of the organization, a Uruguayan national with ties to a guerilla group in that country, will be tried separately, though certain sources say he acted to finance the group and the actual mastermind evaded arrest and is currently in hiding…"

While the news anchor continued, the feed paused on a photo that still chilled Jay. In it, a young boy and young girl, probably not more than twelve, stood hand-in-hand in the middle of the street, their faces painted like the Ghosts' white-and-black skull, while a battalion of riot officers behind shields bore down on them. Jay had seen it a hundred times over the last week, but he kept focusing on their knuckles bone-pale from gripping so hard, the stray threads hanging from the knee of the boy's ripped jeans, and the terrifying determination on the girl's face.

"Hell of a thing, isn't it?" the bartender said, motioning at the screen.

Jay looked up at her, blinked a couple times.

The bartender shook her head as the news surveyed more of the damage. "You believe some people are calling them heroes?"

The screen moved to a field reporter covering the funerals of the slain CEOs, the chyron at the bottom of the screen declaring them unlucky, innocent bystanders caught in a terrorist plot. Jay took a long drink from his beer. "Everyone's got to have one, I guess."

"Yeah, but them? Murderers, terrorists? I don't know, hon. Feels like things got turned upside down at some point, and we're here trying to figure out if we're supposed to right it or if it's been so long, we just forgot which way is up."

"Yeah. Who knows." Jay dropped some bills on the bar and knocked, saying thanks, then left.

The wild, angular guitars of Cave In's first album shredded through Jay's car before they settled into a rhythmic, chugging palm-muted riff, the singer's ragged voice following. Jay had found the CD a couple days ago, a mixtape Sam had made years ago. It hurt part of Jay to listen to it, but at the same time, it felt like a good hurt. Jay couldn't explain it, couldn't stop listening to the tape either.

He drove aimlessly around the city, much the same as he'd done the last ten days, inevitably passing the Harpers' mural several times a day. He wondered if it was a self-imposed purgatory, like revisiting those nights of him and Sam driving around at night, bullshitting and listening to albums, all dressed up with no place to go, just the two of them passing through space in a metal box, their world boiled down to ten square feet. He wondered if a small part of him thought he could find some wrinkle in time and go back there, change things, preserve them.

His phone vibrated in the cup holder.

Dalworth probably, calling to say he'd moved up the IA interview because he was a prick and he could. Or maybe Yemin, double-checking Jay was still helping with the X-wing bed. Or, some weird thought blooming in Jay's skull, it was Vargas, sending the photos of herself she'd joked about two weeks ago.

But when Jay picked up the phone, he saw a random assortment of numbers, too many to be an actual line.

He hit the green button to answer but stayed quiet. Breathing on the other end. His heart pounded in his throat.

The car behind him honked but Jay barely heard it.

A long moment later: "I'm sorry I almost shot you. It was just supposed to be for effect."

Jay swallowed. "It's okay."

Sam coughed out a laugh. "How many families have conversations like this?"

"I don't think our family is any cause for comparison."

"I think you're right on that."

Jay sat quietly on the phone, guiding his car through several streets on autopilot.

"Holy shit," Sam said after what felt like an eternity. "Is that the mixtape I made for your freshman homecoming?"

Jay laughed—snorted, actually. "I had the worst haircut. I can't believe Kelly went with me."

"Probably why she cut you out of all the pictures her friends had."

"Yeah," Jay said. "That kind of hurt."

"You knew she was terrible, right? I mean, she had great tits but she was not a very good person."

"You're only saying that because Peter Gabriel was her favorite musician."

"Which would be reason enough."

"Yeah, well." Jay didn't have to say anything past that. It was part of their shorthand, their shared experience, one he wagered precious few people would ever understand.

"I heard she—"

"What are we doing?" Jay said.

"What?"

"This. Now. This conversation. What is this? What are we doing?"

"Talking?"

"You know what I mean, Sam. You're a wanted felon. A terrorist. If they catch this on my phone, they'll trace it and find you and waterboard you with gasoline."

"You know I'd never let them catch me."

"They're trained professionals. You, sister, sing in a punk band."

Her smile practically beamed through the line. "Maybe. But they never caught me crossing the border."

"Into Mexico?"

"Went out west with Rico for a year or two. He hooked me up with some people who could get me down to Chiapas."

"You smuggled yourself across the border?"

"Getting down isn't hard. Getting back is an ordeal," Sam said. "You don't think I'd give you motherfuckers my photo and prints for a passport, do you? It was all worth it, though."

Something passed over Jay. Realization. "That's where all this came from," he said, everything clicking in real time. "The Ghosts. Everything."

"It's been building for years. Everything I did before led to it. Everything Oscar experienced shaped it." She breathed out a laugh. "'Every person, everything, is connected.'"

Jay's hand gripped the phone hard. When he swallowed, it felt like a rock in his throat.

Sam's breath passed over the mouthpiece. Jay strained to hear any background noise, anything that would give him the slightest hint as to where she was. But as ever, Sam was an enigma. Looking back on it, he realized she'd always been that way. He'd always thought he knew her, thought he'd knew what she'd do, but it was more of an educated guess. He'd use previous actions to guess future ones rather than understanding what caused those actions. He wondered if anyone would truly understand his sister.

"You remember my first day of freshman tryouts, when Coach Slattery said I'd never set foot on the field hockey grass?"

"She was an asshole."

"She was. But what happened?"

Jay's voice went suddenly rote, monotone, rolling out an answer he'd given a hundred times before, and that familiarity now rang a bell of painful nostalgia inside him. "You tried real hard and you didn't bother to make JV because you went straight to varsity."

"You know why I did?"

"Because you were trying to fuck Rachel Marbury?"

Sam barked out a laugh, then bit it back. "Man, we could've been something special, something legendary, but as soon as I got near her, I froze up because I got scared like an asshole. You want to know something? I have always wondered what could've been between me and her. To be honest, as I've gotten older, I've thought about her more often than I feel comfortable admitting, even to you." She paused a moment, lost in some fantasy. "Anyway, that's beside the point. Yes, I was really into her. But no, that's not why. JJ, I have never given a shit about field hockey."

"Then why'd you play?"

"I tried out to get close to Rachel. I made varsity to prove Coach Bitchface wrong, because she said I couldn't. Imagine what I could've done if I actually cared."

Jay didn't know how to respond to that, so he didn't.

"I'm proud of you, JJ," she finally said. "I wish things didn't turn out like they did, but I am proud of you. Despite everything that happened to us, you never let anything stand between you and what you wanted. You look like a fucking reject Old Navy model, but you're still the punk-as-fuck kid I knew growing up. And I respect the hell out of that."

"I wasn't trying to cuff Forlán," Jay blurted out. "I was trying to get you."

As soon as the words left his mouth, he wondered about that. Had he actually been aiming for her? Had she been trying to save him or trying to drown him? Everything in those moments was such a blur, but he'd been through enough training to know that, in situations like that, instinct overrode rational thought.

"I know you were." Her tone was typical Sam: half knowing-smile, half scowl—all enigma. "See you around."

"What?" Jay sat upright. "Sam, hey, what?"

But the line was already dead.

"Fucking asshole," Jay said aloud to no one. Goddamn Sam, still taunting him from wherever she was.

*Hell with it,* Jay thought, and turned up the music louder.

But as he drove, something kept burrowing in his skull. *Imagine what I could've done if I actually cared.*

Jay didn't know where the number Sam used came from, but he had it on his phone, and he could use that. It might take days, might take weeks, and the Bureau might never find her, but Jay would. Somehow. He knew that.

But first, he had something to do.

Jay screeched into the departure drop-off lane at BWI. He glanced at his watch.

Four forty.

He'd missed Vargas's flight by twenty-five minutes. *Goddammit, goddammit, goddammit. Damn traffic.* He banged his head against the steering wheel. So close, yet so far, like so much of his life.

As he began pulling out of the lane, tracing the loop of cars dropping off loved ones, he heard Sam's voice in his head. *As I've gotten older, I've thought about her more often.*

*Imagine what I could've done if I actually cared.*

Then: *So, are you hungry, Jay?*

"Fuck this."

Jay cut across three lanes of traffic, horns blaring, and whipped his car into the short-term parking garage. It was expensive as hell, but a short walk across the skyway to the departure terminals. Jay ran through them, dodging around families carting car seats strapped to roller bags and business travelers bleating into Bluetooth headsets. A few minutes later, he sidled up to the airline counter, out of breath and with nothing in hand but his phone and his wallet, and said, "One ticket for the next flight to Pittsburgh, please."

The man behind the counter gave a practiced, polite smile. "Round-trip or one-way?"

Jay thought for a second. "Surprise me."

# ACKNOWLEDGMENTS

This book wouldn't be possible without a great number of people. Thank you to Stacia Decker, Steve Feldberg, and Eric Campbell and Lance Wright for all the hard work and guidance. Thank you to Chris Irvin for the early reads and Angel Luis Colón for the late texts. Thank you to the Maryland/DC/Virginia writing scene that keeps me inspired, especially Ed Aymar for making it all happen. And thank you to Amanda, Donovan, and Ruby for more things than I could count.

**NIK KORPON** is the author of *The Rebellion's Last Traitor*, *Queen of the Struggle*, and *The Soul Standard*, among others. He lives in Baltimore.

BOOKS

On the following pages are a few
more great titles from the
Down & Out Books publishing family.

For a complete list of books and to
sign up for our newsletter,
go to DownAndOutBooks.com.

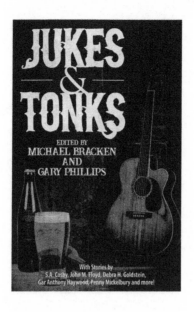

*Jukes & Tonks*
Crime Fiction Inspired by Music
in the Dark and Suspect Choices
Michael Bracken and Gary Phillips, editors

Down & Out Books
April 2021
978-1-64396-184-2

The stories in *Jukes & Tonks* introduce sinners and saints, love begun and love gone wrong, and all manner of unsavory criminal endeavors.

What they have in common is that they plop you down in worlds where the music pulsating from the stage provides the backbeat for tales that are unsparing, heartbreaking, twisty, and a few are as dark as the night.

*Roughhouse*
Jeffery Hess

Down & Out Books
May 2021
978-1-64396-132-3

If Scotland Ross doesn't get $100,000 fast, his wife will die.

A quick heist of a Tampa casino may save her life, while dooming him to life in prison if caught. Scotland never expected his trusted accomplice to go rogue and turn against him.

Betrayal, smoking guns, and a future strangled in revenge's cold grip make it a rough trip home. And the next day, things get worse.

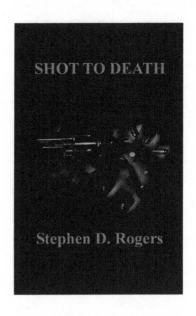

**Shot to Death**
31 Crime Stories
Stephen D. Rogers

All Due Respect, an imprint of
Down & Out Books
April 2021
978-1-64396-193-4

*Thirty-one bullets that will leave you gasping for breath...*

From hardboiled to noir to just plain human, these stories allow you to experience lives you escaped, and to do so with dignity, humor, and an eye toward tomorrow.

*Deemer's Inlet*
Stephen Burdick

Shotgun Honey, an imprint of
Down & Out Books
August 2020
978-1-64396-104-0

Far from the tourist meccas of Ft. Lauderdale and Miami Beach, a chief of police position in the quiet, picturesque town of Deemer's Inlet on the Gulf coast of Florida seemed ideal for El-don Quick—until the first murder.

The crime and a subsequent killing force Quick to call upon his years of experience as a former homicide detective in Miami. Soon after, two more people are murdered and Quick believes a serial killer is on the loose. As Quick works to uncover the iden-tity and motive of the killer, he must contend with an under-staffed police force, small town politics, and curious residents.